Peter Ransley's television play *Minor Complications* won the Royal Television Society's writers' award in 1981. About a woman who fought her own medical negligence case, it showed the odds such a person faces, and led to the formation of a national charity, *Action for the Victims of Medical Accidents.* Another BBC Play for Today, *Kate the Good Neighbour*, won the drama gold medal in the First Commonwealth Film and Television Festival, 1980. More recent TV work has included *The Story of Ruth* and the series *Bread or Blood*, based on W.H. Hudson's *Shepherd's Life*. His stage plays *Ellen* and *Disabled* were performed at Hampstead Theatre Club, and *Runaway* at the Royal Court.

The Price is Peter Ransley's first novel.

The Price

Peter Ransley

CORGI BOOKS

THE PRICE

A CORGI BOOK 0 552 12574 1

First publication in Great Britain

PRINTING HISTORY

Corgi edition published 1984

This book is set in 10/11 Mallard

Corgi Books are published by
Transworld Publishers Ltd.,
Century House, 61–63 Uxbridge Road,
Ealing, London W5 5SA

Made and printed in Great Britain by
Cox & Wyman Ltd., Reading, Berks.

For Cynthia, Nicholas and Rebecca

The Price

1 *Keep a Note of the Damage*

At least there was this to be said for it: other people bought the drinks. There was even some competition.

'What will you have, Frank?'

'No, no, I'll do it. Frank?'

'Orange juice,' he said, in his soft Derry accent. 'Ice if there is any.'

No laughter, no derisive jokes, although everybody in the all-male pub in Northern Ireland's second city had a pint of Guinness or Lager in front of him. There was a little patch of stillness; even the cigarette smoke seemed to stop climbing for a moment. The moment of stillness never failed to gratify him, made him feel taller than his five-feet-five inches. The stillness was because his order meant he was on his way to kill someone.

A moment later he was angry with himself. He was a fool to come here, go through this meaningless ritual. He looked round the nodding, grinning faces. He knew everyone. It was ok, he tried to tell himself. He needed this moment just as others needed a large pull of whiskey. Martin, the barman, was even sycophantically fishing with tongs for a non-existent sliver of ice.

The orange-juice was warm and slightly sickly. His stomach was empty but all he could eat were some crisps from a bag thrust out at him.

A few minutes chatter, slaps on the shoulder and knowing looks sickened him as much as the drink. He put it down. He wouldn't do such a stupid thing again. He, Frank Crossan, didn't need the approval of these idiots.

Only Doherty, a pensioner with a face cracked like old

leather, who had killed a politician famous in the fifties, now forgotten, rolled a cigarette and ignored him. All he talked about was horses and women. That was the way to be. On the way to the door he tried to catch the old man's eye, but Doherty, drawing his tongue across the cigarette paper, seemed unaware of him.

That rattled him. It was unlucky to be ignored by Doherty. The rain blew at him. He dived into a shop doorway to zip up his jacket. He should have refused the job, and bugger the consequences. Who was Tommo to give him orders? A shagged-out pill-head whose nerve had gone!

Frank ran to the other side of the street and hurried down to the Strand Road, clinging to the wall to try and escape the driving rain.

He had it over Tommo. For weeks they had been watching the house of a man serving in the British Army, following a tip-off that he had secretly come home on leave. They had shot the wrong man. Frank had told Tommo, warned him, tried to stop him. Now when the big man came back from Belfast there would be an enquiry, and Tommo would get the chop.

'How are yer?'

A big woman with shopping bags, standing over him as if it wasn't pouring down. Mrs Flynn, lived near his mother on Scotswood Road.

'Are you still at the garage?'

'No no. I left there'

Nor ever worked there. The respectable working life his mother created for him!

By the time he reached the big car park near the Guildhall it was exactly half-past two. No car. No Willy. He bought a Lion bar at the kiosk and chewed it in a doorway, his wet jeans clinging to his knees. He could go. Twenty-to-three now. He decided he'd eat the bar and then go. The rain fell steadily over the straight lines of houses climbing up the opposite bank of the Foyle: Waterside, the Protestant part of Derry.

He was tilting the last crumbs of chocolate into his mouth from the wrapper when the car came. It was not his friend Willy, a solid reliable driver, it was Sean, scarcely eighteen, a tearaway with his brain in his bollocks.

'Willy's sick.'

'What's wrong with him?'

'Food poisoning.'

'Jesus Christ.' Frank looked at the wisps of beard coming out of Sean's chin. 'I don't feel too good myself.'

Sean was bad luck too. He was tempted to go home and take off his wet clothes and have a hot bath.

'It's all set up,' Sean said. He had foggy brown eyes that looked out of the car mockingly at Frank: frightened?

That did it. He got in and Sean drove on up towards Shantallow. Always the job car had a warped door that took some shutting, a tear in the seat and an ashtray that came out when you pulled it.

'Wet?' said Sean.

'You should be in the RUC,' said Frank.

End of conversation. God he was shivering. Blast the rain. Blast the job. Blast Tommo. When the car stopped he should walk away, hitch a lift, get out of Derry. And go where?

He lit a cigarette for Sean, who silently took it.

He knew where, he had it all worked out — in fantasy. Depression gripped him, as the grafitti and the smashed phone boxes of the Shantallow Road blurred past the car windows. He would never get out. He was 24, a good operator, tight muscles, no nerves; he should be running the operations, not a burnt-out bastard like Tommo.

'Go round,' he said to Sean.

'This is the house.'

'Go round!' he snapped.

Sean looked into Frank's eyes and went round the housing estate. It was post-war concrete blocks, built just before they had started piling the blocks on top of one another. The rain kept it deserted, except for kids in a playground shelter and a man removing a tyre from an abandoned car. It was a mile from the exactly similar estate where Frank lived with his wife Ann and daughter Mary.

Often during the day he thought of Mary, the bossy way she had with him — 'Draw this' 'Come here Dad.' She was the reason why he didn't get out.

Get out where? The only way out was in the van to the Kesh. Or a box. Unless . . .

'How many times do you want the guided tour?'

Sean was crawling close to the pavement.

'Here.'

'This isn't the house.'

'It's the one I'm using. Wait round that corner.'

'But —'

Sean did as he was told. Now he was plainly frightened. He lit one cigarette from another. He had some beer in the car. Special Brew.

'Give me that.'

Sean did so without a word.

'You can celebrate afterwards. Don't wait in the fucking car. Wait in that fucking house. When you hear shots, I mean shots, not plastic bullets, do you know the difference, you run the engine and have it in fucking gear.'

On-the-job training! Where were they recruiting them? Before he had been on his first job he had gone to Donegal and stayed with Danny McKee. He'd survived because of Danny. Be unpredictable. Change your plans at the last minute: You're on the ground, you know what's happening. Which was why he was going to another house.

He opened the gate. A neat garden: good. People were easier to deal with when they had neat gardens. He dropped the Special Brew behind the hedge.

'Drink this,' Danny McKee had said. They had been shooting up in the Glendowan mountains and he was bursting with pride: the head of the Para he'd been firing at was more holes than cardboard.

'This' was a mug full of Jameson. He thought it was a reward and swallowed the whiskey obediently, his eyes watering.

'Fire.'

He missed the target altogether. He missed again. The tears in his eyes were now tears of mortification. Danny's hand pulled down the gun barrel.

'You're dead.' He pointed to the cardboard figure. 'He's shot you twice.'

The tears flowed faster: he was just seventeen and he really felt dead. Which was why he now drank orange juice, although Danny would have disapproved of his ostentatious ritual. He must stop that. Danny should have been his father, instead of that bronchitic old fart . . .

'Oh.'

The woman standing on the doorstep was in her thirties, with a plump dead-white face from which a nice smile was vanishing. She was holding a pound note, coins and a receipt book.

'I'm taking over the house for a while.'

She hesitated only a moment, and then mechanically held open the door. He wiped his feet carefully and unzipped his jacket. On the wall was a picture of Jesus with a lettered scroll saying 'Bless this house, Lord.' There was a smell of furniture polish that made him think of incense. Mary always made him come to mass on Sunday. He did it for the child, although to him it had become meaningless. He watched her take the Communion but never joined her. She secreted a fragment for him, and kicked up a scene if he wouldn't eat it. The woman had placed the receipt book and money on a little polished table next to two other small pyramids of money.

'How long will you be?'

'I've no idea.'

From the back room appeared first the face then the body of a boy of about eight. Expecting the insurance man, or whoever the money was for, the moon-face of the small boy stared up at Frank in astonishment.

'Get inside.' As the boy's mouth opened his mother expressed the anger she felt for Frank: 'Inside!'

Yes, he had thought so. From the back bedroom he had a good line on the street corner where the riot would be. He dragged the double-bed to one side and stood in the centre of the room. A good view. Not visible from the street. That would do.

The gun was in a house in the next street, under some potatoes in a plastic bag printed with apples and oranges, forming the slogan Fresh Fruit for Your Health. In the bedroom he unwrapped it and fitted it together. Apart from some rust it was in good condition. Had he used it before? It looked like one of the first Armalites to come to Derry in the late seventies.

He could hear Danny speaking: 'Fits inside a Sunshine Breakfast packet. Single-shot or semi-auto, .233, goes through body armour or an armoured car.'

There was a knock at the door and the woman came in with a cup of tea. There were two biscuits in the saucer, one chocolate. He didn't hide the gun and she didn't seem to see it.

Perhaps it was because he had wiped his feet, perhaps she had thought they were all animals.

'A soldier treats other peoples' houses like his own.' Some people thought Danny was a silly old fart, with his Christmas Cracker mottoes, but Frank hated cynics and needed someone to live up to. Danny had died last year, not violently, but quite unexpectedly, of a heart attack. He was 50.

Frank cradled the hot cup in his red raw hands. He sipped the tea gazing at a plaster statuette of Mary under the cross. There was perhaps an hour to go.

Quite probably nothing would happen. That was how it was nine times out of ten. The Armalite would be ferried back in its plastic bag. He might be in time to collect his daughter from school.

At a house near the crossroads lived — or had lived

— an informer. There had been a riot the day before, when the windows had been broken. A teenager had been arrested and later released with two teeth missing and a broken arm. There was going to be another riot today, and this time it was going to be a tooth for a tooth.

The door-bell went. He crept to the landing holding the Armalite. There was the rattle of coins: the insurance man.

'Quiet today.'

'Yes it is quiet.'

The insurance man tried to linger, but the woman got rid of him quickly. Perhaps Frank was drinking his cup of tea.

The two biscuits made him feel hungry. He regretted not having eaten. Downstairs the television was on. Someone else called for one of the little piles of money.

It happened quite suddenly. The informer's house had been broken into, but it couldn't have been that that drew the army so quickly. They must have anticipated trouble. Two armoured cars appeared. A boy was pulled out of the house. Stone throwing began. A crowd formed near the playground. A soldier was hit by a stone and that started the plastic bullets.

As Frank took up his position the butt of his rifle knocked over the plaster statuette of Mary, which broke into several pieces. The woman must have been in the bathroom, for she appeared at the door.

'My sister brought it back from Lourdes.' Her hands were clasped tight in front of her, her voice high with anger.

'Keep a note of the damage.'

He shut her out, treading on a piece of the statuette as he sighted his rifle over cushions piled on the back of a chair, oblivious now of anything but the view through the open window of figures running, an armoured car rolling slowly forward, a fire flaring up in a rubbish bin in the playground.

There was something going on outside his eyeline.

Shouts and screams. He ought to go to the front of the house to see. But he also ought to keep his rifle trained on the crossroads. The troops had been careful, running round the back of the armoured cars, covering the nearside houses for snipers, crouching low, making themselves as small as possible.

It was only if you stayed long enough that somebody made a mistake. The troops were trained to recce a street and clear it. If you sweated it out, took the risk of a house being searched, then the soldiers relaxed a fraction, just a fraction, their heads came up and they became targets, cardboard paras like Danny used to set up for him. Frank had chosen a good position: they wouldn't be able to judge the angle of fire, tell which street it came from.

But he was a good distance away. Too far? Troops were running back to their carriers. The raid was over. A soldier was putting out the fire. He was just within range. A child ran in front of him. Frank took his hand off the trigger and wiped it on the pillows.

Another soldier ran, weaving. He followed him with his sights. He needed the head. He didn't get it. A wounding wasn't sufficient, he needed a kill, that would put his stock up, that would finish Tommo.

He changed position and more of the statuette ground beneath his heel. He wasn't aware of it. Two troops had lifted a man and were running him towards the carrier, his feet scarcely touching the ground. They were on the right side of the carrier for Frank.

A curious icy thrill ran through him as he followed the three men with his sights. It was like choosing between two reds at snooker. The nearer soldier was a cert, but the bullet might pass through him and into the man they were lifting. He picked the further man.

As he aimed he sensed rather than saw the net curtain that he had draped back dislodge. He had a fraction of a second before it fell back over the window. He was semi-automatic but he fired only two shots. Before the bullets left the barrel he knew, just as a snooker player knows the ball is going to go down when the cue strikes, that the man was dead.

The .233 bullet used in the Armalite causes a tumble shock wave producing extensive wounds. With half the back of his head gone Private Gavin Foster from South Shields, Co. Durham, was dead before his body hit the ground. He was 20, and had joined the army after two years on the dole. He had been in Northern Ireland four months and had married, one week before posting, because his girl friend was pregnant.

Frank didn't wait to see his man fall. He broke the rifle and shoved it into the plastic bag as he ran down the stairs. The woman holding her son was a blur as he ran through the kitchen into the back garden. The gun was taken from him, over the fence, by a boy who looked as if he was still at school.

There was an alley between the two sets of houses. Frank plunged down it, then through an open gate leading to the tiny garden of the next street of houses.

'Mind the bloody crysanths.'

The speaker was an old man in a shirt with rolled-up sleeves in spite of the rain. Frank stumbled against a propped up bike. The old man gripped his arm and propelled him through the small kitchen where his wife was feeding the budgerigar. Seed rattled on the linoleum. When he opened the front door he would be into the get-away car in seconds.

Except that it wasn't there.

At first he thought he had made a mistake. Come through into the wrong street. He stood just inside the front door gasping for breath. Rain streamed from a broken pipe, splashing just in front of his feet. There was no car, but there were two soldiers, nervous, crouching. The three men stared at one another in a stretching moment of stillness.

Frank slammed the door shut, ran back through the kitchen, the budgerigar fluttering in a panic, and grabbed the bike as the old man opened the gate into the alley.

'Mind the bloody —'

It was years since he had been on a bike. His jeans snagged on the chain. His lungs screamed for air as he forced his legs up and down, up and down. The back tyre was soft and bumped jarringly on the stones of the alley. Behind him was the sound of running feet and shouts. He crouched over the handlebars, tried to weave, wobbled, skidded. Perhaps the skid saved his life: fresh white wood suddenly appeared on the fence in front of him. More shots. The alley bent in a dog leg in front of him. He nearly made it. The bullet caught his left arm just as he reached the corner.

The alley led into another, and that into a road on the fringe of the housing estate. It wasn't until then that he was sure he was hit. Instinctively he headed towards home. A woman with a pram was crossing a zebra. He didn't stop. She shouted something. Sirens sounded. His legs went up and down mechanically.

He glimpsed children on the pavement. They were being collected from school. Ignoring the pain in his left arm he turned the bike down a side-street: it was not only a physical but a mental effort: it was away from home. He had been seen, clearly, by the soldiers. They would come, or they would be waiting for him.

Never do the predictable. He could hear Danny's voice through the drumming in his head as he slid off the bike, exhausted, and clattered it against the school railings.

Stupid of him. Well, there had been enough bad luck signs that day. Across the road were two RUC men in an armoured Land Rover, their eyes fixed on him beneath their stiff peaked caps. The shoulder of one of the men dipped slightly as his hand reached into his holster. Frank felt a great weariness, even an urge to walk towards the Land Rover.

'Dad.'

Mary, his daughter, was running towards him from a small group sheltering in the porch. As he leaned, panting, against a gatepost, he saw the RUC men look away, beginning to lose interest.

'Sorry I'm late.'

He forced himself to bring his left hand out of his pocket and catch her when she jumped up at him.

'I didn't know you were coming for me!'

'Sudden inspiration.'

There was blood on her coat and jumper. At first, he could tell, she was cross with him for making her dirty, and then she realized. He pulled her to him, laughing.

'Say nothing. Kiss me.'

They walked through the playground. Soldiers had arrived and were clustered round the RUC car. Frank put his good arm round Mary.

'What did you do at school today?'

2 The Last Place on Earth

'How was school?'

Frances Carr opened the door of her Renault 5 for her daughter. Clare, who had just turned 12, screwed up her face. She knew from her mother's expression she would only half-listen to the answer. Since her mother had remarried she had had many more things and much less of her mother.

The private school in Hampstead, russet red brick, dark green uniforms and a motto *Truth is Glory* was part of the new life.

'Seat belt.'

Clare's lower lip stuck out.

'If you're riding in the front put your seat belt on.'

Her mother's lip was also sticking out. She was thirty-two. Her square, rather heavy face was made striking by a frame of thick black hair and large grey eyes which could be disconcertingly direct.

'What did you do at school?'

'You don't have to make conversation.'

'Sorry, not with it.'

Clare was a little mollified, but only a little. 'Free choice essay,' she said.

'What subject did you choose?'

'Marriage.'

Oh God, Frances thought, I asked for that one. She said: 'That's a fairly large subject.'

They had hit the beginning of the rush hour round Swiss Cottage and a man in a Rover tried to carve across her lane. She accelerated, forcing him to brake.

She didn't do what most drivers did: stare straight ahead as if nothing had happened. She smiled sweetly at his silently cursing face. He smiled back. Oh God, he was one of those.

'Do you want to hear it?'

'What?'

'The essay.'

Frances saw a gap, shot through it, escaping the hooting cars and the Rover and was free down Avenue Road, going against the main stream of traffic.

Clare kicked a muddy shoe against the plastic fascia. She began to recite in a bored, colourless voice, as if she was standing up in a classroom.

'My father died when I was eight in a riding accident. I loved him very much.'

Her voice faltered as the game touched her feelings and suddenly became real, dangerous.

Frances caught the change in tone and slowed down, wanting to put an arm round her daughter but apprehensive of a rebuff.

'Recently mother has married again.'

Frances' grip tightened on the wheel and her lower lip protruded. 'All right.'

'He makes computers. He is very rich. I *hate* him.'

The word carried such venom it stopped her and the car. Frances pulled on the handbrake and turned to Clare. 'Don't you ever say that again.'

Clare's eyes shone with tears that were barely kept back. Frances put her arms round her and held her tightly. But it was no good: Clare had to see that life had changed, she must adjust. 'We like each other very much, very much indeed and if you hurt him, you hurt me, do you understand?'

Clare stared out of the side window for the rest of the journey.

The Renault entered the drive of the large house in St John's Wood. Geoffrey's house. Not what Frances wanted, but it would do for now.

In the darkness of the bag by her side she could see

glittering the seed pearl choker with a diamond and sapphire centrepiece which she had bought at Aspreys that afternoon for £10,950 plus VAT, as if she had been shopping at Sainsburys. The days of poverty were over.

They had driven on side roads until they reached Lough Neagh at Toome Bridge. From there they eventually joined the motorway to Belfast. The car was an old Escort with a bad knock, but at least it wasn't stolen. Willy said little. He had thought Frank mad when he told him to take him to Belfast. He was only doing it because they had been at school together and he always did what Frank told him.

Willy's face was white not from food poisoning, but from fear. He had been ill — flu — but was that the reason why he had been switched from the driving job? Why had the soldiers turned up so quickly? Had they searched the house he was originally going to use?

He winced and held his bandaged arm away from his body as the car jolted.

'I'm going to Danny.'

That was what he had told Mary to say to his wife. Danny was dead, but she would know exactly what he meant. And she would think he had crossed the border into Donegal. So would the police. He hoped.

The rain had gone but a fine drizzle made the wipers squeak. Belfast Lough rose misty on their left.

'Where did you say?'

'Victoria Park.'

Willy's voice rose a notch. 'That's through town.'

Frank made no comment. He closed his eyes. He'd lost blood, was too exhausted to feel much fear. If they took him, they took him. It might even be better for him, to be out of Tommo's reach.

He could swear he hadn't slept, but, when he opened his eyes, car lights were on and the soft beginning of darkness blurred the shapes of big old Victorian houses whose front gardens had mainly been concreted to take cars. They had got through town then. He began to feel fear again, now they had nearly made it.

Never trust anyone — not even yourself. Danny's Christmas cracker mottoes kept coming back to him as he tried to distinguish house numbers in the gloom.

Where was he going? What was he trying to do? The idea now seemed a ridiculous fantasy. He should have stayed in his own back yard. They would have sorted Tommo out. He was a fool, an idiot to run for it. He clenched his good hand impotently.

'Nineteen?'

'Get out and check,' he snapped.

As Willy beckoned, he glimpsed through the rain-speckled windscreen a man in a black great-coat approaching. His heart hammered. The man passed without a glance: a bus-conductor.

The drizzle and the cool wind were refreshing on his muzzy, aching head as they skirted a line of dustbins daubed with flat numbers in white paint which had trickled down the corrugations of each bin. A cat fled as they climbed the steps. A light glowed from the entryphone, faintly illuminating a stained glass picture of birds pecking berries.

Willy's finger found a button labelled *Kate Fanning*.

'Who is it?'

'Frank,' said Willy.

When Willy pushed at the heavy door, she was standing at the entrance to her flat across the dark hall, bigger, heavier than he remembered. As she jabbed at a timeswitch that lit the shabby hall, decorated with meters and a board stuck with undelivered letters and circulars, Willy pushed past her.

'Here!'

She made a grab at him, then saw Frank's bandaged arm and stopped.

'Hello Kate. How are you?'

She would have been attractive but for lines of scepticism, of suspicion that were already notched heavily into the centre of her forehead at the age of what, twenty-seven, twenty eight? She had the plump neck and the milk-white skin he had often noticed in Belfast women. Brought up a Protestant in Antrim, she had become a vehement, outspoken speaker on the Catholic side.

Willy returned. 'It's ok.'

'See you Willy.'

Kate found her voice. 'Wait a minute!'

But Willy was already running down the steps towards the Escort, and was driving away by the time she reached the car.

Frank went in the flat, the warmth making him dizzy. When she came back, specks of rain were gleaming in her cropped, brown hair.

'Shut the fucking door for Christ's sake!'

He stumbled into a room, knocking some papers off the arm of a chair. There were more books then he had ever seen in a house before; enough to stock a library. She picked up the papers.

'Why did you come here?'

'I've run out of things to read.'

Derry flippancy always sank like a stone in Belfast. He fell rather than sat in a settee, biting his lip as he jarred his arm.

'You told me to drop in any time.'

Her eyes kept returning to the bandage. 'You didn't mention that.'

'On the phone?'

The settee was an old leather one with stuffing coming out of it, and still smelt of the junk shop she had picked it up from. His wife wouldn't be found dead with such a thing in the house, but God it was comfortable. He couldn't keep his eyes open. Her voice sounded a long way away.

'How bad is it?'

Tell her it was much worse than it was? No, she knew about wounds.

'It missed the bone. The man said.'

'Why *me*? *Here*?'

The violence in her voice opened his eyes. Hadn't he been asking himself the very same question?

'You're middle-class. No known associate of the wanted man.'

In fumbling for his cigarettes, several fell on the floor. Irritated, she stuck one in his mouth.

'Thanks.'

Her heavy breasts shifted as she struck the match.

'I came because of your talk in Derry.'

That was at least partly true.

'Which one?'

'You said we shouldn't be bombing our own people. We should be hitting the politicians, the rich. You said you wanted to be involved.'

'I said there should be better planning.'

'Which *you* could do.'

For the first time she was on the defensive. She went to the curtains and closed a gap in them.

'I'm a teacher.'

'I'm an electrician. Just talk, was it?'

She whirled round, the notch in her forehead deeper than ever.

'Was it the soldier this afternoon. Don't tell me! You took a chance coming through Belfast! Why didn't you go to Donegal?'

'Because I wanted to see you!'

It sounded pathetic as he said it, but he was so tired, his eyes were flickering again.

'Because I was set up this afternoon? I've left Derry. I've packed it in.'

'You mean you're running from them? As well?'

No no. It was more complicated than that, although no doubt Tommo would blacken him into a cowboy who wouldn't take orders. It was more complicated . . . He no longer knew what to think . . .

She took the cigarette before it slipped from his fingers, and, with distaste, for she hated the smell of tobacco smoke in her flat, stubbed it out. Making a vice with her finger and thumb she prized up his head until his eyes, blind with sleep now, opened.

'I want you out, Frank. First thing in the morning I want you out.'

Frances kept her sister's letter but threw the brochure away. Because there was a colour photograph stuck on it Ida, the au pair, took it out of the wastepaper basket.

'What a lovely place!'

The photograph was of a Georgian mansion set in landscaped parkland running down to the sea. A headline underneath it said: KILNAMEATH CO. WICKLOW IRELAND. FOR SALE BY PUBLIC AUCTION.

Frances held out her hand.

'I didn't mean to throw that away.'

She wished she could.

Now, as they dressed for dinner, the brochure stood in line with the objects ready to go into Geoffrey's dinner jacket: keys, wallet, invitation, his pencil-slim calculator, diary. Even the pearl choker she had bought that afternoon — as an act of defiance to these feelings, was that it? — failed to dispel the black mood that had crept on her ever since the brochure had arrived in the post.

Geoffrey was cleaning his teeth. He somehow managed to scrub and spit while humming Mozart.

She looked from the brochure to the eighteenth century portrait of a man of thirty with a slightly mocking face, hanging incongruously among the white, lime and stainless steel of the bedroom. He was one of the few things she had brought to the house: Charles, the fifth earl, who had plundered Europe to furnish Kilnameath.

The house had gone out of her family when the eighth earl had been shot in the land riots of 1881. She had been brought up near there. Played there. Ran a stables near there.

Her first husband had died there.

She jumped. Geoffrey's hands were on her shoulders. He kissed the top of her head.

'You look . . .'

Their eyes met in the mirror. Although he was fifty,

when he gazed at her like that, the boy of eighteen with his first girl came back into his face.

'Good evening Mrs Carr.'

'Good evening Mr Carr.'

They had been married three months.

He picked up the brochure. 'Did you put this here for me to see?'

'Can we go?'

What was she saying? She didn't want to go there!

'Where?'

'To the auction.'

'To Ireland?'

His eyebrows were lifted. He had a way of making some of her suggestions sound so ludicrous she automatically rejected them herself.

'I suppose it's silly.'

Then she was immediately furious with herself, with him.

'Heavy week next week,' he said.

There was a never-ending stream of dinner parties and trade functions. He briefed her on tonight's as he always did, while he was fastening his tie.

'It's an industry bunfight, top table next to the Minister, don't forget his wife likes porcelain. No, wrong Ministry. She's Save the Children. Perhaps you should sponsor a child. They always like to think computer manufacturers have normal human instincts.'

She slammed the brochure into a drawer. He turned.

'Do we have to go?'

'We should already have gone. Here. Drink up.'

He held out her glass, rattling the slivers of ice in her gin-and-tonic. She had a little moment of insight, an observation trivial in itself, but which hinted at some larger defect.

'You can't bear to leave an unfinished drink, can you?'

The Yorkshire accent crept back into his voice and the embarrassed teenager into his face.

'That's true. I always hear my mother's voice: "Drink

up. You never know when you might need it." '

He winced at himself disarmingly. As he moved to put the glass down she took it and swallowed the gin. They laughed at one another and the danger was over. Another two drinks and the black mood would go. She took the fur wrap from him and gave herself a last triumphant look in the mirror.

After all, the very last place on earth she wanted to go was Ireland.

As a child Kate had been so frightened of the dark she had screamed if the light wasn't on. Once her strict father had taken out the bulb and waited on the stairs to make sure she didn't leave the room. She had screamed until the vomit came, until her mother fought past her father and opened the door.

Now when she couldn't sleep she always put on the light. She was on the leather settee, having given Frank her bed. She had opened the windows and pulled the door vigorously to and fro, but she couldn't get rid of the faint smell of stale tobacco.

Sirens sounded, swelled and faded. Frank cried out. She sat up. Although the walls were thick the neighbours might hear, might have seen. No men stayed in her flat. At one o'clock in the morning she was convinced the neighbours would put two and two together.

It gave her a queer feeling to see him in her bed, sprawled on his right side, away from his injured arm, his shirt twisted up round his neck. A cigarette end floated in the half-finished drink she had made him. This room, too, would have the harsh smell of smoke for days. She pulled his shirt down and the sheets up.

When his mouth opened she put her hand over it. His eyes opened.

'You cried out.'

'Did I?'

The top of his shirt was wet and his forehead was hot. He wasn't going down with something! A slow steady anger built up in her as she tipped two paracetamol into his palm — no, make it three.

She held the water out for him as he swallowed the tablets.

'Go south if you've lost your nerve.'

Drops of water hit her cheek as he shouted back at her.

'I haven't lost my nerve! We're all getting on each others' fucking nerves! I was nearly lifted this afternoon. Someone put the finger on me. All right! I'm going to operate on my own, build up my own unit. I need you but I can do without you!'

'What for?'

His face shone with the look, half-mad, half-desperate that she had seen so many times before, in drinking clubs off the Falls Road, or back rooms in Andersonstown.

'Something big. Something really big.'

She walked out, closing the door behind her. She dare not take a Mogadon so she read the most boring book on her shelves, on the sociological derivations of orange, red and green socialism, but even that would not send her to sleep.

It had been an excellent evening. What a success Frances was turning out to be, Geoffrey reflected as he placed the brush at the correct angle and vigorously flicked his wrist so he could almost feel the plaque falling away from his teeth.

She had charmed the Minister. The schools contract was now virtually certain.

And there was a bonus. He had married Frances because he was tired of being on his own at the dinners and receptions he had to attend now he was a figure not only in computers, but in industry. He had wanted a woman who was good at that sort of thing, and he had chosen her as he would a good designer or engineer — he had poached her.

She had cooked what she called posh lunches for executives in his advertising agency in Manchester

Square. He had doubled her salary and installed her in Beach Yard, where Carr Computers had its city office. This enabled him to satisfy himself that she had the necessary qualities. Within two months they were married.

The last thing he had expected from marriage was satisfactory sex. He had thought that would wane very quickly, partly because that was marriage, and partly because his sexual requirements had been minimal for years. His way of dealing with what he called the itch was Mrs Cooper.

She was the highly respectable wife of a software manufacturer who had been bankrupt twice. At a dreary echo of a banquet at Grosvenor House, where 250 Boeuf à la Ficelle had been followed by 250 Soufflé d' Oranges, he had found himself alone with her, in a corner near the band.

They had been dancing, made one or two jokes, pressed against one another while they laughed. That was all.

'Do you want me?' she said.

'Yes,' he laughed.

'Follow me.'

Bemused, he found himself going past his company table where Lansbury, his PR director said something which was drowned by the band striking up Hard Day's Night (most of the people there had been young in the sixties).

She was staying in the hotel with her husband. The clothes he had changed from were draped over a chair. She was perhaps forty, the skin still tight over her cheeks. The black gloves that ended in a frill at her elbows moved like wings as she took his face and kissed him. She unzipped his fly. He pulled away.

'He won't disturb us,' she said. 'You don't have to worry about that.'

She began taking off her dress. Her breasts were small, with livid purplish aureoles round the erect nipples. As he moved towards her, she turned away.

'Two hundred pounds.'

He sat on the bed staring at her.

'No-one will know, and you'll never see me again. Unless you want to.'

She put away her husband's clothes as she spoke.

'Well make up your mind. This room's not very warm.'

At the time it struck him that she must be in some terrible trouble, but he was incapable of paying out money and getting nothing for it.

That had been four, no five years ago. He saw her once a month, sometimes not for several months, in what she told him was a friend's flat in Pimlico. The same friend — presumably, he had never met her — took his messages when he had the itch. She had refused to see him only once, when one of her children was ill.

He liked to think he was paying for her children's education, because of the software manufacturer's failure, but he really had no idea. Nor did he know if there were others, although he assumed there must be. They used one another and asked no questions. That was the arrangement.

He looked for a similar arrangement in his marriage, but it hadn't worked out like that. Where Mrs Cooper was remote and controlling, which he thought exactly suited his temperament, Frances was wild, demanding and unpredictable.

After the first month of marriage she'd been ill and they'd had no sex for several weeks. Then a burst of activity. Then another fallow period. Then, a week ago, she had begun waking him in the mornings, her mouth exploring his body.

At the climax he had cried, something he had never done with a woman before. He had been late for work, quarter-to-ten, which was also unprecedented.

There she was now, waiting for him, flicking the pages of a magazine impatiently. A delicious shiver ran through him. As he approached she dropped the magazine on the floor — a habit he'd have to get her out of — and got out of bed.

'That was Clare.'

She raised her eyebrows in exasperation, kicked at her slippers, decided not to bother and went up to the next floor.

He turned out the light and sat on the bed waiting. The magazine lay tented next to her slippers; beyond them was her slip, crumpled up with her tights and pants. He tried to ignore them, but eventually got up and put them on a chair. It took him thirty minutes to get to bed; her as many seconds.

He was at the door. The house was silent. He went up the curving flight of stairs. The top of the house was a mysterious shape; a half-landing, then three attic rooms. It was a full moon, and by the light from the landing window he could see into Clare's room.

She was sound asleep. Frances was on a chair by the bed, her face in her hands. Geoffrey was touched. Then as he moved and a board creaked she looked up and he saw there were tears streaming down her face. She wiped them away with her arm and came out of the room. As he put out his hand, she walked past him down the stairs.

He caught her up on the bottom flight where the dimmed hall-lights glinted on the steel-tubed chandelier hanging in the stair-well. She wrenched her arm away.

'I can't bear you touching me!'

Her face was so distorted Geoffrey thought she must be mad or ill as he followed her into the kitchen.

If Geoffrey found it difficult to get on with Clare, he could always ignore her. It was impossible to ignore Henry, Clare's Yorkshire Terrier, which was rising blinking from its basket as Frances switched on the neon strips. She held up a warning finger.

'Henry! You know Geoffrey by now!'

She seemed quite normal again, fully in control of herself. She was switching on the coffee machine. His slipper crunched on a piece of dog biscuit. He really detested having the dirty animal in his house. The dog growled menacingly as he neared Frances.

'In your basket!' she scolded. 'Go on! Naughty dog! He's a friend!'

'That's good to know,' Geoffrey said. 'What is all this?'

'Do you want coffee?'

'No thank you. What is all this?'

'I can't *stand* you!' The words were a vehement explosion, but immediately she clapped her hand over her mouth and her voice rose high, girlish. 'What an awful thing to say!'

She was surprisingly immature in so many ways, he thought. She produced a large bowl-like coffee cup and warmed the milk, her movements now crisp, matter-of-fact.

'I can't stand the way you brush your teeth.'

He laughed, moving to her, keeping the table between him and Henry.

'It's more than that,' she said.

'Teeth don't sound crucial.'

'Don't joke!'

Grinning, he put his arm round her. She pulled away, her voice like ice breaking.

'I really can't bear you touching me.'

'You don't seem to have found it very difficult.'

'I've been trying very hard.'

She didn't stop looking at him after she had said this. Her grey eyes were as cold as the winter sea. For an instant, as she moved to pour her coffee, the shadow of her pubic hair was visible through her night-dress.

He felt sick. For the first time since childhood he did not know what was happening to him, to his own body. He sat down. The dog kept his eyes on him. The faint vinegary smell Henry gave to the kitchen was mingling with the smell of coffee. She brought her cup to the table, her fingers wrapped round it.

'I told you I didn't love you.'

Wasn't this what he had planned? There was always Mrs Cooper. Hadn't he been exhausted by Frances' attentions, his routine disrupted, his creative energy diverted? The anger that was building up inside him was hurt pride, that was all. He controlled himself.

'Love,' he mocked. 'You wanted the money, I wanted a wife.'

'A social asset.'

'What's wrong with that?'

She looked lost, and mumbled something into her coffee.

'What?'

'It's an appalling mistake! I . . . I liked you, I did like you, sometimes I liked you rather a lot. I thought it would work, we had no illusions, I thought we had none but . . . everything's business! We even had our honeymoon at a computer convention!'

'I was with you most of the time.'

'In Cincinnati.'

'I wasn't looking at Cincinnati.'

She grinned and ducked her head between her hands. He shut his eyes for a moment in relief. It was a mood; it was tiresome, but he could handle it. Gradually she would adjust. The first thing that would go was Henry, he promised himself, staring back at the dog. Calmer, more relaxed, he became solicitous.

'Why haven't you said anything before?'

'I tried.'

'When?'

She shook her head. She had curved a piece of her black hair into her mouth. Her face was still, but somehow in movement, like a good portrait which does not freeze but animates. There was a bleakness, a desolation in it. For the first time he was moved to touch her not in lust or friendliness, but in concern. But, wary of her reaction, he kept his hands to himself. Perhaps she read his change of mood. At any rate she spoke slowly, hesitantly, in a tired voice.

'It's only partly business. It's Clare. My first

marriage. Michael died at Kilnameath.'

She shivered. He wanted to put his arm round her, but again stopped himself.

'When I saw the house was for sale all that started coming back to me. I can't explain it.'

'It must be difficult.'

In a few minutes they would be in bed together. The dog grumbled as it settled in its basket. Perhaps he could get used to the animal. The fridge hummed. She put down her cup.

'I'll go away for a while.'

He stared at her in astonishment. 'Where?'

'Ireland.'

Even then he kept his temper, was quiet and reasonable. 'Why go there if it upsets you? What will that solve?'

She got up. As he moved to her she flinched and then at last his anger burst out, a worked-out, controlled anger that forced her back into her chair.

'Sit down Frances, I'm not going to touch you. We've been married three months. Three months! It's not been that bloody easy for me either, what with you, your daughter, your dog! Marriage is a bit of a shock to the system for the first time at fifty. Look at the time! I've a nine-o'clock appointment. I'll cancel tomorrow evening. Well I'll cancel the second part. We'll have a late dinner. Alone. Really talk this out. All right?'

She walked to the door. He stopped her.

'All right?'

'I'll sleep in the spare room.'

Now he touched her, held her. Now he understood. It was all part of some complicated sexual game they had not played before.

'Frances, you're just feeling —'

'You haven't been listening to me have you!' she shouted.

The violence excited him, and his grip tightened the more she struggled. She got an arm loose and lashed out, catching him a stinging blow on the ear. Now there was no control. He grabbed her, forcing her against the table, the coffee cup rolling off and breaking. He had been dimly aware of the dog, barking in the background, snapping from under the table. It went for him. He lashed out, his slipper flying across the room. He had a moment of primitive satisfaction as the dog yelped, paws skittering across the tiled floor. Frances snatched the dog up and comforted him.

There was a short, appalling silence. The dog was against her breasts, whimpering. Geoffrey rubbed his ear, dazed not by the blow but by the feeling that he had stumbled into some mad world that was not subject to good sense or reason. She had had all the credentials. He had been congratulating himself on his choice. Then Clare had called out . . . no . . . but now she really was calling out . . .

'Mummy? Mummy!'

As he opened the door, he was amazed to see how much his hand was shaking.

'It's all right, Clare,' he said. 'Henry mistook me for an intruder.'

Frank didn't feel too bad when he awoke. His fever had gone. It wasn't until he swung his legs out of bed that he realised how weak he was. It took him ten slow minutes to dress, although he only had to put on his trousers, jacket and shoes.

Kate was asleep on the sofa, the notch quite shallow in her forehead. He saw the title of the book she was reading: 'The Colours of Irish Socialism'. No wonder she was sleeping soundly. He went into the kitchen, holding on to the edge of the door and then the table.

He took out his cigarettes. No. Better not smoke. He drank milk straight from a bottle because it would take too much of his energy to find a mug. He gazed round, looking for a bag or purse. He searched a drawer: bills, letters, a clothes-peg holding money-off offers on soap powder and muesli. Then above his head he saw what he was looking for: a board of hooks containing keys.

Didn't she drive a Beetle? Yes, here was a VW key.

As he turned to shut the drawer, a phrase in a letter caught his eye. 'We regret there is no vacancy at the moment'. There were a number of similar letters.

'BRIGHT PARK SCHOOL. Dear Ms. Fanning, We regret that the post you applied for has now been filled, but must . . .'

He didn't hear her come up behind him in her bare feet. She snatched the letter from him and slammed the drawer.

'Are you out of a job too?' he said.

She didn't reply. He finished the milk and tried to zip up his jacket.

'Where are you going?'

'South.'

'How?'

He shrugged and gave up the zip. It was amazing. You could shoot a man with one hand, but you couldn't do up a zip. He went past her to the door. Her face was distorted with anger.

'You can't go out on the streets!'

'You want me out.'

'You need a car. Get one! Phone someone!'

'And end up in Derry doing another shit job on my way to the Maze? I'll take a chance.' He smiled suddenly, charmingly. 'Ah, it was a bastard thing to do, landing myself on you Kate. Thanks for the bed. And the breakfast.'

He flinched as she came over, but she was only doing his zip. She did it with rough resentful movements, reminding him of his mother when she used to check him before school. He almost expected her to tug a comb through his hair.

'Thanks.'

'Do you know a safe way over?'

She said the words as if they were teeth being drawn out.

'Near Monaghan. An old smuggler's route.'

'I'll take you.'

His legs were crumpling and he sat down, trying not to show the triumph and relief he felt.

He could see she was angry with herself immediately she'd agreed to take him. Then a thought struck her. She looked up at the board of keys.

He knew her now — or thought he did. He put on the hang-dog boy's look that used to work with his mother, preparing to absorb her anger because he knew he would eventually get his own way, and slid the key across the table.

Frances slept in the spare room where Clare found her.

'You're on my side,' she said.

Just as she used to before Geoffrey. Frances was glad of the comfort. There had been no relief in having it out with him, only the cold fear that they would soon be living from hand to mouth again.

In the morning light it all made no sense. It had all started with that brochure. Kilnameath. Again.

'That house destroys everybody who owns it,' said her sister Margaret, a normally prosaic farmer's wife.

Had she sent it knowing it would bring her back? What rubbish she was thinking! Margaret could hardly not send it! Still, she could picture her sister's face as she put the brochure in the envelope . . .

'Come on Mummy!'

Normally it was Frances dragging the sheets off Clare. Clare pulled her out of bed and did something she hadn't done for years. She took her by the hand and led her down to her and Geoffrey's bedroom. There was no sign of him. He must have gone. Half-past-eight. Her clothes had been tidied away. Charles, the fifth earl, looked down at her from the picture, lips pursed above his frothing cravat, as if he was saying:

'Where next?'

'What are you going to wear?' Clare said.

'Don't be silly! You'll be late for school!'

But she submitted while Clare dressed her like a doll.

Clare would be soon leaving that school, anyway. They were still laughing when they went downstairs. Geoffrey was in his study: forbidden territory. The door was open, and she caught the green glow of the monitor on his computer as she passed. He didn't come out when he spoke.

'Frances.'

They were like two girls before the head-teacher's study. Frances stifled Clare's giggles.

'See if the book's in the car.'

'What book?'

Frances gave her a shove as Geoffrey came out of his room. Clare ran out of the house and banged the door. Except for last night, she had never seen Geoffrey when he wasn't urbane and in charge of himself and others; even the embarrassed teenager, she now realised, was put-on, controlled. But now his face was wooden, his hands clenched. He seemed to speak with a tremendous effort.

'I'll come with you.'

She stared at him, bewildered. 'To school?'

'No no no! To Ireland.'

Although she had suggested it, she was appalled at the prospect. 'You can't!'

'I know I can't,' he said, 'but I'll cancel a couple of trips. Clare can go to your aunt's. And take that dog with her.' Then, stiff with an awful, genuine embarrassment he added, before plunging back into his study: 'We can have some time to ourselves. Call it a second honeymoon.'

3 *A Kiss for the Bride*

Is this the country we want to unite with? Kate always found the question in her head whenever she drove from Belfast to Dublin, through the small grey towns and flat landscape of the N1. In that morning's *Irish Times* there was a report of a doctor fined for supplying condoms to a patient one evening, when it was too late to take his prescription to the chemist.

'I did it to prevent an unwanted pregnancy,' the doctor said.

'There is another way of doing that,' the judge said. 'By not indulging in sex outside marriage.'

What was the point of throwing out the Brits to join a society suffocated by the Catholic Church and sucked dry by speculators? It was because she wanted to hit out against that society, as much as against British rule in the north, that she was on this road. On her way to Frank.

Well, it wasn't as simple as that. She had taken Frank over the border. He had tried to involve her in his crazy scheme but she had refused and returned to Belfast, determined to get a job, to teach. She had every expectation of landing a job at a school where the head-teacher had similar views to her, but between the application and the interview he was injured in a car accident. His deputy saw her. She didn't get the job.

Angry and bitter she had made enquiries about Frank. And then she had begun buying glossy society magazines like *Tatler*. A pile of them lay in the grip on the seat beside her.

The day was windy and the glimpses of the sea at Balbriggan — she took the longer coast road, for she liked the sea, and it gave her time to think — matched her mood.

She stopped at Skerries and scrambled over the rocks until the spray was hitting her face. A mist shut out the line between the sea and the sky, and she couldn't see St Patrick's Isle. Ireland was the most wonderful country in the world, she thought, when you were looking out to sea. She had been born in a small village not far from the Giant's Causeway, and had had this sound in her ears every day when she had walked to school. A voice inside her was telling her to go back. She shut it out. By the time she got back to the car, her coat was soaked with spray. She didn't mind. In Dublin she would be able to smell the salt.

The street was of red-brick Edwardian houses with flowered tiles in the porch. She pressed the bell marked Stephens and stood back so he could see her through the grimy net curtains.

He was overjoyed.

'Why didn't you tell me you were coming?'

'I didn't want to phone.'

But not for security reasons. Because she wanted to analyse her feelings, analyse him, catch him unawares. How a man lived was how he was. She took in his flat while he made a pot of tea and coffee for her. He never drank coffee.

The two rooms were furnished with job lots which landlords pick up at auctions. On the mantelpiece, grey with dust, was a card with clasped hands on the front and a heading: In Sincere Sympathy. The tea, sugar, milk and brown sauce were in a permanent arc on the table, bounding an area within which Frank evidently read the paper and had his meals.

'Who's died?'

'My wife.'

'I'm sorry.'

He burst out laughing. She stared at him.

'Your're swallowing my cover story.' He picked up the dusty card. 'This was left by the last tenant.'

She was annoyed at being taken in and drank her coffee in silence. Picking up her mood he sat quietly, smoking, watching her. He was no longer wearing a bandage. There was no sign of drink. That was unusual. And good. She wouldn't work with a drinker. He began to make small talk about Dublin. He disliked the south as much as she did.

He had discarded the black jacket and drainpipes, the macho clothes they all wore, and had on shapeless brown trousers and a check shirt he had probably bought at Dunne's. She was not unimpressed: the room and his outfit all added up to Catholic working-man on his own since his wife had died.

Only the meticulously trimmed moustache and the black nervous eyes that reacted to every sound in the house and street conflicted with this portrait, with the relaxed small talk which always made her feel uneasy, out of her depth, for she felt awkward chatting, and hated gossip.

She interrupted him in the middle of a sentence.

'If we did work together . . .'

He had draped her wet coat over a chair in front of a two-bar electric fire. It must have been its sea-weed-like smell that made her feel for an instant the spray stinging her face and hear the abrasive rasp of the gulls in her ears. He was staring at her oddly. It was the most important moment of her life and she had to force herself to concentrate.

'What would you do with the money?' she said.

By contrast he was very relaxed. His wrists dangled loosely.

'Supply arms. I have a contact who does container freight between France and Rosslare.'

The huge containers that were swung from ship to lorry were a nightmare for customs and police. Kate knew of two arms shipments that had got in that way.

He smiled and lit a fresh cigarette.

'What do you want? My career to date?'
'I know it.'
'You've checked me out?'
'Haven't you?'
Abruptly she opened the grip. For the first time she felt in control as he saw the glossy magazines and his eyes gaped.
'Porn?'
'I think it is.'
She opened the pages of Tatler at a report on the Royal Dublin Horse Show. Bemused, he read an account of a ball at which two officers of the Queen's Dragoon Guards threw baked alaska at one another and then solemnly waltzed across the floor. Frank dropped the magazine.
'And then they wonder why we throw bombs at them! What are you doing with these?'
'You're interested in the rich aren't you?'
She flicked over pages of society weddings, dinners and balls; pages of elegant clothes and flashbulb smiles. Now she spoke with assurance.
'These just give you leads. But they can give you an indication of who's rich, who's poor, where they live when they're in Ireland . . .'
Kate went on to show him the research she had done from following up these leads. After months without a job she had worked with enthusiam. It was amazing how cooperative Chambers of Commerce, Trade organizations and even Government bodies could be.
'I'm doing a thesis on foreign investment in Ireland and I wonder if . . .'
People who had never met her would chat freely on the phone.
'Oh yes he's certainly involved in the culture of the country — he has a house here.'
An estimate of the money people had could be made from company reports and newspaper speculations. She was astonished at the number of millionaires she uncovered.

Frank turned the pages of the loose-leaf file she handed him with undisguised admiration.

'I knew you were smart, Kate, I knew it! Jesus! There are more millionaires in Wicklow than there are pints of Guinness!'

He could not have told from her expression whether she was pleased or not. Her coat was dry and she brushed at it fussily for it was stiff with salt. She had enjoyed the research more than anything she had done for a long time.

'I'm going home,' Frances told Charles, the fifth earl, which was ridiculous, for she'd never lived at Kilnameath.

It was also ridiculous that she had bought this plum-coloured suit and matching bow-tie, and that she felt so excited, as if she really was going on honeymoon. Or was it the spell of that place?

As a child, her father had told her stories about it which became all mixed up with dragons and fairies. There had been a family book. She remembered phrases as she put on lipstick. Arthur Compton, under Cromwell 'acquired much merit by reducing the Irish to submit to the Government of the Commonwealth.' He served in the storming of Wexford in 1649 when Cromwell 'pased like lightning thru' Ireland.' For his services, he was granted lands in Wicklow where he built Kilnameath.

She pressed a tissue on her lips and glanced at the fifth earl. He had built the magnificient Georgian mansion that still stood there, 'ransacking Europe' as her father had told her when she was an open-mouthed little girl, to fill it with treasures. It was also filled with ghosts.

She shivered. Had he told her about a headless horseman, or was she making that up? A busy rural doctor, he had always seemed to have time to tell her stories. They had been very close. When he had died two years ago she had left Ireland, she thought for good.

On her way downstairs she could see Geoffrey in his study. She couldn't believe it. He was filling a despatch case with papers and computer disks, as if he was going on one of his usual business trips.

Since that morning when he had proposed the holiday he had been quiet and distant. They hadn't slept together. They discussed nothing. He was out by the time she got up, and often didn't get back until she had gone to bed.

She walked past Geoffrey's study. He was too absorbed in fussily making sure he packed the right disks to look up.

Well, that suited her. He could stay in the hotel room, which from what she had gathered was all he saw of any place he stayed. She would go to Kilnameath.

Outside the sun was bright and last night's wind had covered the drive with leaves. It was cold, but some people passing were still wearing T-shirts, as if they didn't want to believe the weather had changed.

Henry and Clare capered round her.

'You look terrific!'

At least she had managed to give Clare plenty of attention.

'Are you sure you'll be all right?'

'I'm not a baby, mother. You enjoy yourself. Where's your lover?'

Michael, the chauffeur, was loading the car. She glimpsed him hiding a grin.

'Saying goodbye to his computer?' Clare said.

She shrieked as Frances chased her round the car. Henry joined in, jumping up at them. Geoffrey came out. Frances stopped fooling about, and was immediately annoyed with herself for doing so. He *had* a sense of — well perhaps not fun but at least humour — why did he never show it when Clare was there? Henry was growling in the back of his throat.

'Sshh!'

Clare was standing to attention. She gave her a fierce warning look, and immediately Clare's body drooped sulkily and she trailed her feet through the leaves. Oh no! She didn't want to leave Clare like that!

Geoffrey put the despatch case in the boot and went to talk to Michael. On a sudden, angry impulse Frances snatched up the case and passed it to Clare, gesturing urgently towards the larch tree. Clare blinked at her, and then her eyes gleamed and her face brightened as she dropped the case behind the tree.

Everybody on the plane stared at Frances. Geoffrey felt proud and happy. Really, after what he called (but only to himself) the dog-fight evening, he had handled things rather well. He had kept cool and distant. Getting things done before the holiday had kept him busy. And he had planned things so he could work on essential projects in Dublin. What was the use of being in computers if you were tied to the office? He had virtually an office-full of files on the disks in his despatch case.

Except it wasn't on the carousel at arrivals. Only a forlorn cardboard box and an uncollected set of golf-clubs kept circling.

'Ah, if it's not at Cork it will be at Shannon,' the waiting porter said helpfully.

Ireland!

'After all, there's always me,' said Frances in the taxi.

She was quiet and concerned about it, where normally she would have been irritated at him making a fuss. He felt better, closer to her than at any moment since the dog-fight. In fact, she looked frightened — no, that was too strong a word — apprehensive, as she stared out of the car windows. Still, he was wary of touching her.

'Clare was born there.' She indicated the bulk of a large Hospital.

He glimpsed posters stuck near the General Post Office. *Remember the men of 1916.* A gaunt old woman in a black beret with the orange green and white tricolour twisted round a crucifix was arguing with three young men.

'What's going on?'

She shook her head.

'Will you try to like it?'

Huddled in his corner, he nodded. Ireland always seemed to him more a foreign country than France or Germany. The cab went over the Liffey, and drew up at the Shelbourne on St Stephen's Green.

'There are two telephones in the suite?' he asked the receptionist, as he filled in the card she gave him.

'Yes sir.'

'I shall want one to be a computer link to London.'

The receptionist had the blank face of a doll. He slid the card across the counter.

'Ask the manager to see me when it's convenient.'

He felt very pleased with himself. He hated inefficiency and normally he would still be angry about the case. But he had thought ahead. He beamed at his wife.

'I have duplicates of all the disks, of course. I can hire a Carr micro-three, dial London and copy a fresh set of disks in minutes. That's the beauty of computers!'

'How wonderful,' she smiled.

He had been meaning to work before lunch — there were some sales forecasts he must check — but perhaps they should have a drink. It took him a few moments to realise what Frances was saying to the receptionist.

'You haven't given me a card. I'm Mr Carr's secretary.'

'I'm sorry, madam, I thought Mrs Carr was coming.'

'So did I.'

Frances began filling in a card with her huge sprawling writing. A porter took their bags to the lifts. Geoffrey was first bewildered then angry.

'I thought you'd be pleased!' he exploded.

'Pleased?'

'How I've handled the situation. Not letting it spoil our day.'

He collided with the porter who was assembling the bags in the lift. The man had a face as blank as the receptionist's as he studied the numbers on the way up, while they carried on a violent, hissed conversation.

'How long are you going to keep this nonsense up?'

'As long as you are.'

He lost his temper completely.

'For God's sake! I am managing director of a major company in a major industry and I must do *some* work! A few hours in the morning —'

The lift stopped and they got out. It was appalling! Her eyes were blazing. Another dog-fight and in public! And what was he doing, responding like a child in a playground!

'We are on our second honeymoon!' she said.

'We've had one honeymoon.'

'We've had this one too.'

As if nothing had happened, the porter picked up the cases Frances indicated. 'You're this way, madam. I shan't keep you a moment, sir.'

When she was half-way down the corridor she turned and said: 'Your missing case is behind the larch tree in the front garden.'

Frances hired a car and took the familiar road south through Bray and into Wicklow. She felt she was behaving like a stupid teenager but what the hell! She could now see that Clare had been reacting for her. Now her daughter wasn't here she could really let herself go.

Let him stew! If all she was was a business decoration then she would stick to that brief. Turn up at his bloody functions. When she felt like it. Bed was out. She'd find somebody else for that. There was never any shortage of contenders. The only trouble was Clare; she was such a bossy, moral, yes an extraordinarily moral little bitch.

Her thoughts boiled over as she turned off at Enniskerry and put her foot down. She hadn't had such a good rage, such a vindictive hate-session for months. Since she had married that berk, to be precise. To think that she had been planning to leave him, let him off the hook! She must be mad! She would take him for all she could get.

Was that why she had been buying jewellrey? He could scarcely take that back. Well, knowing Geoffrey, he could. As the mountains rose on her right, her spirits rose with them. Up there was Sally Gap, nothing but thin winding roads, streams that were dried up in summer and rushing little torrents in winter, where she used to ride with her first husband, Michael.

What a contrast! All of a sudden she felt his thin, bony cheeks between her fingers and tears sprang to her eyes. She had to stop the car and walk. She had a craving for a cigarette. She hadn't smoked for years. Not since that night, or soon afterwards. Everything had stopped the night that Michael died. She stopped at Roundwood and bought a packet. She couldn't stand the taste and had to put it out after a few puffs. The acrid smell of the black, pulped cigarette brought the night back. There had been a fancy dress party at Kilnameath, and Michael had been dressed as Charles, the fifth earl. She saw him lounging, a smile on his thin cheeks, anachronistically smoking a cigarette.

Now she drove so slowly that a lorry hooted and people glanced at her impatiently as they passed her. In a way she was putting all this on, wallowing in her feelings, but wasn't that understandable, after the last few months?

In Laragh someone shouted and she kept on driving as if she hadn't heard but in the mirror she glimpsed a familiar white head: Joe, the barman at the Grand Hotel, Ballyglen.

All this way and she wanted to see no-one. Nor would she. Except Margaret, her sister, she would have to see her.

Watch, Margaret's dog, was blind and smelt of rotten

apples. Frances knelt, rubbing the hard top of his head.

'Ah you stupid old thing stop barking! Don't you recognize me?'

There was some kind of canker in the animal's ear; like the farm it seemed to be decaying as she watched. She heard the tread of Margaret's wellies but didn't look up until her sister was standing over her. She wore an enormous baggy sweater covering her hips and her large hands were white with flour.

Frances got up awkwardly, always nervous when meeting her elder sister after a long gap, and irritated with herself for being so.

'Why didn't you tell me you were coming?'

'I didn't know I'd be welcome.'

'Jesus Frances, don't be stupid!'

Margaret hugged her. She smelt faintly of the dog and fresh baking and the spontaneous warmth of her welcome brought a lump to Frances's throat.

The kitchen was so hot Frances immediately began to sweat. On the huge table, scrubbed bone-white, were batches of bread and scones, just turned out.

'Oh . . . can I just smell them?'

'You can even eat one if you like.'

Why did her sister's tone always imply she was putting on an act when her reaction, now at least, was perfectly genuine? It always drove her to actually putting on the act: little sister returning from London, uttering false longings for the simple life.

'If only I could live here again!' Frances sighed.

There. She'd already started.

'You wouldn't last a week.' Margaret filled a kettle. 'Or do you want something stronger?'

'No. I don't drink much now.'

'Do you not,' Margaret said evenly.

In silence she took bone china cups, her best, from the dresser, where stood a row of family photographs, including one of Michael riding. She might have taken that down, Frances thought bitterly. Margaret passed her butter.

'Was it a nice wedding?'

'I'm sorry you weren't invited. No-one was. It was such a rush . . . such a . . .'

'A sudden romance.'

Frances felt the blood rising in her cheeks. All right! If she wanted her to play the wild unpredictable little sister, she would, she would!

'My heart stood still, that sort of thing, yes.'

She knifed up an enormous hunk of butter. Margaret was always going on at her children for taking more butter than they needed.

'Where is he?'

'Oh . . .' She watched the butter melting in the still warm scone. 'We've separated.'

Margaret almost dropped one of her precious bone-china cups.

'Jesus Frances, I can't do with you! You're joking!'

The scone was perfect, as always. A trickle of butter ran down her chin as she chewed with malicious enjoyment. She indicated the picture on the dresser, her words coming through the crumbs.

'Well, I married Michael for love. So this time I thought I'd try money.'

'It sounds as though you've made an even greater mess of it.'

Frances swallowed before replying, and now her voice was flat and hard.

'It was not a mess. And as far as the present situation is concerned, I don't stay with someone I can't stand.'

'Nonsense.'

'It's not nonsense! You can't stand him!'

'Him' was Robert, who was more often to be found in Leeson's Bar, discussing why farming was unprofitable than on the farm. Frances licked the butter from the corners of her mouth and looked at the crumbs on her plate.

'That's beautiful. That's home.'

Margaret put her elbows on the table, which was

scored with hundreds of knife-marks. Her voice was slow and tired. 'Home? It's a scone. You should try making some!'

Frances burst out laughing and stretched out her hands across the table. Margaret gripped them tightly.

'Ah, in five minutes we can drive each other up the wall, but it's grand to see you!'

They relaxed and drank the tea and gossiped until Margaret went over to a fat blue jug on the dresser and pulled out a bunch of keys, each with a crumpled brown label attached.

'Kilnameath. I keep a set for the agents.'

Frances stared at them, her face rigid. Although she'd taken off her coat and blouse, it was stifling, and a trickle of sweat ran down her back.

'Well, that's what you came for, isn't it?'

The road began to climb. It was more heath than parkland. Now the wooded bit. She had the curious feeling that the place would not be there; her father had told her so many stories about it, and so much had happened to her there that it often seemed to be a product of imagination rather than reality.

Now the abrupt patch of gloom where the trees bent over the bridge crossing the stream.

Now the planks creaking under the car's weight.

Now the rooks' tree, round which they always seemed to be wheeling and calling.

Now the great wall of rhododendrons, red blooms browned and rotting, blown into drifts at the side of the gravel drive.

Now.

With a mixture of fear and joy, she saw it. The great sweep of the terraces affected her like music. The lines could have been put down only in an age of great certainty and arrogance; an arrogance which also led to the family's downfall when Arthur, the sixth earl, whose lack of sympathy to the labourers in the famine years led one member of the United Irishmen to say 'he is as elegant as he is much hated' and another to shoot him.

The vision was deceptive. Only when she got closer did she see the crumbling stonework, smashed windows, the brown and green lichen spreading up the pillars of the porch. A fire had blackened the steps, and beer and wine bottles were littered about.

She leaned against a pillar in despair. When she had last been here two years ago it had been neglected but lived in; now it was rapidly becoming a ruin.

She found the front door key. Miraculously, the Georgian fanlight was unbroken. In the hall, the dust she kicked up made her nose prick. There was a sound from one of the rooms. She froze. She was stupid to come here alone. To this place. She pinched her nostrils as she had a sudden desire to sneeze, but only succeeded in making the explosion more violent when it came. She cried out when a cat shot from the room, veered away from her and leapt through a broken window.

She laughed and told herself not to be stupid, but on her way upstairs her jumpiness returned. She stuck close to the wall as notices said: CAUTION! BANISTERS UNSAFE. From an upstairs bedroom, where draughts billowed the paper coming away from the wall, she could see the copse where Michael had ridden that night.

The light was beginning to go. The paper flapped. She was suddenly calm. If there were such things as ghosts, they should certainly appear now. She grinned as she momentarily visualised a motley collection of nuns, horsemen and earls coming across the park.

She lit a cigarette. Now, oddly, for no reason, it tasted all right. She wandered through the house, leaving the big room downstairs until last, afraid of the state it would be in. She pushed open the double doors and caught her breath.

Even neglected it was a magnificent room, as big as a small ballroom. It was said that Adam himself had never created a better ceiling; in his style, it was decorated with acanthus, griffins and winged sphinxes, and what must have been a brilliant blue had faded to a delicate egg-shell shade.

She clasped her hands in delight, walking in a dream round the wall, touching remembered furniture as if it was still there.

Then she heard the hooves. At first she though they were part of her fantasy, but they grew louder as though the horse was going to jump through the shattered windows into the house.

She started to walk from the room, then hurried, then ran across the hall to a door at the back of the house. It was locked. Where were the keys?

Someone was calling her name. It wasn't Michael, don't be stupid, she sobbed to herself, Michael is dead, Michael is dead.

The door was opening.

In a blind panic she ran up the stairs, leaping up, grabbing the banisters. They slewed outwards. She screamed, held on for a moment and fell on whoever or whatever it was. She scrambled up, turning, ready to run, to see the dazed face of Geoffrey staring at her. Sobbing, she buried her face into his familiar, everyday shoulder.

'Frances! What's wrong? What is it?'

'That wasn't you?'

'What?'

'The horse.'

'Don't be ridiculous.'

'I heard a horse.'

'Of course you heard a horse. There is a horse. Bloody maniac cut right across my taxi.'

'That would be me.'

Frances walked unsteadily towards the open door as the speaker came up the steps. Yes, of course, it would be Andrew, grinning all over his face as usual, sweeping off his peaked cap. Tethered behind him was a wiry brown horse with an odd white blaze on its forehead; bred from the same stock, it might have been the horse Michael rode that night.

'Joe saw you in Laragh and I knew where you were heading.'

She put a hand on a pillar to steady herself. Geoffrey emerged from the gloom of the hall, dusting his suit.

'Andrew Paget. My husband.'

She had never actually seen anyone's jaw drop before. Andrew took a full second to recover — a long time for him. He slapped his dirty brown cords and the huge grin came back.

'Well would you credit that now! Beaten again to the first prize!'

Geoffrey could not recall the last day when he had done no work whatsoever. He had not even called the office! Now here he was in — where was it? — the Grand Hotel Ballyglen, with Frances hunched up in a high-backed chair staring at the flames of a log fire.

He had had to go after her — God knows what would have happened to her — it was the same kind of madness she had had that night in the kitchen.

Now he felt guilty at spending a wasted pointless day. Some musicians had arrived to play what was advertised as Genuine Irish Music. There was some kind of a drum, an accordion and a fiddle. Andrew was having a heated argument with the fiddle player. Geoffrey indicated him.

'Who is he?'

'He used to ride with us. Michael and me.'

She didn't move, or look from the fire.

'When did you live at the house?'

'I've never lived there! You don't listen.'

She snarled at him. Her hair was tangled and her clothes still dusty. He felt his cheeks flush: nobody ever talked to him like that.

'You never tell a straight story,' he retorted.

'There are no straight stories in Ireland.'

Andrew had come up. He must have been Frances's age. He wore a green quilted waistcoat and the peaked cap, which seemed a permanent feature, was slipping from the back of his head. He bent deferentially over Frances's glass.

'Was that a Jameson in there?'

'Bushmills.'

'Black Bush, it's the sight of you that destroys my memory! Kiss for the bride.'

She raised her face and he kissed her with enthusiasm on the cheek. She pulled away.

'You smell of horses.'

'You used to like them.'

'Get my drink Andrew will you.'

'Verrr . . . moot, Geoffrey?'

'I'm driving.'

'I am driving,' Frances said.

She could make him livid with rage and then, as now, hunched up, staring at the fire again, switch him to concern. A log crackled and flared. The firelight hollowed her cheeks. He remembered her clinging to him in the house. He felt awkward and ill-at-ease, as if he was trying to open a conversation with someone he'd never met before.

'Crooked or straight . . .' he began.

'What?'

'The story. Tell me it.'

At first she didn't move and talked in a monotone.

'Michael and I had our stables near Kilnameath. It was owned by a judge, a great character. We used to go there for parties. We practically lived there. Like we did as children.'

She poked the fire with a fresh log and dropped it on, sparks shooting up the chimney. She spoke so softly he had to bend over to listen.

'It was a great dream we had that one day we would buy Kilnameath.'

There were groans and shouts of laughter from the bar, where Andrew had picked up the fiddle and was attempting to play it. Frances looked towards him.

'The three of us . . .'

She stopped. She was clenching the arm of her chair.

'If it upsets you . . .'

'Of course it upsets me!' she blazed.

For a moment he was angry again.

'I should be in Tokyo.'

Not in Ireland, where, in his experience, people promised everything and delivered half of it too late if you were lucky, not in the Grand Hotel Ballyglen where the accordion was striking up under the tasselated lampshades, burnt where the bulbs had touched them.

Then she spoke as if she was talking to herself.

'There was just moon enough to see. We were drunk. The three of us went riding, riding, riding. Over the bridge. Towards the copse, the copse on top of the hill. There's a high hedge. He would go over it. He was thrown and broke his neck.'

She clasped her hands round her knees and rocked herself slowly, gently. There was more laughter from the bar, drowning the accordion. She turned to him, eyes dark with pain, swallowing, lips moving as if she was preparing to say something more.

Then, so abruptly she made him jump she shouted: 'Paget! are you bringing that bloody drink?'

They were shouting for the glasses when Frances came out of the Ladies. She stood in the shadow of a curtain and watched Andrew drinking with Geoffrey, just as he had drunk with Michael. It was a bizarre feeling, added to which she had never seen Geoffrey drunk before.

Andrew's Ver. . . moot, which he described as a closely-guarded family recipe, was famous for miles around the Grand Hotel Ballyglen. She was surprised Geoffrey was still on his feet, let alone talking in his familiar relentless fashion to Andrew and another farmer Tom.

'Hello darling,' he said, waving his calculator, that

bloody calculator that was always in his inside pocket. She blinked at him. The other two, drinks untouched, were gazing at figures and graphs scribbled on note-paper torn from the pad Geoffrey always kept in his other inside pocket.

'Course of action,' said Geoffrey to the two men. 'Lease out the land for grazing until you accumulate enough capital to restock your cows. Here's the results for differing areas of leasing and interest rates.'

He was so enthusiastic and eager that for an instant Frances felt a fond pride, as if he was a son who had done particularly well at school.

Andrew gazed at the hieroglyphics in awe. 'Blessed angel of mercy. And you've never farmed?'

'We've done software for farmers.' Geoffrey picked up Andrew's drink. 'You know what Lord Kelvin said.'

'Ah no, now, I can't say I recall that.'

'When you can describe a thing in figures, you know something about it.'

'Is that a fact.'

Tom quickly picked up his drink as Geoffrey finished Andrew's.

'Everything is figures.'

'The man's right there, Tom.'

'Dead on,' agreed Tom.

Frances was holding Geoffrey's coat. Andrew put his arm round her. 'Your man here's right Frances! Everything is figures!'

Outside in the car park his drunkenness and a thin, cold drizzle rapidly made her sober. When he stumbled, she caught his arm.

'Sorry . . .'

'The car's this way.'

As she took his arm again he pulled away and mumbled: 'Mustn't touch you . . . mustn't touch you.'

She held open the car door. He stood there, rain gleaming on his face, suddenly stiff and formal.

'I'm afraid I'm in no condition to drive.'

'That's all right,' she said, catching some of his formality.

He'd never let her drive him before. He fumbled for the unfamiliar seat belt.

'The vermouth is rather strong here.'

She couldn't tell from his expression whether he was joking or not.

'Are you sure you'll be all right?'

'I know the road well,' she said.

Too well. She stared across the car park where people were shouting goodbye. What got into her, had driven her here in spite of all her foreboding? There seemed two different people in her, one who had come here, the other who had married Geoffrey.

He was still fumbling doggedly with the seat belt. He would never give up, never ask for help, not even with the smallest thing. She did it.

'Thank you.'

His voice really was slurred now. She started the car and then turned back to him.

'Thank you for coming for me.'

'Oh well . . . thought . . . I thought, on a honeymoon people are usually together.'

She laughed and kissed him.

'I thought you couldn't bear to touch me.'

'Sometimes I can. Sometimes I can't.'

He sat up, his face distorted, as if there was a tremendous struggle going on inside him. As he spoke, he felt automatically in his pockets to reassure himself that his calculator and note-pad were there.

'I . . . I'm not used to . . . I've never . . . I can't talk about what I feel.'

Her voice was soft, but she knew there was a glint in her eyes, a mocking glint exactly like that of Charles, the fifth earl.

'What do you feel?'

He couldn't speak. She took his face between her hands, like an offering.

'Come here. Open your mouth.'

Her tongue darted. He moaned, his hands reaching out for her, like those of a man falling, clutching for the only thing that can save him. A thunderous hammering on the car roof snapped them apart. Bobbing down in front of the rain-streaked windscreen appeared Andrew's grinning face, only the peaked cap, still at a precarious angle, preventing it from looking like a devil in a medieval painting.

'A kiss for the bride!' he shouted, and leapt off, vanishing into the darkness.

She drove quickly back towards Dublin, not because there was any hurry, but because it stopped her thinking. At first he gripped the side of his seat but eventually he relaxed and she thought he was asleep.

It was not until they were through Roundwood, passing the reservoir, that he spoke.

'Do you want it?'

She dipped her lights as a car approached. 'Mmmm?'

'Kilnameath.'

4 *It Will Wear Off*

Daly, the auctioneer of Kevin Mahon and Partners had done well: there was a traffic jam in Ballyglen. It was always difficult to decide whether to sell a property like Kilnameath in Dublin, on site or in a nearby hotel.

He'd plumped for the Grand Hotel Ballyglen, and he reckoned he'd backed a winner. There would only be three or four serious bidders. The art was in building up an atmosphere, an audience. The hotel was full of farmers who'd come in to drink, gossip, and find out how much the land would fetch.

Other people had been drawn to the village hotel.

Frank sat in an old Cortina and watched people arriving. He had been drawn by a paragraph in the *Evening Herald* which said 'computer millionaire's wife here to bid for ancestral home.'

The report went on: 'Mrs Carr laughed at the suggestion, which she called bizarre. "It's far too ancestral for me," she said.'

Frank was despondent. He was in his element when things were happening. He could not stand the apparent inactivity of planning. Hadn't his big scheme been practically taken over by Kate, who was still in Belfast, while he did the leg work down here?

She said it would take at least a year to find the target, plan, and then find the resources the plan demanded. She talked like a television documentary.

Meanwhile what did he live on? Kate had given him a little. With Ronan, who was sitting beside him now, he had stolen this Cortina, against Kate's instructions.

Her instructions! Who did she think she was?

Ronan, who was twenty, wanted action too. Willy, who had driven Frank from Derry to Belfast, would be the fourth member of the unit — if there ever was one. He and Ronan found themselves drifting from the paramilitaries and ex-paras in Dublin to the crime scene. However moralistic Kate might get, they would have to do a post office. He'd already staked one out, in Dun Laoghaire.

Geoffrey was in his element. In the lounge of the Grand Hotel, at the very table where he had calculated Andrew's farming future, he pored over a survey of Kilnameath with Costello, a Jewish solicitor with greased hair and wire-framed spectacles. Costello passed over a sheaf of Polaroid photographs.

'That man would find you a worm in a mansion, Mr Carr.'

Geoffrey turned pages quickly, his face expressionless. He looked at Frances who was crouched by the unlit fire, piled with logs for the evening.

'I would have to weigh it against the investment it would replace,' he said.

Her legs were crossed awkwardly. Her grey trousers were splashed with mud: that morning she'd been riding at Kilnameath.

'Oh darling! I know! It's a crazy idea!'

'Not crazy,' he corrected her. 'If we can sell that land —'

She combed her hair away from her face with her fingers and leaned forward in excitement, upsetting the photographs.

'You're not *really* thinking of buying it!' she said.

He couldn't help being sharp with her. She was a liability at something like this. There was that silly interview she'd given to the newspaper!

'Don't get excited! Don't let people see you want it!'

'Sorry. Sorry.'

'Now who's going to be bidding?' Geoffrey asked Costello.

Frances wandered through the crowded bar not so much in a dream, as in a dream that might come true; a dream she had with one husband which might come true with a second.

She was bewildered, smiling mechanically at people who welcomed her back, as if she had bought the place already. She passed near a group round O'Leary, the farmer who owned the land adjoining Kilnameath, whom Costello had said was sure to bid.

He was about seventy, with a huge callous on his right thumb where he was constantly flicking at the wheel of his old metal lighter as he lit and relit his pipe. He sucked, flicked and laughed.

'Not me Sean! Who has the loose cash these days? In the fifties three acres of potatoes bought you a tractor — now you're lucky if it buys you the back wheels!'

So he was out. Perhaps she should tell Geoffrey. On her way to him she saw Margaret.

'Come and meet my husband,'

'Oh Frances, I can't keep up with you. Let me do my face. Here.'

Always embarrassed at giving gifts, Margaret shoved the envelope at her sister, saying before she went: 'When they sold the contents, they found it in a cupboard. I kept it for you.'

It was a faded blue booklet, the cover woolly with age. She read: CHRISTIES. Sale of Silver, Porcelain, Paintings and Fine Furniture, Being the Contents of Kilnameath. September 20th, 1883, at Kilnameath.

She turned the pages. There were line drawings and prices marked in the margins in brown ink. Pair of George II giltwood sidetables . . . Chandelier, Waterford glass . . . Three pillar Sheraton dining table in mahogany . . .

The book was knocked from her hand by the swirl of people going into the auction. She cried out as it fell in

front of approaching boots. A hand rescued it.
'Thank you.'
'You're welcome.'
She fleetingly noted the man because he was young among the mainly middle-aged and old audience, and because his accent wasn't local, but from one of the northern counties, perhaps even from the north. Then she forgot all about him.

As Daly commenced the auction a man with a rolled umbrella squeezed into the back row.
'Can't place him,' muttered Costello to Geoffrey.
'Now ladies and gentlemen,' Daly said, 'Kilnameath is a 192 acre 4 roods and 2 perches property, land registry number . . .'
He asked the audience for £300,000 and not a muscle moved until he patiently got down to £100,000.
'Thank you Mr Wainwright.'
A man with red-veined cheeks holding the hand of a blond woman in a tight, electric-blue dress.
'Impressing his dolly bird,' whispered Costello. 'He'll not stay.'
Geoffrey loved auctions, bridge and poker. He had given up the card games as too frivolous, but he had bought all the modern paintings at Apex Road at auctions in London and New York. He was oblivious to Frances beside him and, under a casual, apparently bored exterior, registered every nuance, every hesitation of the bidders.
There were only two, Wainwright and a solicitor, McCarthy, acting for a German — Costello had told him that rich Germans, Dutch and Swiss were increasingly buying Irish properties because they would be outside the European fall-out area if the bomb dropped. It seemed that O'Leary was not bidding as his solicitor was not there.
Daly looked at his audience and shook his head reproachfully.
'We're at 180,000 to Mr McCarthy, let me remind

you that it's a piece of history we're selling here, with one of the finest landscaped parks in County Wicklow. Just in case,' he added, making the possibility seem remote, 'you're not interested in any of that, thrown in with it is 80% — 155 acres — of prime agricultural land.'

The audience laughed and warmed to him.

'I'm going to ask you for £200,000 Mr Wainwright.'

Wainwright shook his head. Geoffrey glanced at Costello, who raised his prospectus.

'Thank you Mr Costello . . . 220 . . . 240 . . . 260 . . .'

Geoffrey smiled inwardly. It was like runners pacing one another. It was often not the amount, but the actual number of bids a man had made that determined whether he stayed or not. McCarthy and his German client were finished. It was going to be his for 260. A good buy. A very good buy indeed.

'260,000 to Mr Costello . . . 270,000, gentleman over there.'

Daly was pointing to the man with the rolled umbrella. Geoffrey could see him only as a blur out of the corner of his eye. Other people turned, chairs scraping.

'275 . . . 280 . . . 285 . . . 290 . . . will you give me 295 Mr Costello?'

Costello looked at Geoffrey who remained still. Daly pointed to the man with the rolled umbrella.

'290,000 over there . . . I will call it three times . . .'

'Geoffrey!'

Frances was gripping his arm, actually shaking him! If anything more was needed to stop him bidding, that was it.

'290,000 twice . . . 290,000!'

The hammer came down, there was an enormous sigh, and everyone began talking at once. O'Leary got up from what had seemed to be his afternoon nap and shook hands with the man with the rolled umbrella.

'Would you look at the old divil!' Costello exploded. 'He got a different solicitor. From Dublin. I know the face now.'

Frank looked at O'Leary's seamed face and threw

away a newspaper. It was the *Evening Herald* which contained Frances's interview and photograph.

'Come on,' he said to Ronan, 'let's go to Dun Laoghaire.'

'Dun Laoghaire?'

'I need to buy some stamps.'

Everybody in the room was standing chatting except Frances. Geoffrey touched her on the shoulder. He had to bend to hear what she was saying.

'Could you have bought it?'

'Of course I could have bought it,' he smiled. 'But it's not worth it at that price.'

'Except to him.' Costello indicated O'Leary.

'Didn't you think it might be worth it to me?'

Frances was standing now, shaking her hair back from her blazing eyes. People going out from the room to the bar stopped to look at them.

'I didn't realise you'd be this upset.'

'You didn't!' Her voice was incredulous.

'Why didn't you tell me?'

'I did, you know I —'

'You said it was a crazy idea.'

'That was just . . . just . . .'

She stopped, confused, unable to speak. He took her hand, but she pulled it violently away.

'Oh, you shouldn't have said you'd buy me it, that's all! I'd no idea you could! Just like that!'

He only ever lost his temper with her.

'I told you! I have to look at these things as an investment!'

'Investment!'

She spat the word out and a woman in a baggy sweater stopped, realised it was too late to turn away, and gave them a nervous smile.

'My sister Margaret. Geoffrey. Margaret has invited us to tea.'

'I must phone London first.'

'That will take an hour. I'll see you at the hotel.'

She walked away. Margaret looked at him helplessly. 'Well. Nice to meet you.'

He had to stop himself from shouting after them. She was immature, unpredictable, selfish — he had never hated, yes hated, anyone so much in all his life. She had left something on her seat — not surprising! She was always leaving things and losing things.

He picked up the blue catalogue and turned the pages. Pieter Syners, picture, fox attacking poultry . . . Apple Green four poster by Angelica Kaufmann hung with . . .

He stared at the drawings, the crabbed brown writing in the margins. Wasn't he so used to being his own master that he found it difficult to see anyone else's point of view? She was all those things he had called her, but on the other hand, what was he?

For a whole week he'd done no work. They'd been round the quays in Dublin, in the mountains, at Kilnameath. One mad day she and Andrew had even persuaded him to sit on a horse. He had the photograph to prove it . . . not that he would ever dream of showing it to anyone!

He turned the pages of the catalogue again, going over their conversations about the house. From feeling unquestioningly that he'd done the right thing, he began to have the icy fear that he had not only done something wrong, but something irreparable.

A tiny snapping noise broke into his thoughts. He looked up to see that the room was almost empty. One of the people left was O'Leary, and the noise came from him lighting his pipe. As Geoffrey stared across the skewed rows of chairs at him, O'Leary puffed smoke and smiled the slightest of enquiring smiles.

From his office window Geoffrey could see St Pauls and glimpse Tower Bridge. Ireland and what had happened there seemed a long way away. He was at his own desk with the micro-computer he had designed built into it. On the wall was a map of the world dotted with the Carr Micro logo, where he had companies or agencies.

'How much did this O'Leary take you for?' Richard Lefray asked.

Geoffrey winced at the phrase. 'I don't want this getting about.'

'Of course not.'

Lefray's bland exterior concealed a sharp financial brain which enabled him to put venture capital into risky projects which the bigger City groups wouldn't look at. Some failed but the profits of the successes more than compensated for them. His real name was Brown. At school he had added an 'e' on the end, but had metamorphosised in the City as Lefray, on the principle that people had an unconscious faith in financial houses with Jewish-Continental names, like Lazards, Kleinworts and Rothschilds. Browns did not have the same kind of ring.

Geoffrey had been his biggest success, and their long friendship was all the closer for being based on mutual distrust.

Geoffrey stared at the map, his empire. It was unbelievable.

'Three hundred thousand.'

Lefray's lips pursed minutely.

'I got the house, Kilnameath, and he got the farmland he wanted. For nothing! I still wake up sweating about it! A *farmer*! An *Irish* farmer!'

'Does he need a merchant banker?'

It was said with sympathetic flippancy, but it would probably end up being a serious question, Geoffrey thought sourly. He picked up his coffee, and spilt it.

'What the hell is happening to me!'

Lefray's tone remained flippant. 'Well. It is unusual.'

'What?'

'To be in love with one's own wife.'

'Don't be bloody silly!'

Lefray flushed, smiled uneasily, and tapped the file he was carrying on the knife-edge crease of his trousers. Geoffrey walked to the window, staring down at the familiar streets. Neither of them really knew how to handle this conversation. In all the years they had known one another, had they really only talked about these streets, money, people going up and coming down?

'It'll wear off,' Lefray said.

'Will it?'

Now Lefray became as awkward as Geoffrey. They glanced away from each other, fiddling with things, a paper-clip, a tea-spoon. It was odd, pathetic, Geoffrey thought, that they could deal with millions of pounds with assurance, but flounder in the face of this tiny emotional problem.

Lefray fashioned the paper-clip into a hook.

'Well, I mean . . . you must have been . . . this sort of thing must have happened to you before.'

'I suppose so. When I was sixteen.'

'Is Frances back?'

'No. Still over there. She's just found the original chandelier.' He opened a folder and stared into space. 'Me. An Irish landowner!'

Lefray abruptly burst out laughing and couldn't stop. Geoffrey looked aggrieved, then grinned.

'It's not that bloody funny.'

He opened the folder and their uneasiness evaporated as they moved on to the familiar ground of legal documents. The first page was headed: An Agreement between Carr Computers PLC and Lefray Eagle Holdings. Geoffrey picked up a pen.

'It's cost me three per cent of my shareholding.'

Richard's eyes were focussed on the nib of Geoffrey's pen.

'You can afford it. This only brings me up to twenty-nine per cent. You're still by far the biggest shareholder.'

Looking as if he was having a tooth extracted, Geoffrey signed.

5 The Irish Folly

John Lansbury, public relations director of Carr Computers, gazed round in amazement and pique at the mass of people filling the great room at Kilnameath, eating boar's head under the glittering chandelier and restored, bright blue Adam ceiling.

'So this is where Geoffrey spends his week-ends,' he said to Richard Lefray.

If Lefray believed he had created Geoffrey financially, Lansbury believed he had created Geoffrey.

Over ten years of press stories, drinks and junkets, Lansbury had assiduously built up the idea that Geoffrey was a unique combination of innovator and developer. When Geoffrey discussed the state of British industry on television, his off-the-cuff remarks were carefully scripted by Lansbury.

Now here he was, in a role someone else had scripted for him, a country landlord entertaining the county, for God's sake! The first shock came when they had arrived, and Geoffrey had actually met them on horseback!

Lefray covered his face as Geoffrey tried to turn the horse and was nearly thrown.

'Nearly thirty pence off the share price,' Lansbury murmured.

Neither Lefray nor Alan Tyndall, the financial director of Carr Computers, had laughed.

They weren't laughing now as Geoffrey handed them drinks from a wine-cooler. He might have been one of those frightful-looking earls staring out from the walls with their long jaws and their arrogant eyes.

'What can another take-over do for us, John?' he said.

'Make money, master?' said Lansbury, innocently.

Now Tyndall and Lefray laughed, but apprehensively as Geoffrey's eyes burnt with, well it wasn't arrogance, but something worse — enthusiasm, a new hobby horse.

'I want to get back to ideas! Research! Tomorrow's products!'

'Such as?'

'How do I know? I want laboratories. A computer research centre. Here.'

The three stared at him, their glasses frozen on the way to their mouths.

'We'll walk over tomorrow. I'll show you the site.'

Tyndall was another man who thought himself largely responsible for Geoffrey's success. He had plodded behind him all his working career, keeping the books, not creating anything, but preventing the mistakes, the foolish ventures.

'How will this be financed?' he asked.

'Let me introduce you,' said Geoffrey.

As if responding to a cue, two Japanese had entered the room and were staring around, blinking in the bright lights.

There was always a wind at Kilnameath. It came in from the sea, smelling of salt. The heater in the Garda car had been reported, but still wasn't working properly.

Guarda O'Keefe got stiffer and stiffer with the cold. If he knew Inspector O'Hanlon he wouldn't be leaving the hooley until the early hours.

He rubbed his waxy white hands. Who was going to rob the place with all these people around? And didn't the Carrs have their own security man, Pat Shaw, an ex-policeman who doubled as chauffeur?

He picked up his flashlight and got out of the car. The

windows of the house were open and the din was terrific. Did they have a full orchestra in there? He took a nip from his flask. If O'Hanlon was drinking in the line of duty, why shouldn't he?

He wished he was tucked up with his new wife. She would be too tired when he got in. The bloody hours of this job — but what else was there? It was better than Tallaght, in the biscuit factory.

He walked round the back of the house. The wind was stripping clouds from the moon, and he could just about see without his torch. Here it was still neglected, and he picked his way over fallen masonry.

He shivered, and took another nip. He would get promotion, that was the answer, he would capture a wanted man and they would make him an inspector on the spot and send him to grand houses where he would drink with the nobs and eat boar's head.

'Can I introduce Inspector O'Keefe? He captured the most wanted —'

Something moved. Or was it the shadows, as the wind whipped the branches of a tree against the wall? Fear dried his mouth. He was near the kitchens, light coming from the partly-open door, but the movement had been near the tree.

For a moment he nearly succumbed to the urge to walk away and pretend he had seen nothing. Then, ashamed of himself, he crept forward. There was someone there, black against the blackness of the tree. His hands were shaking so much that when he switched on the torch he had to hold it in two hands, like a gun.

He almost laughed out loud. The one person was two: a man in a black anorak pressed against a girl who, from her apron, must be a maid from the kitchen.

On the way back to the car he finished his flask. The image in the flashlight had really turned him on. Tired or not, he would have his wife when he got in.

Andrew had seized a fiddle and played to Geoffrey and Frances who grabbed the bewildered Japanese and led them in a hokey-cokey round the room.

From the safety of a corner table, Lefray, Tyndall and Lansbury gazed at the scene.

'Katsushomo!' Tyndall exploded. 'What happens to our shares if the Japanese come in?'

'Research!' said Lefray. 'That could suck up millions.'

'He refuses to recognize he's no longer a scientist,' Tyndall said.

'Nor ever was,' said Lansbury sadly. 'The oldest hazard in the business. You create an image of someone, and he comes to believe in it.'

Kieran Malone wiped his hand over his mouth, still greasy with the maid's lipstick. That was the easiest, most enjoyable hundred pounds he had ever earned!

'I like your eyes.'

'Get on.'

'That's not the only thing I like.'

'Get on!'

'You should be running this place. You're more beautiful than she is.'

'Get on.'

If Norma's vocabulary was restricted, her hands and lips were not. His moans of pleasure had been genuine. It had been difficult to keep to the job in hand.

'I hear the chandelier took eight men . . .'

'That's nothing! You should see the silver . . .'

He would like to. But it wouldn't be him. He wasn't in that league. Yet. Your man was the thief, the stranger who was paying him the hundred for information. Fifty down, fifty when he delivered.

It had been throwing-out time in Mickey's Bar. He had been talking about the wonders of the house, from what Norma had told him. Tom, who had done a job with him once, had brought the man over.

'Can you keep your ears open and your mouth shut?'

There was something about the eyes of the man, the memory of which made him stop, suddenly afraid of the dark. The trees loomed round him and the wind carried the faint sound of music from the house.

'My friend needs to know their movements. When they're going out, when they're away. That's very important.'

He wanted a cigarette but it was too dangerous. There might be more guards around. He went over what he had said to Norma.

'Ah, I don't suppose they're ever there . . .'

'It's not true! They . . .'

He was safe enough! No-one would connect him. She was as thick as a ditch. He gazed back through the trees at the lighted house. So what if they lost a few pictures, some of their fine silver? The insurance would pay.

He slipped over the stream and cut through the wood to get back onto the Ballyglen road.

Streamers exploded and the dancers screamed and scrambled for them. Lansbury could see fragmented little pictures of the scene — bursts of movement and colour — reflected in the drops and pendants of the chandelier.

There was a word for places like this. It escaped him, nagged at him. Hadn't the word been coined, in fact, at around the same time as the house had been built?

He found it, and a smile of pleasure crossed his face. Words were his job, and finding the right name for any problem was the beginning of dealing with it.

'Folly,' he said.

Lefray and Tyndall looked up from their whispered conversation. Lansbury joined them.

'The Irish Folly.'

Geoffrey packed one small case, and didn't put much in that.

'Aren't you taking the other case?'

'No. I'll be back on Friday.'

'Oh. Will you? Good.'

Frances turned away and sat down on the bed, where

she was writing a shopping list. That was all she said: 'good'. He read a tremendous amount, probably a foolish amount, into even a single word she said.

Was she, like him, afraid to express her feelings, afraid that their happiness might break?

Happiness!

The word came surprisingly, independently, into his head. He looked out of the window, up towards the wooded copse. They had ridden off the party up there. Well, he hadn't ridden. Gone at a sedate walk, more like. Even so his back was still stiff.

'It is the nine-ten plane you're getting?'

'Yes.'

He watched her write, combing her hair back from her face with her fingers.

'Could you remind me? I must collect Clare's asthma stuff from the chemist after we've seen you off.'

Her voice was so abstracted, casual, that a chill ran through him. Did she really care whether he went or stayed?

'It'll wear off,' Lefray had said.

Ironic that his feelings had grown stronger whereas . . . He'd bought this place, that's why she'd been so nice to him, simply that, that was their relationship, it was their agreement . . . was that only a year ago? . . . he mustn't put more into it than that.

'Damn!'

'What?'

She was holding the pill dispenser which she'd taken from the bedside drawer.

'I'm getting awfully scatty about the pill.'

She threw the dispenser back in the drawer, among a jumble of make-up and tissues.

'Oh well. It doesn't matter.'

'Doesn't it?' he said.

She turned to look at him. He might as well look in the sea as in those eyes, but the words hung in the air between them.

'Does it?'

That was all. The happiness, why shouldn't he use the word, it had always seemed such a silly sentimental word, but why shouldn't he use it, it was the only word, the happiness was so unbearable he had to leave the room.

At the airport he kissed Frances and Clare with all his old awkwardness and formality but it was the glow of that moment between them which he carried on to the plane.

Until she threw the pill dispenser into the drawer Frances did not know she wanted a son by Geoffrey.

Wanted, or was going to have? It was a premonition, rather than a desire. She huddled in a corner of the Mercedes as Pat drove her and Clare through Dublin on their way home.

Premonition implied that she would just let it happen, but that wasn't really true. Her attitude to Geoffrey had changed completely. She might not love him, but she respected him enormously. With all his achievements, of which she was proud, there was something stunted inside him, a seed that had never grown, that was beginning to emerge into the light.

It was the shy, kind, gentle, feeling part of himself.

She had discovered that his business had become a treadmill, that he looked nostalgically back to the beginning, when he had invented and designed the product, instead of marketing and financing it.

Or was that her description which she was selling to him? It didn't matter. One night after making love she struggled to put it into words. To her own surprise, she found herself complaining not about what his work did to her, but what it did to him.

The floodgates opened. He talked endlessly about his early difficulties, of the vulnerability of beginnings. The next day he thought of a research centre at Kilnameath.

They were leaving Bray and climbing up into the hills. She always went this longer route, never on the main road. The dog was barking as Clare rooted through the parcels, looking for sweets.

'Where's the chocs?'

'Don't give the dog any more,' she said mechanically.

It was so hot her eyes kept closing. She envied women who could say positively, with no doubts: I want a child.

In the early days of her first pregnancy she had had bleeds and had been advised to lay in bed.

She had gone about normally, even riding. Secretly, hadn't she wanted to get rid of it? Hadn't she been testing fate just as she did the night Michael died?

The car stopped and her eyes opened. There were roadworks. A labourer was holding a red stop notice. Somewhere ahead a drill hammered.

'You forgot to get the pill.'

She sat up, startled. Clare was holding the shopping list on which she had crossed out everything else.

'Damn. So I did.'

Sometimes looking into Clare's eyes was like looking at herself in the mirror.

'Are you getting broody?'

She laughed. 'That'll be the day.'

Pat opened a window and tried to flick out a wasp with his newspaper. Clare crumpled the shopping list into a ball and shoved it at Henry, teasing him into snapping for it.

'Do you want a brother?'

'How sexist!'

'Or sister.'

'You said brother mumm —'

The car shot forward, throwing them back. As Frances picked Henry off her, the brakes were slammed on. Her head hit the seat in front of her. Dazed, she glimpsed a white van blocking the narrow road.

A nightmare face, eyes and mouth in a balaclava appeared at the window and then was snatched away as Pat reversed off the road. Another man in a balaclava was running towards them, holding a gun.

Henry was barking and Clare screaming as Pat shoved the car into first and wrenched at the wheel. Frances tried to put her arm round Clare but was thrown off, this time against the side-window as the car slewed round and she could momentarily glimpse what Pat was trying to do: drive over the narrow verge, squeezing between the white van and a brick wall.

The car grated against the wall, the wing-mirror bent, and she thought he was going to make it when the windscreen exploded and the car crashed.

She blacked out for an instant. The dog was barking in her ear. She felt for Clare's hand, but it wasn't Clare's hand.

Frank pulled out the woman, and threw her to Willy, who bundled her into the van. It was speed speed speed that counted now. Pity he'd had to shoot the driver, but they'd allowed for that.

The roaring of the drill drowned the screams of the wee girl. He thought nothing about her as her leg caught in the seat belt and he wrenched at it. Speed speed speed.

The dog went for him, its teeth breaking flesh. He let go of the girl and flung off the dog. As it scrambled back on to its feet, yelping among the broken glass, he shot it. Pity he had to do it in front of the berserk girl, but they couldn't leave it, it would mean quicker detection. Speed speed speed.

His hand went over the girl's mouth as he spun her round into Willy's arms and Willy ran with her into the van. Her screams died as the gag went in. Good. He switched off the stereo-recorder which was playing the drilling noise.

In the sudden intense silence he registered that Ronan had collected the pick-axes and spades; Kate was bringing up the car which had blocked the escape from the rear. The men with the stop-go poles holding up any traffic would dump them.

Speed speed speed! He and Ronan, without speaking, snatched up a tarpaulin, stretching it out as they ran to the Mercedes. The chauffeur's eyes were staring open; among the rivulets of blood running from his nostrils, fragments of broken glass gleamed like ice-crystals.

The tarpaulin fitted perfectly over the car. They wedged it into position with stones, and put cones and a roadworks notice round it. Speed speed speed! Willy was revving up the van, Ronan running to the car. Kate was doing a last minute check. He joined her, removing his balaclava as she had just done.

He was by the gate in the wall, about to jump into the van reversing towards him when he saw the boy. He was sitting on the back of a horse, about half a field's length away staring straight at him. Frank could have sworn there was no gate at the top of the field, he'd checked it — the boy must have come through a gap in the hedge.

After the frenetic activity, there was a moment of absolute stillness. Frank could feel the movement of sweat on his face. The horse tossed its head.

'Shoot!'

Kate had appeared behind him, rolling her balaclava back on.

It was as if every bone in his body was paralysed. Kate fired. She was no shot at that range. The horse bolted, the boy pulling round its head. By the time Frank brought his gun up and aimed to bring the horse down it was too late. The boy was through the hedge.

'Go after him!' Kate shouted.

The only answer he gave her was to run her to the car. He jumped in the van. That was a pity. That was a pity. But you were lucky if only one thing went wrong. That was what Danny had taught him. Dismiss it and get on with it. They'd got them, that was the main thing.

They might only have half-an-hour because of the boy. Less. But twenty minutes away there was another car, another van. Willy had tied and gagged the woman and the girl. As they bumped down the mountain road he taped padded spectacles round their eyes and put plugs of cotton wool into their ears. They'd got them, that was the main thing.

6 *Everything Happens at Five O'Clock*

At 16.45 Bennet saw the story on the news-agency tape. '16.04 Computer King's Wife Snatched.'

He swore to himself as the paper jerked through his fingers. 'A chauffeur was shot and killed near Auchterloy, Co. Wicklow, today . . .'

Well, perhaps it wasn't a problem; but because he didn't want one at this precise moment he'd bet it was. Carr was rich; if you were rich, and particularly if you were in a risk area like Ireland you took out a kidnap and ransom policy, which more than likely was with Lloyds.

And if the policy had been written by a syndicate at Lloyds then the problem might finish up on Bennet's polished desk in his office in York Row, a narrow little street running into Lime Street, near Lloyds.

Bennet had no idea whether Carr was a client or not. K and R policies were secret, hand-written policies, known only to the broker, the senior underwriter and the man himself.

Unless there was a kidnap.

Then a firm like Bennet's Security Assessment came in. Bennet, an ex-major in his forties who, in his dark suit and striped shirt looked more like a merchant banker, ran a group of ex-Guards, ex-SAS officers who specialised in the crimes that threatened the rich and large multinationals: espionage, kidnap and extortion.

They were retained by insurance syndicates, and an operator was always standing by, ready to fly anywhere in the world at a moment's notice. Or at least that was the theory.

Bennet crossed the thick carpet into his secretary's office. Round the panelled walls were old prints of his regiment's battles: Waterloo, The Crimea, Ladysmith.

'Who's on standby, Lucy?'

Lucy, who had a Gucci scarf slung round her neck and nails varnished like little mirrors, looked up uncertainly from her electronic typewriter.

'Simon,' she said.

Bennet looked sadly at a gallant lancer impaling one of Ney's men. 'Who comes home?'

Lucy didn't need to look at the coded board behind her.

'Paul is on the extortion in Brazil. Peter and John are negotiating the kidnap ransoms in Italy. Peter is due back on Wednesday . . .?'

'Give me the letter,' he said.

'Dear Simon,' he read, 'Please regard yourself as from the receipt of this letter as on a month's leave. You are not to interpret this as a suspension . . .'

Bennet thought: it's not my fault. There's just too much business. Kidnaps were a boom industry. He tore up the letter.

'I have to go round the corner. Get Simon to meet me on the floor at Lloyds asap.'

Not for the first time he thought that the impaled French soldier had Simon's face: long, handsome, and unlucky.

At 17.20, the Aer Lingus plane carrying Geoffrey and Lansbury touched down in Dublin fifteen minutes late. It was eight hours since he had kissed Frances and Clare goodbye.

Reporters and cameramen met the plane, some carrying pictures of Geoffrey to identify him. Passengers were jostled as the reporters crowded round them. One glimpsed a man ducking away, hat pulled low over his head, another, dashing after the first, spotted the letters G.A.C on the man's despatch case.

'Mr Carr! Sir!'

'Has there been a ransom demand?'

'Not to my knowledge,' said Lansbury, as his hat slipped off and cameras flashed.

Geoffrey was already being shown into an unmarked Garda car with an armed escort.

'Where are you taking me?'

'Ballyglen sir.'

There was already a piece in the stop press of the *Evening Herald*. Geoffrey stared at the smudged words: 'IRA suspected.'

Soon they were leaving the airport on the Nl. There was an accident at Drumcondra. The rush hour traffic congealed and it took them more than an hour to get through Dublin. It was the longest journey of Geoffrey's life.

At 17.40 Detective Inspector Kearney from Dublin's Special Branch arrived at the incident room which had been set up at Ballyglen Garda station. Forty, with thin receding hair, he was originally from Cork, and had been looking forward to a week's fishing holiday on the Blackwater with his son when the phone rang.

The local inspector, O'Hanlon, met him as a switchboard, a long table and a typewriter were being carried in. Already photographs of Frances and Clare were pinned up next to ordnance maps of Wicklow and Dublin.

A phone on a chair rang. A guard carrying the typewriter picked it up.

'Yes madam . . . What time was this?'

'Anything solid?' Kearney asked.

'An astrologer says they're in Newry,' O'Hanlon answered. 'That's as solid as any . . .'

'Nobody saw anything? Heard anything?'

'Nobody's come forward . . . No prints, except for family and chauffeur. One bullet recovered, from a Browning nine milly. The body and the car were found by a lorrydriver. I think he stopped to see what he could pick up . . .'

As soon as the guard put the phone down it started ringing again. Kearney stepped over the typewriter and gazed at the maps. The kidnap spot and possible get-away routes were marked.

'How much time did they have before the body was discovered?'

'Two hours? Maybe a little more. They just might have made the border before the alarm went out.'

Kearney's finger travelled up to Dundalk, then Armagh in the north.

'They wouldn't bank on it,' he said. 'I'll bet they're still in the south.'

At about quarter-to-six Kate's hands began to shake and she had to sit down. Until then she had been perfectly calm. She gave a quick, guilty glance out of the window to see if Frank had seen her.

He was in the garden of Annacloy, the house they had rented, swishing with a stick at the long grass. She watched him check the gate. Trees and overgrown shrubs hid the old estate house from the road.

She had rented the place for two months. That should be more than enough.

'I'm a writer . . . I need something off the beaten track . . .'

'North Leitrim's your place . . . There's few tracks there, beaten or unbeaten . . .'

The guide-book said: has a secret, forgotten feel to it; a good place for a quiet holiday. It was fishing country: pike, salmon and trout. They had passed many small lakes, each with its lone angler, before reaching Annacloy, set at the head of a narrow valley, whose steep grassy slopes terminated in limestone crags. It was twenty miles from the sea, and about the same distance from the border.

It was the place she would have chosen, if she had wanted to write something. If Frank was not particularly brilliant in thinking ahead, he had more than made up for it in recruiting her. She would do the shopping, ramble about. The middle-class writer — who would suspect her?

She made tea, and sipped it scalding hot. Her hands were still trembling. She had not expected this. She had been involved in interrogations, one of which had led to a girl losing her baby. You had to steel yourself; the girl had been going with a soldier, and it was presumably his child. But she had never seen anyone shot before. The plan had been to release the chauffeur. Of course Frank had had to shoot him. He'd had no option.

But then she had shot at the boy. She must stop these thoughts, they were no good, they were rendering her inefficient.

Frank was returning. Her mouth burning from the tea, she pulled back a curtain and opened the door to the cellar. She picked up a tray on which was a sandwich, a packet of biscuits and a mug of tea, put it down, picked up her gun, put it on the tray, that was unprofessional, started to put it in the belt of her trousers . . . was the safety catch on . . .?

Calm down!

The cellar ran under the whole house. A whitewashed corridor led to three rooms. The first she passed had no door and was full of rubble and old cans of paint. She rolled down her balaclava, turned the key in the heavy door and unbolted it.

The woman might rush her. Frank had untied her and taken off the spectacles before Kate had realised what he was doing. She thought it was better that they saw nothing, heard nothing. Still, it was done now. All that planning, and things kept cropping up that they had not foreseen.

She brought up the gun in two hands, kicked open the door, and pushed the tray along the stone floor with her foot. Were her hands shaking?

The woman didn't rush her. She was crouched on the bed, her shocked eyes staring out from a face smudged with dirt and grease from the sacks on the floor of the van. A large bruise had swollen up the side of her forehead.

Kate lowered the gun and pushed the tray into the room, tea slopping.

'Where's my daughter,' the woman whispered, 'please what have you done with my daughter?'

No words, no conversation beyond the absolute minimum, that's what they had agreed. They mustn't see them as persons, feel in any way sorry for them, that would be fatal. It had been a mistake to take off those padded spectacles, uncover those wild pleading eyes.

The woman clasped her hands together. 'She's twelve, twelve, she'll be terrified, please let me see her, you must let me see her!'

At least Kate had got her own way there. The girl was in another house up the valley, with Willy and Ronan. That gave them an extra chance if anything went wrong and the police found one of them.

As Kate opened the door to leave the woman screamed violently and jumped up from the bed. 'Please answer me! Why won't you answer me!'

Kate jerked the gun up, stopping the woman. 'She's all right. She won't be harmed.'

'Let me see her. Please let me see her.'

Kate slammed the door shut and locked and bolted it. Her hands were shaking. This was no good. No good at all.

The woman's hammering on the door followed her all the way upstairs until she closed the door at the top and drew the heavy curtain. As she peeled off her balaclava Frank's voice coming from nowhere made her jump.

'Don't miss —'

'What?'

He was stretched out on the settee, reading one of the brochures which were spread out in a neat fan for holidaymakers, together with a local map, shells and bits of coloured rock which a previous tenant had collected. There were even toy spades, a bucket, and sand in one of the mugs.

'Are you a nature trailer?' Frank asked. 'Don't miss Lough Key Forest Park, the bog gardens are a must!'

She realised how wild and distorted her face must have been when he dropped the brochure and came over to her.

'You'll get used to it.'

This was patronising, this really upset her, him playing the cool macho man, they were always talking about being real *Men*!

'What do you mean?' she said.

Even worse, he put his hands on her shoulders and said: 'Don't let her upset you.'

And, worse still, much worse, for a fleeting moment she just wanted him to hold her, not that she fancied him, she just wanted him to hold her, and that had never happened with a man for a very long time. She enjoyed, needed, her independence.

In the early days of their relationship he had taken it for granted that she would sleep with him; if you took to the gun women were regarded as one of the fringe benefits. One night in the Dublin flat, when he had had a few drinks he had tried to stop her going back to Belfast.

'It's a long drive,' he had said.

'I like driving.'

'In this?'

It was pouring down. She had nodded. 'Alone, don't tell me I'm funny, or strange, or cold, I've heard it all before.'

Had she actually patted his cheek and smiled, rather patronisingly? At any rate she had been cool then, in control. Now she exploded, walking into a chair without seeing it.

'That bitch doesn't upset me! It's the boy!'

'I don't shoot children.' His voice was as cold as one of the mountain streams they had driven over.

'I don't mean that! You should have gone after him!'

'We'd never have got away!'

Her usual calm deserted her. He didn't seem surprised, which made it worse. She found herself yelling until her throat hurt.

'You don't shoot civilians! What about her? The girl?'

'They're different.'

'How different?'

'They're responsible for the soldiers in north, for the shit state here.'

She sat down. He lit a cigarette and began flicking through the pages of the brochure. She realised that the question she had been asking was not 'would you shoot them?' but 'could I?'. He was apparently able to contemplate the possibility. But it wouldn't come to that. She must keep a tighter control over herself: she was going to be no use if she didn't. She forced herself to finish the by now cold tea before speaking again.

'The boy . . .'

'He caught a glimpse. Across a field.'

'A glimpse!' She nearly lost her temper again, but then put on the manner of a policeman questioning the boy. 'How old, son? As old as me? As your dad? Straight or curly hair? Eyes like this or . . .'

He had too little imagination, and she had too much. He was inclined to hope for the best, while she prepared for the worst. At least she had his attention now.

'The Garda will have him,' he said.

'They won't lock him up, will they? Send Ronan. He can pick up his driver pal in Dundalk. Find out what's happening. Put pressure on the family. If it looks bad, lift the boy.'

Frank lit one cigarette from the other and went over to the window. After the sunny day, cloud had built up, and in fact drops were already falling on the window.

At 18.10 it was still a fine warm day further east when Geoffrey arrived at the Garda station at Ballyglen. He was ushered down a long green-painted corridor where a man was raising his voice.

'There was the drill and two shots. Then the drill stopped — and then another two shots!'

Geoffrey glimpsed that the man was a labourer, with mud caked on his wellingtons, talking to O'Hanlon and another man and then, through an open door he saw something that stopped him dead. Between Guards on the phone and workmen putting in a new switchboard he saw pinned on a notice board, photographs of Frances and Clare. Before this he had been numb, as if under an anaesthetic, clinging on to the idea that there had been somehow a mistake, there had been a car accident, they had been taken for shelter somewhere.

O'Hanlon touched his arm. The last time he had seen him had been drinking at the party. He introduced him to Kearney and they took him to a small bare room and gave him thick, stewed tea.

'No news of them?'

'No.'

'It is the IRA?'

'Both the Provos and INLA have already denied involvement,' Kearney said.

'Does that mean anything?'

'Yes.'

Geoffrey felt a fraction relieved: if it involved money, that was something he understood. He looked up to see Kearney watching him. He had soft, light-blue eyes and a habit of pulling at a lock of his hair, as if trying to cover his growing baldness.

'It might be a breakaway group,' O'Hanlon said.

'Cowboys, criminals, same difference.' Kearney wrote on a card and slid it across the table, the grain of which, like a school-desk, was inked with countless biros. 'If anyone approaches you, please get in touch with us immediately, Mr Carr.' He pulled at his hair. 'They may threaten to harm your wife and daughter if you tell the Guardia.'

Geoffrey was suddenly tired of everyone, including

himself, walking round the subject, like doctors not mentioning cancer.

'By harm you mean kill.'

O'Hanlon actually smiled. Yes, he was exactly like a doctor, able to talk about everything except death.

'They will be bluffing Geoffrey. They're not going to kill someone who is worth money to them.'

'I'll bear that in mind. Thank you.' He put the card in his wallet.

Again he felt Kearney studying him, then abruptly the policeman rose and picked up a brown envelope from the windowsill. Without saying a word he took out a photograph and put it in front of Geoffrey. It was a picture taken through the smashed windscreen of the Mercedes. Pat's sightless eyes stared out at Geoffrey. The dead dog lay on the back seat among broken glass, jumbled parcels and a hat and scarf he recognized. He stood up, lurching away, bile burning his mouth, as O'Hanlon glared angrily at Kearney.

Kearney brushed the lock of hair delicately over his smooth, shining forehead.

'I'm sorry, Mr Carr. But I have to make you realise the kind of people we're dealing with. If you do pay a ransom, there's no guarantee they will honour the deal.'

Geoffrey covered his mouth with his handkerchief and spat into it. O'Hanlon rested his hand on his shoulder. Geoffrey returned the handkerchief to his pocket.

'I understand,' he said.

'Carr is insured,' Bennet said to Simon Mitchell. 'Took out a kidnap and ransom policy when he travelled in South America and half the world's business executives were in People's Prisons. The silly fellow didn't tell us he'd moved to Ireland, acquired a family, small details like that.'

'Does that affect the policy?' Simon asked.

'Technically. But the underwriters will fork out.'

'How much?'

'He's probably under-insured at today's rates. He's covered for two million dollars.'

They had met at Lloyds, where Bennet had been to a meeting, and were walking in the gallery, looking down at the now-silent floor of the vast hall. Bennet liked to come here, particularly at the height of the day's business, when the rows and rows of 'boxes', circular booths ringed with chairs, were surrounded by brokers laying off millions of pounds worth of business, at the fall of a rubber stamp bearing the syndicate's name and the anchor symbol of Lloyd's.

Simon looked more and more like the dying French soldier in the print in his office, with his St Bernard eyes, his suit that could do with a press, and his untrimmed moustache. Bennet liked his men to keep a military cut.

'How are things on the home front?'

Simon's eyes smouldered. Good, thought Bennet. At least there was a bit of spirit there.

'We've separated,' Simon said. 'I've moved out.'

'Access?' Bennet said. 'Weren't you worried about that?' Needle the bloody man, get him fighting.

'I can see my son twice a week.'

'Good, good, excellent.'

Blood coloured Simon's cheeks. 'Italy wasn't because of the home front,' he said bitterly. 'The hostage had a heart attack and died while the ransom was being paid.'

'Well it's a moot point how long he'd been dead, Simon. Underwriters do wince a little when they pay a large amount of money out for a corpse.'

'I did a proof of life!'

A photograph of the hostage, usually taken holding a daily paper, to prove he was alive.

'Water under the bridge, Simon, all I'm saying is it would be a bit bloody silly if I sent you over there to save someone's wife when all you could think about was saving your own marriage.'

'There's nothing left to save.'

'Good.'

Now he was really angry, his cheeks dull red. Sometimes the man with his back against the wall was the best one to send. A phone was ringing in an empty box behind them. Some people below were leaving, their voices echoing across the deserted floor. Well, decisions were what he was paid to make.

'Packed your razor?' Bennet said, handing Simon an envelope.

Simon instinctively felt at his moustache. Bennet knew that Simon loathed him, but knew that he would trim the drooping moustache. Once in the army . . .

'Sorry it's Ireland,' he said as they left the building. 'Hope you have a good mac. It's a lousy forecast.'

In Wicklow clouds streaked the setting sun, but there was no rain yet. The kidnap gang crept up the lane to St Edna's farm. They had been chased away from the big car with the shattered windscreen by a guard. They were putting up lights, and going over the ground for clues, Denis said.

He was the big boy, nine last August, the leader. With him was his sister Colette and Mark, whose prize possession was a fragment of glass from the windscreen.

They slipped into the farm yard calling softly: 'Kevin, Kevin, Kev Kev Kev.'

'Kevin saw the kidnap!' Denis kicked a stone across the yard. He didn't believe a word of it, but it was his job as leader to check.

'Did they use laser guns?' Mark shouted.

Colette spread her arms below a first-floor window. 'Are you coming to kidnap me Kev?'

The kitchen door was wrenched open and they ran screaming as a woman came out.

'Wait until I see your mother!', she shouted. 'You should be in bed!'

The woman, Eileen Synott, who was plaiting the wet tea-towel she would have brought down on their backs if she could, was not only angry, she was terrified. She closed the door and went into the damp-smelling hall. She could visualise the scene in the front room.

Kevin was standing before his grandma. Mrs Spencer, stiff with arthritis, never moved from her chair except to be helped into bed. A coal fire burned although it was warm, lighting up the gloomy room, where the furnishing had stopped in 1920.

On the mantelpiece and on a shelf next to her rug-covered chair, were lines of faded brown photographs, most including a jaunty, youngish man in a twenties peaked cap. In one he was a member of an IRA flying column, holding a gun. In another he followed a funeral cortege. Both had the republican colours pasted in the corner.

Her rigid, bony fingers dug into Kevin's arm, but he dare not move, although her smell choked him. Her cheeks fell in fold after fold close to his eyes and there were two large spots, one on each side of her nose from which hairs grew.

'He was the hero of Wicklow,' she said pointing to the jaunty man. Her old cracked voice rang out proudly. 'C company, Sixth Battalion.

'He shot the Brits,' said Kevin, repeating a lesson.

'He did he did!' The old woman laughed in delight. 'And they were all there to bury him: Tom Barry, Dan Breen, Ernie O'Malley.' She drew him closer. He fought to hold his breath, in a panic lest she might kiss him. 'And it's still going on, you see. Enniskerry and Bray are run by Brits. It will all go on, he used to say, until we have one Ireland, sea to sea.' She pulled him in front of her, her voice hardening.

'You saw nothing, d'you hear me?'

He nodded dumbly.

'He tells me everything. If you open your mouth he'll come out of his grave and tell me.'

The door opened and the terrified child ran to his mother.

'I've told the police we heard and saw nothing!'

Eileen shouted. 'Now will you leave the boy alone!'

The kidnap gang had run to the road, where they saw yet another car, crawling along to the scene of the great ambush. As the man in the passenger seat wound down the window, Denis ran alongside and shouted: 'Down there mister! By those lights!'

Lansbury stopped the car and Geoffrey stared at his Mercedes. A wing was crumpled. Glass had been removed from the shattered windscreen. Further up the field, in a slowly moving arc of light, men were searching.

A scream made him jump. In the ditch the girl Colette was being kidnapped by Denis, a dirty handkerchief wrapped round her mouth. The other boy, Mark, ran up to Geoffrey.

'They shot him here mister. Give me a pound and I'll tell you.'

'He never saw it,' Denis said, aggrieved that he'd not been smart enough to think of this.

'I know someone who did!' said Mark heatedly.

'Who?' said Geoffrey.

'Kevin,' answered Denis. 'He saw a space ship last week.'

The three shouted with laughter and ran screaming away into the gloom.

As Lansbury drove Geoffrey over the heath towards Kilnameath, the first spots of rain fell on the windscreen. The rooks were settling in their trees. Red rhododendron petals were beginning to cover the drive.

'What are all those lights?' Geoffrey asked.

Lansbury swallowed. 'The press, master.' He glanced nervously at Geoffrey's rigid face, staring straight ahead at the cars and vans drawn up in front of his house. He cleared his throat. 'However I put this it is going to seem highly inappropriate but these, er events are bound to have repercussions on the company. If you make a statement —'

'I do not care nor wish to talk about the company.'

Lansbury smiled. 'Frequently what I feel myself, master, but —'

He stopped as Geoffrey's eyes blazed angrily at him. 'They are on my land. Get them off.'

Lansbury slowed down as they approached the house. There was an RTE television van, and they could see the cameraman, camera over his shoulder, the sound man following with the boom. A group of other reporters were coming towards them from the steps.

'We need their cooperation,' Lansbury said. 'I told them there would be a statement.'

Geoffrey wrenched open the door of the car, his anger boiling. Lansbury followed, struggling to protect him and clear a way through the reporters. In the criss-cross of car headlights, voices shouted at him from all directions.

'Has there been any approach from the kidnappers, Mr Carr?'

'Have the police any leads?'

'Do they think they're in the north?'

'Are you politically involved Mr —'

'Have you anything to say to the kidnappers, sir?'

Geoffrey had reached the top of the steps. Flash bulbs went. Behind him the door opened and he heard Margaret's voice, but the last question made him suddenly realise that there was a way to reach Frances. As soon as he opened his mouth there was a hushed silence.

'To say to them? Ask them please not to harm my wife and daughter.'

A woman prised herself up, using the shoulder of the reporter in front. 'Have you any message for them, Mr Carr?'

He looked down at the upturned faces, bemused. He could say something to Frances? His voice dropped to a whisper, as if everyone had vanished, and he was speaking through the silence directly to her.

'Just — I love you.'

The silence lengthened. For a moment no-one moved. Then a flash bulb went off in his face followed by another and another. Geoffrey glared angrily and went inside, the door closing, Lansbury remaining to fend off the questions.

'Your company Mr Carr!'

'Please! You can see what Mr Carr is going through!'

'Is he selling shares?'

'He's no plans to do so.'

'What's he worth?'

'No idea,' Lansbury said.

'Six million?'

Inside the house, Margaret put her arms round Geoffrey as the barrage of questions continued. She had a sheaf of scribbled notes and messages in her hand. She read the question in his eyes and shook her head.

'They're all calls from friends. Press. Lunatics.'

Outside they heard Lansbury call to one of the reporters: 'Would you know what you're worth, Stephen?'

'That's easy.' There was the ring of coins on the step. 'I can count it.'

Geoffrey stepped angrily to the door, but before he could open it the phone rang. He stared at it.

'I've got Maire taking them,' Margaret said. 'She'll put anything important through to the study.'

He seemed unable to move. She took his hand and led him through to the study like a child. Maire, the housekeeper, brought in soup and French bread but Geoffrey walked about the room, unable to sit or eat. Eventually Lansbury joined them.

'Have the vultures gone?' Geoffrey asked.

'Settled in the trees,' Lansbury replied. 'I'm worried that if we're not more cooperative they'll speculate about what you're worth . . .'

Geoffrey wasn't listening. The rain was falling steadily now and he felt savagely glad that the vultures were wet and hungry. Abruptly he covered his face in his hands.

'How ridiculous!'

They stared at him. The phone rang. They all looked at the extension on Geoffrey's desk, waiting, waiting. When it clicked without ringing, Margaret said: 'What's ridiculous?'

'Oh . . .' He flushed. For years he had hated displaying emotion, even to himself. Now what a public spectacle he had made of himself! 'All that out there. On the steps.'

'It wasn't,' Margaret said softly. 'It wasn't ridiculous at all.'

The phone began ringing again, and again their eyes swivelled to the extension.

Geoffrey tore a hunk of bread to pieces. He couldn't stop talking, it was as if he had to confess. 'I've never said it to her, do you know that, Margaret. I've never said it to anyone. Before tonight.' He tried to smile but it came out as more of a grimace. 'And even then I didn't say it to anyone.'

'If you're not going to eat that bread then drink something,' she said, pouring out a Bushmills.

'Isn't this Protestant whiskey?' said Lansbury.

'I have my confession tomorrow,' she said as the extension phone rang. They stared at it. Half-way through the second ring Geoffrey picked it up.

'It's Stephen Bennet, Mr Carr, one 't'. We met while you were on a South American licencing trip. Security aspects.'

Geoffrey's face was a frozen mask. Then he placed the assured, plummy voice.

'Do you remember the procedure?'

It was the worst, most agonizing day of his life and he felt he was playing in some bizarre farce. 'Procedure. Mmm. Yes.'

'Our man will be in La Paz tomorrow.'

'La Paz,' Geoffrey repeated, dumbly. Lansbury's glass stopped half-way to his lips.

'Mitchell, very sound, reliable chap . . .' The voice took on some of the manufactured sorrow of an undertaker. 'I'm deeply sorry to hear of your present misfortune, and hope our matter reaches a satisfactory conclusion.'

'Thank you . . .' Geoffrey put down the phone and swallowed the whiskey. 'It's the bloody insurance man,' he said.

What Kate needed was a good screw to calm her down, Frank thought. She was great at the bits of paper and timetables, but a bit of a liability in action. And she thought too much. She had just returned from the other house, where the girl was coughing and unwell, complaining that everything had gone wrong.

What she meant was it hadn't gone to plan. Nothing ever goes to plan: that was another of Danny's sayings.

'Oh stuff Danny!'

She had stormed out, and was now prowling round the house in all this rain, looking for the Garda under every stone, while he watched the ads on the old black and white telly with a pack of Smithwick's and a bottle of Jameson on the table next to him. He'd been dry for two weeks before the action. Now he was going to make up for it.

An electric fire with a buzzing element was warming his legs and he must have dozed off, for suddenly there was Carr on the screen. He jumped up to turn up the sound and lost the picture. He flung open the door and was about to shout when he saw Kate, leaning just inside the porch, staring at the rain.

He banged the set with the flat of his hand and got back the picture.

'Ask them please not to harm my . . .'

The sound crackled, and it looked as if Carr was talking in the middle of a snowstorm.

'Any message for . . .'

Frank put his arm round Kate.

'Just — I love you,' Carr said.

Frank danced and hugged Kate.

'Stop it!'

'What do you mean stop it, we've done it! This'll make those bastards in Derry sit up! He's easy! You heard him! I told you! Didn't I? Didn't I? We chose the right one! We'll have the money in a week. On come on, admit I was right — don't be so bloody grudging!'

She grinned. She still had her coat on and her cheeks were streaked with rain. It was always the same after a killing: first the running, then the exultation of escape, then the drink, then the woman. It wasn't just the sex, it was a desperate craving to be inside her, to fall asleep inside her, to literally fall, to drown in that cry, that sweat, that smell.

Sometimes he would go to Deirdre, whose husband was in the Kesh. She was a good laugh, you needed that, she understood, while his wife was always mute and passive. He would pull her on top of him, burying his face in her breasts, shaking as days of tension finally drained out of him. She always knew from that that he had been on a job, just as the orange juice told the pub he was going on one.

He always knew when a woman wanted him. Kate was still cold from outside, smelling of the rain, her short hair gleaming with it. Smiling, he slipped his hands inside her coat. Yes, she was coming to him, her breasts touching him. As his arms went round her, suddenly she wasn't there but behind him twisting his arm in a lock which made him gasp with pain.

She released him. He sat, gripping his wrist. She put on the kettle and then said, as if nothing had happened: 'Will you do the first watch, or shall I?'

It was after one o'clock that night when Geoffrey finally went upstairs. Maire was making the bed. She apologised: the day had been such a dreadful confusion, the room had been forgotten. In fact, it was just as they had left it when they had gone out in a hurry that morning.

He told her to leave it. She dropped a pillow and then began picking up Frances's clothes, which, as usual were strewn about the floor.

'I said leave it, leave everything!' he shouted.

He sat on the bed. Some powder was spilt on top of the bedside cabinet.

'Where will you be sleeping, sir?'

'Here. I'm . . . sorry I shouted. I . . . I want this room left exactly as it is until Mrs Carr returns. Do you understand?'

When Maire had gone he opened Frances's bedside drawer and pulled out of the familiar jumble the pill dispenser she had sworn at.

'Oh well. It doesn't matter,' she had said.

'Doesn't it?'

'Does it?'

He lay down fully dressed on the still crumpled bed, pulling the counterpane over himself, listening to the wind blowing the rain against the windows. He dozed and woke several times, convinced that the phone was ringing. For an instant, he couldn't believe it when it was. In fumbling for the light switch, he knocked his pen and note-pad on the floor.

'Mr Carr?'

It was a man, a tense, jerky Irish voice.

'We have your wife and daughter. They will cost you a quarter-of-a-million.'

He fought to be calm. He couldn't see where the pen had gone, and he couldn't talk on the phone without a pen in his hand.

'How do I know you have them?'

'We need money tomorrow.'

The man was ridiculous. But perhaps they didn't understand anything about money. 'I can't raise —' he began.

'Shut up. Listen. Deliver twenty thousand tomorrow for starters or they'll suffer.'

This is a hoax, Geoffrey told himself, this is a hoax.

'Whoever you are,' he said, 'you must prove to me —'

The voice cut in, ugly, blunt. 'In thirty seconds I'm putting this phone down, Mr Carr. Be in the phone box at Drumlogeigh at eleven tomorrow morning. Alone.'

Geoffrey crawled on his hands and knees, found the pen.

'Drum —'

'Drumlogeigh, Kildare. The money —'

The phone toppled and he caught it as it was falling to the floor. For a moment he thought he had lost the call.

'What? What?'

'. . . used fives and tens. If you don't turn up, or tell the police, they will be shot.'

'How do I know you have her? You'll get nothing unless you ask her a question.'

Something that was known only to the two of them. His mind was a blank. Stupid! He should have thought of this! His eye caught a photograph, one taken at the party of Margaret with Frances.

'What's her sister's name? Her married name? Hello? Hello?'

Why hadn't he asked where they had spent their first honeymoon? Or where he had first met her . . . Where they had first gone to dinner . . . I always see you as lunch she had said when he asked her . . . There were hundreds of better questions!

'Hello? Hello? Hello?' he shouted into the crackling phone.

'Margaret Healey,' the voice said.

It was a shock that he'd got that right. 'Ask her where we spent —'

'This isn't a bloody quiz show, Mr Carr.'

The line went dead. He stayed by it, hoping it would ring again. He was unable to sit down, let alone sleep. He went from thinking it was a hoax, to the near certainty that it was not. Why hadn't he asked a more sensible question?

It was possible it was someone with local knowledge. But then they hadn't known what question he would ask. He took Inspector Kearney's card out of his wallet, and half-a-dozen times picked up the phone and replaced it. Once he got as far as dialling the number.

Eventually, as the darkness seeped out of the sky, he put on his outdoor coat and walked down to the stream. The rooks were wheeling, calling. The rain had stopped, but the wind blew drops from the trees onto his bare head. There was supposed to be a police guard about, but he couldn't see one.

When his mother had died and he had kissed her cold face, he had felt desolate, lonely, deserted. Perhaps the desolation had been so much it had prevented him from ever entering into such a close relationship again. He had plunged into business, then money, and forgotten all about those feelings. Now they came back: the awful chapel of rest, the plastic flowers in the window, the unctuous smiles, the open coffin smelling like a hospital corridor, the cold waxen cheek.

Although it was a long, uphill walk, he went up to the copse because it was the place where Frances most often went.

7 *And Have Things Changed At All?*

Simon Mitchell caught the last plane to Dublin where he picked up a hire car. Bennet told him that Carr was expecting him at ten the next morning.

Before leaving his hotel, he shaved and trimmed his moustache, smarting as he did so over what Bennet had said to him. It amounted to giving him a last chance, didn't it?

Well, he wasn't so interested in staying with the bloody firm. He could start up his own security outfit: it was a booming industry, which would grow as Britain became more and more divided into haves and have-nots. There would be more have-nots grabbing people like Frances Carr.

It was something of a fantasy, starting his own outfit. But there was a real reason why he might chuck the firm, get out of this particular job. He'd lied to Bennet.

He didn't have access to his son Christopher. They'd fought over everything, he and his wife Carol — house, money, child.

Christopher was five. On the cheap dressing table (things were so tight he stayed in dumps and claimed for expensive places) was a photograph of him proudly holding up Christopher. He kissed the picture and put it in his case.

He ought to be in London fighting, Bennet was quite right. He'd nearly agreed with him. At the same time, he wanted to show the bastard . . . he didn't want to leave a failure . . .

He felt just that when he arrived at Kilnameath at

ten o'clock to find Carr gone. He could have got down there much earlier! He should have anticipated this! He really had lost his touch!

'What time did the man tell him to be at Drumlogeigh?'

He was in the hall, talking to Lansbury, with Maire hovering, mute and scared in the background.

'Eleven o'clock.'

What a start! What a balls-up! He told Lansbury, whom he immediately decided he wouldn't trust an inch, to phone the police.

'He doesn't want them informed.'

'They're informed! They've probably followed him from here. Anyway the phone's tapped. The Garda's very good at it. He might walk into a shoot-out.'

That shook Lansbury, but he still dithered. Simon dialled the number Maire gave him and threw the receiver at Lansbury.

Lansbury said: 'You speak to them if —'

'I'm only here in an advisory capacity,' Simon said.

'Oh. Is that what you're doing.'

Lansbury's acidic niceties were lost on Simon. After Lansbury had told the Garda, Simon ran him down to his car and drove with his foot on the floor, up the mountains, through the Wicklow Gap, heading towards where Lansbury thought he was drawing the money.

As he skidded through hairpin bends, Lansbury hanging on to the strap and begging him to slow down, he felt exhilaration to be in action again after weeks of dry legal wrangling over his child.

It was what his wife, as acid as Lansbury, called White Knight Time. She hated him being a hero to his son, disliked him even buying pistols or soldiers for presents.

Well, he would rescue the Lady in Distress, regain his confidence, and then, perhaps, Christopher.

'There he is!' Lansbury shouted.

They had joined the N 81 at the small town of Hollywood and were just parking outside the bank. Lansbury was pointing to a car driving off in the opposite direction.

Simon, half out of the car, leapt back in. Lansbury had time to get back in but not to close the door as Simon slammed in reverse, bumping over the kerb. The half-open door caught empty fruit boxes stacked outside a greengrocer and sent them flying.

Lansbury shut the door and was hurled forward as Simon passed traffic on the wrong side of the road, heading straight for a lorry. He got to the head of the traffic just in time, wrenching the wheel over.

Lansbury opened his eyes to fasten his seat belt. 'And I thought you were the man from the Pru,' he said.

A lorry backing across the road lost them precious minutes, and by the time they got to Drumlogeigh Geoffrey was in the small village's only phone box. Outside a group of children were pitching stones into a tin can.

The few shops looked as if they'd had the same things in their windows for years. Geoffrey's car was parked outside *Shirley, Beauty Specialist and Hair Stylist*. The trade cards of permed heads were so faded the models looked like ghosts.

Simon tried the door of Geoffrey's car. It was open.

'Get in.'

Lansbury protested. Simon shoved him in. The period of exhilaration had vanished. He could see Geoffrey waiting for the phone to ring. Simon never ate breakfast, and now his empty stomach contracted. Suppose he was wrong?

There was a car parked further back. The driver had his head bent into a newspaper.

'Do you recognize him?'

'All I can recognize is the Irish Times.' Lansbury's voice was querulous. 'Mr Carr can be a man of very short temper —'

Simon gripped his arm. Geoffrey had picked up the phone. He probably only spoke for a few seconds, and then came straight to the car, carrying a despatch case. He stopped when he saw people in it. Simon thought he was going to have a heart attack. Poor bastard, he hadn't shaved and looked haggard and drawn.

'The insurance man cometh,' said Lansbury, as Geoffrey wrenched open the car door.

'Get out!'

Simon thought he was going to be pulled out. 'In the car sir, please.'

'You are risking my wife's life!'

'It's a fake call.'

'How the hell do you know?'

A vein had burst in the corner of Geoffrey's eye, spreading a tiny delta of red across the white.

'Twenty thousand? They sound like professionals. They wouldn't risk a drop for that.'

Geoffrey got in the car. 'They gave me proof.'

Simon's heart lurched. When you made an error of judgement in this business, someone might die. He heard Bennet's sarcastic voice in his head as he said: 'What proof?'

'I told him to ask her a question. Her sister's name.'

Simon turned away in case Geoffrey should see the relief on his face. He pulled out his cigarettes.

Lansbury said apologetically: 'Scarcely an intimate secret between the two of you, master.'

'I know. I couldn't think . . . I suppose I wanted to believe it. To do something.'

He was still holding the piece of paper on which he had scribbled a note in the phone box.

'Is that another box?' Simon asked. 'Tell the police.'

'Are you sure?'

'No. But you haven't much option.'

He indicated the driving mirror. As the man turned a page of the newspaper, Geoffrey saw it was Kearney.

Geoffrey lived in a world of advisers. He could not function if he did not have accountants, solicitors, bankers to throw problems at. The confident face of this young man with a military moustache restored him to something like normality.

The police laid a trap. Geoffrey's despatch case of money was picked up by a motorcyclist, who was then picked up by Kearney. Geoffrey saw him and his girl-friend at Ballyglen Garda station. They were not more than twenty: Dublin junkies, Kearney told him. The girl had read stories about Frances restoring Kilnameath, and, seemingly, weaved fantasies about being her: a wall of her flat in Drimnagh was pasted with pictures of Frances, the great room, the parkland.

Later that day, he slept, shaved, had a bath and then saw Simon. The rest had done him good: he was able to think rationally for the first time since the kidnap. Together they went through the newspapers. 'I Love You' was a headline in many of them. What wasn't good was that one journalist had estimated he was worth six and a half million.

And while he was glad to lean on Simon and use his expertise, he was acutely aware of his role as a rather grisly form of claims assessor.

He made it clear, in the politest possible way, that Geoffrey would not get the insurance money until the ransom had been paid in full. And the kidnap and ransom policy had to be kept secret — there could be no borrowing from the bank on the strength of it. He would have to raise it all from his own resources.

How much? Simon shrugged. 'In Milan a man whose wife was kidnapped wasn't too keen on having her back. She was returned unharmed.'

'I see. I shouldn't love her. I gave away a prime negotiating point.'

He felt sick. Simon was right. He should never have given way to his feelings like that. Ever since he had met Frances he seemed to have been gradually losing his business-sense. But then what did money matter? They could take everything so long as he got her back.

It was a bizarre interview. They were in his study at Kilnameath, the desk scattered with newspapers and telephone messages. The phone continued to ring, and was answered by Lansbury or Maire. Geoffrey knotted his hands together, and rested his head on them.

'How would you write your job description, Mr Mitchell? In one sentence?'

'The operative's function is to recover the hostages, alive, for the least possible ransom.'

It was as if he was quoting from a manual.

'Are those two objectives in any particular order?'

Simon's voice became chilly. 'Mr Carr, our concern is for your family. The underwriters have already written off the one million pounds.'

'I'm glad to hear it,' Geoffrey said. 'But presumably they'd rather I paid half-a-million than a million. I'm not haggling. I've seen that in South America. When the demand comes, I pay! Do you understand? I want them back if it takes every penny I've got!'

Because there were no better leads, Kearney and O'Hanlon went to St Edna's farm. O'Hanlon was sceptical: Carr had reported to them that a child might have seen the kidnapping. They'd had two hundred calls, and none had led anywhere.

Kearney, too, went up the gravel path to the front door with little hope. All the cottages and farms had been checked. Yet there was the mystery of the shots. The labourer they had interviewed had sworn there had been four shots. Only two bullets had been found, in spite of a thorough search.

Eileen Synott answered the door, wiping her hands continually on a tea-towel.

'Not again!'

'Kevin about, Mrs Synott?' O'Hanlon asked.

'He's away with his aunt in Lismore.'

'Bring them in here!' shouted Mrs Spencer from the front room.

The old woman was crouched in her chair by the blazing fire, her small shrewd eyes peering out from folds of skin as brown as the photographs that surrounded her.

'Will you take some tay?' Eileen asked.

'Thank you.'

'We're out of tay,' the old woman snapped.

'Then we won't take any,' Kearney said, his eyes taking in the heavy old furniture, the photographs of the man in the jaunty moustache.

'My husband,' Mrs Spencer said. 'He was killed for the ground you're walking on. And you won't know who they're burying there?'

She pointed at a coffin smothered in flowers and drawn by horses. Among the long line of mourners slowly following was the man with the jaunty moustache.

'Terence MacSwiney, Mayor of Cork, died after a hunger strike in a British prison,' Kearney answered.

'Murdered. At least they taught you something at school.'

'There was a murder down the road,' Kearney said.

There was silence in the sweltering room. The coals settled and one fell into the hearth, smoking.

'We think Kevin saw it.'

As Eileen moved to the coal Mrs Spencer snapped: 'I can do it! Think I'm helpless?'

With painful slowness she gripped a pair of blackened tongs between her rigid hands and, after letting it slip once, manoeuvred the dull red coal back into the fire. Abruptly she began to laugh, a wheezing bronchial laugh.

'Indeed and he did see it and he saw the spaceman that took them away as well! They had three legs and one eye in the middle here.'

Eileen grinned. 'He was with me in the kitchen when it happened. Baking scones. He loves baking.'

'And making up stories.'

O'Hanlon was moving towards the door. Kearney touched the thinning flap of hair falling over his forehead, tired and depressed. It was suffocating and he longed to be out in the fresh air. 'We'd still like to —'

The siren on the Garda car blared out. Kearney

pushed past Eileen, sent a fishing-rod and basket flying as he ran through the hall. The car door was open, the car empty. At first he could see no-one. Squawking chickens drew his eyes to a gate, still swinging.

O'Hanlon following, he ran into the stubble-covered field. There was a movement in the grass under the hedge.

'Kevin!'

The boy scrambled away, brambles tearing at his pullover. They caught him as he was trying to get through the hedge.

'We're not going to hurt you.'

Blood oozed from a scratch on the boy's white, terrified face.

'I saw nothing! I saw nothing!'

'Stealing a Garda car is a serious crime,' said Kearney.

'I was only looking sir.'

O'Hanlon knelt down and said gently: 'Would you like a ride in it, Kevin?'

Kevin wrenched up a clump of grass, and looked from the squatting, smiling policeman to the tall, stern statue above him. He pulled the grass to pieces, his face clouded and confused.

'Were there two men or three, Kevin?' asked the smiling one.

'Four!'

Kevin clapped his hand over his mouth in terror as a figure appeared round the hedge. He shut his eyes, convinced that it was his grandfather, risen from the grave, and ready to carry him back into it. Only when he heard his mother's familiar voice did he open his eyes and fling himself, shaking, into her arms. She rubbed his hair and crooned gently, reassuringly to him.

Kearney bit his lip and then said quietly: 'Mrs Synott, a man has been killed. A woman and her daughter, who is a few years older than your son have been abducted. They may be killed.'

Rage broke out of Eileen Synott's bony frame like a wild animal from its cage. 'Why should I care about her? She's rich! They'll get out of it! He'll pay! He'll not miss the money! Why should we be frightened to sleep at night?'

Kearney thought that the gaunt, bitter face might have come straight out of one of those daguerreotypes of the famine, showing a family crouched over black potatoes.

O'Hanlon was never troubled by such fancies. 'You've got nothing to worry about here, Mrs Synott,' he soothed.

'You'll protect us.'

'Of course. If Kevin —'

The look she gave him stopped him. She pushed the boy towards the house, and then turned back to the two men. Her voice was flat, without emotion. She indicated the black-stoned farmhouse, towards which the boy was trudging.

'The old woman and her pictures.' She was silent for a moment. 'Her husband was killed all right. He was shot for informing. The grand man. Oh, he was a grand man all right. He was shot by the IRA or was it the IRB then? It doesn't matter.'

The boy was calling for his mother. Kearney felt extraordinarily helpless. They were obstructing the course of justice, but if the boy didn't want to identify the men, he couldn't make him.

'That was a very long time ago, Mrs Synott,' he said.

'Aye,' she said, 'It was, it was. And have things changed at all?'

She went back to the boy and the house.

8 *Asthma Can't Kill You*

It was the cold that was the worst, the cold and the damp. Frances felt that she had never been warm since she had been put in the cellar. After a while they put in a paraffin stove which poisoned the foul air, but at least she could crouch over it.

Once a little warmth had crept into her numbed limbs, anxiety grew about Clare. However much she pleaded with them and beat on the door they remained unmoved.

She forced herself to construct a routine, without which she would have gone mad. She had no idea whether it was day or night; her only clock was the meals which they slid along the floor on a tin tray bearing a faded map of the counties of Ireland.

She marked each meal with a scratch on the stone wall, putting a longer mark after each group of three to represent a day. Each day after breakfast she walked fifty times round the cellar. Her only contact with the outside world was the food: she would linger for an hour over the feel and smell of an apple before eating it.

After the evening meal she would try to remember every poem she had learned by heart as a child. To her amazement, what she thought had been totally lost came back to her.

It was, she thought, Wednesday afternoon, two days after the kidnap. She was sitting on the bed, a blanket wrapped round her, reciting.

'The camel's hump is an ugly bump . . . or was it

lump? . . . which you will see at the Zoo. But even uglier is the lump . . . bump? which you get from nothing . . . from having nothing to do! Cameelious —'

She stopped. Footsteps on the stairs. She'd had her meal. The tray had been taken back, the bucket emptied. Two pairs of footsteps. Her stomach contracted as the door opened. It was the woman and the man, both hooded. The woman was holding a gun.

'What are you going to do?'

He sat her on the bed, saying nothing. He was doing something at the back of her — hanging a blanket on hooks on the wall. She was paralysed with fear. The girl was obscured by the man, his eyes elongated in the balaclava. Something was thrust into her hands. There was a click. Her mind was screaming.

There was a flash, and she found herself staring into the lens of a Polaroid camera, the slowly developing film bending out in front of her.

The thing in her hands was a newspaper. Stupidly, she stared at it. There was a photograph of her and Geoffrey, outside Kilnameath. The headline was: I LOVE YOU.

They will cost you 3 million. Contact small ad Irish Times — Tom Ring Diamond. No police or you won't see them again. Tom.

The letters, cut from different magazines, were pasted under a photograph of Frances, her terrified eyes staring out above the top of the newspaper.

'Don't touch it,' Simon said.

He, Geoffrey, Lansbury and Margaret were in the big room at Kilnameath. Geoffrey kept turning away from the photograph and returning to it.

'Three million,' he said. 'That's absurd. I can't pay that.

He caught Margaret's expression. There were a pile of newspapers on the table, the top one of which had a headline: CARR WORTH 6.5 MILLION.

'Don't believe what you read in the papers,' he said.

'That's good public relations,' said Lansbury. 'Or bad, in the circumstances.'

Geoffrey felt sick and dizzy. 'I've had to borrow heavily to keep control of my company,' he said. 'I could just about raise one million, not three.

Margaret was crying silently. Geoffrey put his arms round her. He wished he could cry. It might release the awful emptiness and desolation inside him.

Frank emptied the bucket and flushed the lavatory. He had never been a gaoler before and he wasn't particularly enjoying it. It was all taking more time than he expected. They hadn't heard from Ronan, who had gone down to Ballyglen to sus out the boy who had seen him.

Did the Garda know anything or not? He was cooped up here, unable to go out until he was sure.

And now there was another unforeseen problem.

He took back the bucket. The woman was staring into space. She looked like she was going loopy. He didn't care. She was a thing, an object. The bucket smelt foul. He dropped it in a corner and turned to the woman.

'The wee girl's ill.'

Instantly she was alive, jumping up.

'She's having some kind of fit,' he added.

'Asthma. Let me go to her. She can't breathe. She's wheezing. Like this?'

'Dead on.'

Before he could react she'd run through the open door. He was taken by surprise and she reached the bottom of the stone steps before he caught up with her.

Kate was coming down, her balaclava rolled up. Frank caught the woman. She dug her nails into his cheek, drawing blood. He roared, arm-locked her and threw her on to the bed in the cellar.

Kate, her balaclava on, screamed: 'She saw me!'

'She did not!' Frank tried to calm her. 'All the girl's got is asthma.'

'She could die!' yelled Frances.

'Asthma can't kill you,' said Frank.

'Of course it can you —'

Frank looked uncertainly at Kate and then back at the woman, who had suddenly become a human being again.

'She won't be able to breathe!' Frances said wildly. 'Why won't you take me to her?'

Kate put her gun into the belt of her trousers. 'Tell us what we can do, give her.'

The woman's hands shook continually. Frank found it hard to believe that it was the same woman he had seen at the auction, self-assured, arrogant. Yet wasn't some of that arrogance creeping back now?

'When did the attack start?'

'Last night.'

The woman stood up. Frank gripped her arm. She met his eyes.

'She has had one serious attack before. If you just leave her the air passages will swell up and fill with mucus and she will go into a coma in which she will need a hospital ventilator to get her breathing again and without that she will die and if she dies I will kill myself, I swear to God I will. You can't watch me all the time, I will kill myself and then you will have nothing, nothing, nothing.'

Frank released her. He looked at Kate, who said: 'Tell us what to do.'

The woman sat down. Her hands had stopped shaking. 'You must let me see her.'

It was a dreadful journey from the other house. Willy drove. Frank kept the girl under a blanket in the back of the car: she musn't see the location, which she could describe to the Garda when she was released — if she was released.

She was coughing and wheezing and fighting for breath. Frank really thought she was going to die. He couldn't distance himself from the girl as he could from the woman; she was too much like his own daughter

Mary. His fear that the child would die came out in anger as he rushed her into the house, the blanket over her face.

'All right! You're here now! Stop all that! Stop it! You'll soon be with your bloody mother.'

The woman was very calm as she took the child, Frank had to give her that.

'I'm here, yes it is me darling, it's mummy. You're quite safe now. Could you leave us please?' she said to Frank and Kate. 'You frighten her. Please.'

Frank moved to the door with Kate, then stopped. What the hell were they doing, doing what she told them?

The girl fought for breath which wheezed out, in crackling short bursts. She sat down and couldn't get her breath at all. Her mother made her stand.

'Remember your exercises. Hands down. Down! Clench your fists. Good. Hold. Relax. Good. Hold, relax.'

Frank stared at the small white, straining face and went out and got a bowl of water and a sponge.

The woman actually smiled at him, a calm smile of acceptance. 'Thank you. Clench, hold, relax. She needs a doctor,' she said aside to Frank and Kate.

'Impossible,' Kate said.

'She needs a doctor. Relax. Good. Getting better.'

She negated her last statement with a furious shake of her head at Frank and Kate.

Kate tried to draw Frank away. 'She's fooling us.'

'Is there any medicine, pills,' Frank asked.

'No! She must see a doctor!'

The girl's breath crackled. She was trying to say something. Frank saw the woman shake her head pleadingly, warningly at her, and went to the girl. He found himself squatting, talking to her softly, as he would to his own daughter. Perhaps that reassured her, in spite of the mask, for she managed to cough out the word.

'Vent-to-lin.'

Kate's eyes gleamed with triumph. Frank started to go as the woman shouted.

'They're only on prescription. Why won't you take her to a doctor? You'd still have me. He'll pay you what you want!'

Simon felt much more in control after the two hoaxers had been arrested. Geoffrey didn't like him, but then the family's relationship to any kidnap negotiator was a difficult one. He was either a saviour who was going to bring the victim back, or the man whose wrong advice killed her.

The first thing always was to get the family together, to form what Bennet called the KCC — the Kidnap Crisis Committee.

They sat round the mahogany table, which Frances had found in a hotel in Kinsale. As well as Geoffrey and Margaret, there was Andrew and Lansbury.

In a kidnap, everything is laid bare, Simon thought as he looked round the faces while Geoffrey outlined his financial position.

Money, how much a man was actually worth, was an intimate secret, often not known to his closest family and friends. Whether it was in Italy, France or here, the faces, the fingers fiddling with keys or pens, always betrayed signs of voyeuristic curiosity.

He told them that his assets apart from Kilnameath and the St John's Wood house, were all in shares. As more shares came on to the market for a rights issue, he had had to borrow to take up enough shares to keep a controlling interest.

Tyndall, the financial director of Carr Computers, had estimated that by selling everything, at current market values he could raise one and a half million.

Simon looked up from the scratch pad on which he had been making notes. 'Then I suggest we offer them a quarter of a million for starters.'

'Starters?' Andrew sat forward. He looked out of place in that room, in his dirty sweater and baggy cords. 'It sounds like a bloody auction.'

'I'm afraid that's exactly what it is,' Simon replied.

'Holy mother.'

Margaret dipped her head, searching in her bag for a handkerchief.

'But Tom thinks I have six million,' Geoffrey objected.

As Andrew put his elbows on the table, they poked through holes in his sweater. 'Tom? Who the hell's Tom?'

'The kidnapper,' Simon said. 'He'll have to be told the truth.'

'Suppose he doesn't believe you?' Andrew said.

'Of course he won't believe me at first,' Geoffrey said impatiently. 'But —'

'They'll kill them!' Margaret interjected, and then they were all talking at once, Andrew hitting the table and Margaret, keeping back tears, pleading with Geoffrey to pay what he could now.

'Then where do you go,' put in Simon quietly, 'when Tom comes back for more?'

Geoffrey poured a glass of water. He drank it all before speaking. 'He's right. It will take time to convince them I haven't three million. How do I start negotiating?'

'You don't.' Simon badly wanted a cigarette, but never felt he could smoke at these first meetings. 'The person who speaks to Tom must not have the authority to agree to his demands. He must be forced to refer them back to you.'

'And if he doesn't?' Andrew was still belligerent, unconvinced.

'He will. You think Tom has all the cards. He hasn't. As negotiations go on, his money will be running out. The police may be getting closer.'

Andrew laughed, tilting his chair back and almost falling over. 'Jimmy O'Hanlon! He can't even find his trousers in the morning!'

Laughter erupted, died quickly.

'And their demands will go down, is that the idea?'

Margaret's voice was soft, but with a bitter edge. Simon had been watching her, summing up this woman so different from her sister, the one who had stayed at home, little style, rough chapped hands, very solid and dependable, but could let herself go, he thought.

He nodded to Margaret. 'That is the usual pattern. Perhaps you would like to negotiate?'

'Me?'

'We need someone who can turn on the emotions.'

'Ah.' She looked down at her big hands. 'Is that what I've been doing?'

Simon cursed himself for being clumsy. 'I'm sorry. But either we manipulate them, or they manipulate us.'

Margaret looked at him steadily. 'How experienced are you at . . . this sort of thing?'

Simon had taken out a cigarette before he remembered it was against his personal rules.

'I've advised on nine of these operations and lost one client. He was a middle-aged man who died of a heart attack.'

He rolled the unlit cigarette between his fingers in the silence that followed. Nobody looked at one another.

'So.' Geoffrey ran the point of his pen down the list he had made, and looked at Lansbury. 'John you'll try and get the press to back-pedal on my assets. Margaret will negotiate. I will go to the City to raise the money.'

'And what,' said Andrew, 'do I do?'

Geoffrey picked up his papers. 'We wondered if you'd like to deliver it?'

Frances got Clare leaning forward over two pillows. She was coughing up mucus and still wheezing, but less badly. The Ventolin had done the trick. She gathered from the whispered conversation between the two hooded figures that the man had broken into a chemist's shop.

On the small table by the bed lay both tablets and an

inhaler. She wiped away the mucus from Clare's lips with the wet cloth the man had given her. That small gesture had been enormously encouraging to her. But she was terrified they would separate them again. The two of them were arguing about it by the door. She pretended to concentrate on Clare, but she strained to catch every word.

'Once you start giving in to them . . .' the woman was saying.

Clare's coughing subsided. The woman whirled round, realising Frances could hear. She walked towards them.

'You're not taking her away from me!' Frances cried. 'She'll have another attack!'

The man strode over and put his hand on the woman's shoulder. She twisted away from him and left the room. Frances put her arms round Clare and rocked her as she hadn't done since she was a baby. The hooded man picked up the cloth and the water.

'Thank you,' she said.

The crouching figure whirled round and, holding the bowl of water like a discus, hurled it past them, whipping their faces with water before it smashed against the stone wall. The hooded angry eyes were inches from their white faces.

'Don't thank me,' the figure snarled. 'Don't *you* thank me! I'm just protecting my investment!'

9 *People Will Stick By You*

The portraits of three kindly old men smiled benignly down on Peter Greaves, managing director of the Three Cities Bank in Lombard Street. They were the founding fathers of the bank, painted with beautiful strands of white hair and delicate pink faces, rather as the Victorians used to portray God.

Greaves might be painted and put up there one day, thought Geoffrey: perhaps tomorrow. He was old enough and slow enough.

He knew what the old fool was going to do! Why didn't he get on with it?

How many times had he been in this room to borrow money? Greaves had always got it back. With interest. Well no. There was a considerable loan outstanding, but it was well secured against shares.

He wiped his sweating palms. It was a considerable loan. Suppose Greaves refused . . . He saw Frances's haunted face in the Polaroid they had sent . . .

Miss Vincent came in with more papers and smiled warmly at Geoffrey. Greaves looked up after she had gone out.

'Thank you er . . .'

He didn't even remember the name of his secretary who had been with him God knows how long! Come on! Come on!

Did he even remember what he had come about? Frances was not only in the hands of kidnappers, but in the hands of people like this. Greaves cleared his throat. His eyes were as dry as the digestive biscuits which had been provided with the coffee.

'Absolutely terrible thing,' he said. 'Incomprehensible, Ireland, absolutely incomprehensible. Coffee all right?'

Although they were in the heart of the city, there was no sound in the wood-panelled room, except for the tinkle of Greaves's coffee-spoon. The light on a desk-phone flickered, glowed, went out.

'You already owe us . . .'

Geoffrey watched him shuffle papers with agonising slowness. 'Two million.'

'Mmmm.' Greaves adjusted heavy library-frame spectacles over his protruding pink ears. 'And you're now seeking to borrow . . .'

'One and a half million.'

'For?'

'Two . . . three months?'

'Against the security of your remaining uncharged shares which total . . .'

'A million and a half.'

'Mmmm.' He couldn't find what he was looking for. 'And last night's close was . . .'

'146p. They're worth two million one hundred and thirty thousand.'

Greaves sipped coffee, took off his spectacles and stared into the middle distance. He grimaced and Geoffrey's stomach lurched. He'd had little rest or sleep since landing from Dublin yesterday; he had been phoning, consulting, evading reporters. Greaves turned to him.

'Over-roasted for my taste,' He put down the coffee cup. 'Shares'll go down a bit more, I expect?'

'They'll come back when the Japanese deal goes through. I'm seeing the Japanese tonight. They're on their way from Dusseldorf.'

'What stage are you at?'

'Final draft contract.'

The telephone light glowed again. Again the staring, the looping of the heavy spectacles round his fingers.

'Look, I tell you what I'll do, Geoffrey. I'll recommend we loan you a million, and then when our Japanese friends sign on the dotted, I'll reconsider the other half.'

Geoffrey sighed. His bones felt like rubber.

'Subject to my loans committee, of course.' He shrugged to indicate the formality. 'Is that what you expected me to say?'

'Hoped.'

The old man rose and smiled, looking more than ever like the pictures on the wall. 'Least we can do, flesh and blood being involved. People in the City will stick by you, Geoffrey.'

Suddenly moved, Geoffrey took the outstretched hand.

The loan was the best tonic he could have had. He felt on form. He thought of all his contacts like Greaves, all his resources, and confidence flowed through him. It was going to be all right. He could raise the money and she, they could be back with him in a week!

People were on his side. Since the press were watching his house, friends two doors up let him through their garden. Once in his house he phoned his secretary Janice, to learn the not very good news that the Japanese delegation had been delayed in Dusseldorf. He needed the deal to get the extra half-million from Greaves.

But even that didn't depress him.

'Book me on the late afternoon flight to Dusseldorf tomorrow.'

While he was talking to Janice, there was a tapping on the window. Gesturing outside was a florid-faced fat man with thick wavy hair and an inch of snow-white shirt cuff protruding from the sleeves of his dark grey suit. He brushed leaves from it as Geoffrey slid back the patio door.

'I'm sorry to give you all that exercise, Mr Jacobs.'

'Estate agents need it Mr Carr,' said the fat man, pulling down his cuffs.

'For the purpose of this transaction my name is Bolton,' said Geoffrey.

He opened his mail and made coffee while Jacobs walked through the house. As the heavy man moved from room to room above him, Geoffrey felt a pang. He remembered the day, a rainy one, when he had bought the place, staring through the patio doors into the garden, big for the area, and had had the feeling — I could live here.

'Beautiful, Mr Bolton.' Jacobs had come quietly into the room. 'An exceptional property.'

'How much?'

'I suggest an asking price of —'

'There's no time to ask. It's worth nine hundred thousand.'

'I wouldn't dispute it.'

'You've a week to sell it.'

Jacobs laughed. 'Mr Carr, a studio flat I couldn't sell in a week.'

Geoffrey's voice was flat and hard. Any business was dirty, but property was the dirtiest. Smiles, handshakes, promises: all were worthless. The only thing that counted was what he knew and could manipulate better than anyone else: money.

'You must have several customers, with the sort of money I want, ready to exchange contracts?'

Jacobs shrugged: of course. He dealt only with the rich.

'Offer them my property instead.'

Without hesitation Jacobs shook his head decisively. 'I'm sorry Mr Carr. I don't do business in that way.'

Geoffrey went right up to him. 'I want seven hundred and fifty thousand. Sell it for that and you get ten percent commission. That's £75,000, in case you have trouble with the noughts. If you have to drop fifty thousand to sell it, you get eight percent — £56,000, and so on.'

There was a long silence. Geoffrey slid open the patio door. It had begun to spit with rain out of a grey sky, a similar day, in fact, to the day on which he had bought the house. It took him a moment to register that Jacobs was speaking.

'Mr Carr, we have a code of business ethics. You make it extremely difficult to practice.'

It was bright and clear in Wicklow. Ronan squatted in a group of trees, watching St Edna's farm. It hadn't taken him long to find out what was happening: he'd seen an Inspector and a Special Branch man go in there and pick up the boy. That was yesterday. Another plain-clothes Johnny had stayed the night.

He chewed a cold bacon roll. By his side was a fishing-rod case. There would be trouble if he shot the Johnny. There were IRA standing orders forbidding the use of firearms in the twenty-six counties, except for training. But there would be trouble from Frank if he didn't lift the boy, more immediate trouble. Ronan was nineteen and confused. He admired and feared Frank. He wanted to free his country. But, on the other hand, the big man coming out from the farmhouse and enjoying the sun on his face was Irish. Armed. Ronan had excellent eye-sight and could see the bulge pushing out his cheap suit.

The boy was coming out. He had his fishing rod. They weren't taking him fishing? What the hell was going on?

He froze. Johnny was looking up, straight at him. He knew he had good cover, but it was a nerve-racking moment. It steeled Ronan. He'd try and jump him, but if he had to disable him . . .

He pulled aside his mac, to reveal a Ruger Mini-14 and rolled a balaclava down his face. He signalled to Martin who was in a battered Ford Granada round the bend from the farmhouse. The car chugged into sight. Johnny was waiting impatiently for the boy, who had gone back for something.

As the Granada came into sight, Johnny went to the farm gate. The car spluttered, stopped, just past the farm-house. Martin got out and opened the bonnet.

Johnny was suspicious, had sent the boy back inside.

Ronan slipped silently from tree to tree. The time for doubts was over. It was hunter and hunted. 150 yards. 100 yards. The T/O at his training camp had said he was no marksman, but he could carry out a good snipe.

He stopped. He didn't believe it! He slid down behind a tree, gripping the Ruger in frustration. Cows were being driven up from a field. The first one was already approaching, head swaying low towards Martin and the Granada. Soon he would be surrounded.

Ronan stripped the rifle, putting part in a flap sown in his mac, and part in the fishing-rod case.

Everyone was going fishing.

When Geoffrey got back from St John's Wood his office looked like the incident room at the Ballyglen Garda station. An extra desk had been brought in and Lansbury and his financial director Alan Tyndall were both on the phone.

'What had they marked the price down to?' Tyndall was saying.

'I can't talk about ransom demands.' Lansbury was in his shirt-sleeves, his untouched coffee growing a puckering skin. 'Harry, you know we've asked for a press silence for the sake of . . .'

'How much?' said Tyndall.

Geoffrey tried to decipher the scribble on his pad. 'What's going on, Alan?'

Janice who had followed him in, handed him a pile of letters. 'There's one from the Minister. I can handle the rest myself.'

'Not true Harry,' Lansbury said. 'Not true.'

'Down to what?' Tyndall's voice was incredulous.

'Thank you, Harry I'll buy you a large one.' Lansbury fished the skin from his coffee. 'We progress, master. The —' His phone rang.

The worse the crisis, the stiller and calmer Tyndall usually became. Geoffrey had never seen him like this. He covered the phone and said: 'The stock market is going —' He went back to the phone. 'Yes Terry. I'm here.'

'I can assure you Mr Carr is not pulling out of his company,' Lansbury said. 'God knows who started that one.'

'Who's selling?' Geoffrey asked Tyndall.

'How much actual business is there, Terry, can you tell me?'

Janice's voice came over the intercom. 'David in our press office, Mr Carr.'

'Yes David.'

'And I suppose Mr Carr shot the chauffeur,' Lansbury was saying.

'I have the Mail and the FT hanging on sir,' David said. 'One understands you've been asked for five million, the other for two.'

'The market is going bloody mad,' Tyndall said.

'There's a rumour you're about to off-load your personal holding,' David said.

Geoffrey bent over the intercom. 'Deny it.'

'Hang on,' Lansbury said to his caller and turned to Geoffrey. He'd pulled his tie away from his collar, as if he'd gone back to his early days as a reporter. 'It's no use just denying it.'

'129,' said Alan.

'129!' Geoffrey crossed over to him. When he had talked to Greaves, before the market had opened the share price had been 146. All his calculations were based on that. The whole rescue operation, Frances's life perhaps, was based on something that was slipping and sliding away from him.

Tyndall covered the phone, on which he had an open line to the company's brokers. 'It's mostly small sellers,' he told Geoffrey. 'Unit trusts who move in and out. There's not much volume yet. The jobbers marked us down to 135 before business opened.'

'Why?'

'To cover themselves. To deter potential sellers from getting out because they were afraid you would offload and drive down the price. Unfortunately, it's had the opposite effect. People thought the jobbers knew something. On top of this the rumour that you are getting out —'

'Who started that?'

'You did, master. By saying that you wanted to concentrate on research. We must have a press conference today.'

'No John!' Geoffrey sat at his desk, upsetting the pile of letters. 'I must go to Dusseldorf. I must have that Japanese contract in my pocket before I talk to the press. Put out a categorical denial that I am selling out. Stress that I will remain in charge of my company —' He stopped himself. 'I can't do that.'

'Why not?'

'The kidnappers.' Geoffrey walked round his desk, unaware he was treading on the spilt letters. 'I've sworn to the kidnappers I will sell everything. If I put out a statement denying I am selling out, God knows what they will do!'

'If you don't,' Tyndall said, 'the price will go through the floor.'

'And I won't have the money to pay the ransom anyway,' Geoffrey whispered.

There seemed no way out of the dilemma. His brain was jammed. David called on the intercom. Lansbury told him to wait. Tyndall was still hanging on to the broker.

Geoffrey went to the window. Over the roofs and between the skyscrapers he could see St Pauls. He concentrated on the dome, shutting out the men behind him. He wasn't praying. He was doing what you had to do when a computer programme jammed: reset, get rid of the input and start again. He was at the window one minute before he turned round.

'We'll hold a press conference in two days time. There will be a statement later today. Did you hear that, David?'

'Yes sir.'

Geoffrey snapped at the intercom button. 'Janice . . . Ask — no tell, repeat tell, Richard Lefray to meet me at the Long Room by the Stock Exchange at one o'clock. And, just in case he's unaware of it, tell him he's lost half-a-million pounds since breakfast.'

Kearney was going fishing. O'Hanlon thought he was crazy or had given up, and was determined to get some of the holiday he had missed. They had got nowhere with the boy. They couldn't even be sure he had seen anything relevant. Kearney had seen his white, mute face in his dreams.

Then he had remembered tripping over the rod in the hall. The boy, he had discovered, was mad about fishing.

So he had bought a beautiful rod, all on expenses. Perhaps, later, he could buy it cheap, he thought, as he parked the car near the bridge. He had some difficulty. The fine, slightly muggy morning had brought out a number of anglers. Paddy who was guarding the boy, looked bored to death, and was glad to leave.

Kevin, who was sitting on a little camp stool, ignored Kearney. In his bait tin, brown grubs poured over one another. Trees and shrubs came right down to the opposite bank, dangling their leaves into the water.

Kearney fitted together the beautiful rod. Kevin steadfastly kept his eye on his float.

'I was going to the Blackwater for salmon,' Kearney said. 'Before this job came up.'

Kevin looked at him, and saw the rod. He said nothing, but couldn't stop glancing at it.

'What sort of fly?'

Kevin's eyes bulged, and his hand came out involuntarily towards the gleaming, bright-coloured flies.

'It's bait,' Kearney had told the sceptical O'Hanlon. 'What do you think it is?'

Kevin's mouth opened, drawing out a thin thread of spittle between his teeth.

'Whiskey?' Kearney touched a fly. 'Or Black Chenille?'

He had never been so tense with a fishing rod in his hands. If the boy did know anything, the kidnappers might try and snatch him. He was exposing both the boy and himself: bait too. He comforted himself with the thought that he had Paddy and two other men in the woods, and fitted the fly to his hook. It danced, black and red in the sun, before it hit the water.

Kevin spoke for the first time, scornfully. 'They'll follow that, but they won't take it.'

On the bridge above them, Paddy watched. It was a quiet, peaceful boring scene. He was a restless, ambitious Special Branch man from Dublin, who hated the country. He thought that Kearney was wasting his time. Either the boy hadn't seen anything that mattered, or if he had, he'd been brainwashed by his family. Show him the photo-fits and he'd identify the wrong people.

But he was a meticulous man. He'd checked the line of cars parked by the anglers. He went past them again, looking inside, checking numbers. As he was turning back, something glinted ahead of him, from the woods, so briefly that he repeated the movement to make sure that it had happened.

He walked casually along the road, then took out his gun. It was a car. The glint came from a wing mirror. There was no-one in it. It was an old Ford Granada. For a moment he stood there. Then he remembered. It was the car which had broken down outside the farm that morning.

Geoffrey's Rolls arrived outside the Stock Exchange at the same time as Richard Lefray's taxi. Geoffrey instructed his driver to go and have a coffee. He didn't care whether the Rolls was ticketed, clamped or even towed away. He was here to make a display.

From the moment they walked down the glass-panelled corridor he and Lefray argued. He was surprised. He had expected Lefray to be all sympathy, all support — at least on the surface. But he launched an attack: Geoffrey had over-borrowed, was vulnerable.

'Temporarily.'

'Storms are temporary. People still drown,' Richard said.

People passing caught Geoffrey by the hand. He was not only moved by the good wishes, he thought: I could raise the money in this corridor several times over.

'I can't afford to be financially sound anyway,' he told Richard. 'The kidnappers will up their demands. You must support the share price.'

'Eagle already owns 29%. If we reach 30 I'll have to go to the take-over panel. And we can't afford to take you over.'

Geoffrey knew that. He also knew that the financial press were often surprisingly thick. As they walked he outlined his plan. Eagle's intention of buying all the shares would be announced. That would counteract the fall. Then, like the brilliant conjuror he had once been described as (by Lansbury, actually, who had put the image into the head of a drunken journalist) he would produce out of his financial hat the Japanese deal. The press loved excitement, conjuring tricks. They talked a lot of clap-trap about social responsibility, but sell them a good story and they'd swallow anything.

'That will bring the price back to 150. How are you Charlie?' He greeted a plump broker, hammered last year by the Exchange, and looking to be doing very well out of it. 'Then I announce Kilnameath Research Centre, new products in the pipe-line.'

'What new products?' asked Richard, trying to keep up.

'Really Richard you're a man of too much detail. I'll think of something. Holographic applications, computerised electric runabouts.'

People passing were astonished. He could see it in their faces. They thought he'd be a beaten depressed man! Rumours! He'd give them bloody rumours!

'What about Frances?' Richard said. 'I thought you were here to raise money for . . .'

'I've done that. Got that from the bank.'

A camera flashed. Good, good. It was all working. A young man, looked just out of school, was pushing a cassette recorder at him.

'Haines FT, Mr Carr. Any comments on this morning's dealings?'

'Yes. Buy. You'll make a bloody packet.'

The salmon soared into the air, scales gleaming, water spraying from its lashing tail. For the first time since the kidnap Kearney forgot about the Carrs, forgot about danger, forgot about everything but the leaping straining fish, pulling at the line.

Kevin wedged his rod, forgetting their enmity in the excitement of landing the fish.

'A seven pounder!' he cried.

'Six,' said Kearney. 'Hold my rod a minute.'

By the time he had removed the hook and fly from the mouth already gaping in death, Kevin was already making little whipping movements with the rod, casting imaginary flies.

'Would you like a go?' Kearney said casually.

Kevin shook his head, but his hands still gripped the rod. Kearney waited. As a boy Kevin's age he had begun fishing in a small river that went into the Blackwater, doing a paper round to buy the rod, sitting hunched for hours in the dawn mists every Sunday. He had never been happier. He knew Kevin wanted to use the rod more than anything else in the world. The boy pushed the rod towards him. Kearney took it.

'I didn't see their faces,' Kevin whispered.

He turned away to his own cheap rod, but the magic and pride of owning it had gone now he had held the other, and he didn't pick it up. Kearney felt ashamed and stupid: he should have known. In Ireland, even for an eight-year-old boy, fear was always stronger than desire.

The shot was like a whip cracking across the river. Kearney flung himself at the boy and rolled over on top of him, into the muddy reeds, almost in the river itself. I'm hit, he thought to himself, they can't miss at that range or the boy is, but Kevin's head was rising, he was crying out, his mouth full of mud, there were people running, feet at his eye-level, faces above him and surely that was Paddy's voice?

Among the trees opposite Paddy was pulling someone by the legs back on the bank. As he turned the man over, Kearney could see he was hooded.

At the incident room, a sergeant brought out mouths, moustaches, eyes from which Identikit pictures could be assembled. Eileen Synott and Kevin sat opposite Kearney. Her face was white with shock, but the boy seemed quite calm, even enjoying the experience, sucking a sweet he had been given.

'He's a good memory,' Eileen said. 'He'll remember. You'll remember won't you? Then we'll go away. They were going to take him?' Her hard, knotted fingers rubbed the boy's hair, her voice was vengeful. 'He'll remember. They were going to take him? They should have let him fish.'

There were eight groups of three scratches on the wall of the cellar. Frances walked Clare round the perimeter. Her confidence had kept up since winning the battle to keep her. The main battles now were how to keep clean: the dirt was engrained in her hands and finger nails, and her greasy hair itched. Clare moved to slump on the bed.

'Twice more!' ordered Frances. 'Come on! Left right left right. Mind the bucket, stupid!'

Clare kicked at their primitive toilet. Liquid slopped. As she aimed another kick at it Frances grabbed her. Clare screamed, on and on and on. Frances held on to her as Clare hammered at her with her fists. Eventually her breath crackled and Frances groped for the asthma spray.

She had managed to keep the attacks under control. The worst thing was finding something to do. The best standby was still remembering poetry. She stroked Clare's hair.

'Dylan Thomas,' she said.

After a silence, Clare spoke in a halting, faded voice. 'When I was young and easy under the apple boughs.' Her mother pulled the blankets over them. 'Around the lilting house, happy as —'

She began to cry. Frances continued: 'Happy as the grass is green.'

'He's forgotten about us.'

'Don't be silly! I told you about the newspaper headline!' At night, well she supposed it was night, she lay awake thinking about it, picturing the newspaper page, the heavy black type. 'I love you. He said — I love you.'

'Do you love him?'

'Yes.'

Her answer amazed her. It came out without her thinking. She rocked her daughter.

'More than Daddy?'

'More? You can't weigh it like apples. You just love. We plan to have a baby.'

Again, it was amazing how easily that came out! Clare was sitting up now and staring at her with such a comical expression she laughed.

'Do you mind?'

'No. No.'

'My period's late, in fact. Probably the change in routine.'

Now they both laughed. Clare cuddled into her. Soon she would sleep. Years had dropped away in the cellar, and her teenager had fallen back into being a child again, a toddler, a baby sometimes. Her voice sank to a murmur.

'When we're back in Kilnameath I'll —'

'Not there,' Clare said. 'Not there.'

'All right. We'll go to the apple country, to that cottage. The apples must be ready to pick.' She was silent for a moment. 'And honoured among the wagons, I was prince of the . . .'

Now Frances began to cry, the tears oozing slowly and quietly, but it didn't matter, for Clare had fallen asleep.

The shots rang out over the grave. Earth hit the coffin. Kearney sat in the viewing room and looked at the flickering pictures, trying to identify Frank Crossan. They were sure now. It all hung together. He was missing from Derry. Ronan Flynn, whose body they had fished from the river, was a known associate. And, most of all, the boy had been very positive.

They'd phoned up from the Castle to congratulate him: everybody thought Kearney was a genius except Kearney; he felt lucky to be alive, lucky that, by their action against the boy, the kidnappers had identified themselves.

But where were they?

Blank film and then numbers on the film leader flashed on the screen. The big man sitting next to Kearney grunted: 'Frank Crossan, family man.'

Jack Watson was from the RUC in Belfast. He had hands so large a cigarette looked like a match between his fingers. There was usually one there and he smoked them down to a small butt, so his finger and thumb were stained almost black. He had been cordial enough, but Kearney knew that sooner or later he would get the line that, so far as terrorism was concerned, the Garda were babes in arms compared with the RUC.

The secretly taken film was of the Diamond in Derry and showed Crossan chasing his daughter and scooping her up, laughing.

'He's shot three and blown up ten to my knowledge,' said Watson.

'Anything on the woman?' Kearney asked.

Watson sucked in smoke and shook his head. The film ended and the two men turned to O'Hanlon, who switched on a tape recorder. Margaret Healey's sobbing voice came out of it full volume before O'Hanlon turned it down.

'Tom, listen, please listen —'

The man's voice was blurred with shouting anger. 'He's a bloody swindler! Half a million! The bastard's loaded! You have can have your fucking sister back! In a fucking coffin!'

'Wait until he get's back!'

The phone was slammed down. The policemen heard Margaret breaking down and being comforted by an unknown voice before the receiver was replaced. There was a silence. Watson lit a fresh cigarette.

'Will the family cooperate with us?' he asked.

'They will, they will.' O'Hanlon slipped the tape recording into a case with others.

'To a point,' said Kearney.

'What point?'

Neither Kearney nor O'Hanlon answered. Watson levered himself up. He never sat still for long and was constantly glancing about him, or looking out of windows. He had a livid scar on his neck, which looked like an extra mouth when he was talking.

'Crossan fell out with the people he was working with,' he said. 'He's on the run from them as well as us. Mrs Carr and her daughter are his return ticket to Londonderry. The grapevine says he's fixed up a big arms deal. If he fails, he's a cowboy. If he pulls it off they'll love him and none of your rich industrialists down here will be safe.'

Watson straddled a chair which creaked under his weight. Ash bounced and dribbled on his jacket as his strong Belfast accent became even harsher. 'Mr Kearney, I have every sympathy with that poor lady and her wee girl, but under no circumstances must Carr be allowed to pay that ransom.'

* * *

Frances was just beginning to fall asleep when they came for her. Although an extra mattress had been brought in, she slept curled up round Clare.

The man entered, hooded. At first she thought he was going to take Clare who was asleep but he motioned her out of the door. What was the point of resisting? She would only wake Clare and distress her. As soon as she was in the corridor the man pinned her arms and then she began struggling, but the woman put the padded spectacles on her face and bound them into place with adhesive tape.

They wouldn't answer her questions. She stumbled as they went up some steps and the man saved her from falling. A blanket brushed against her face and a door closed. Warm air met her, amazing warmth after that damp cellar. They left her abruptly. She took a step or two, blind, put her hands out, clawing air.

'There's a chair behind you,' the man said.

The woman's voice, coming like a lash from a different direction, made her jump. 'They shot one of our people. They shot him!'

Frances, feeling for the chair, said: 'I'm sorry.'

Now the voice was in her ear. 'You're sorry! You're sorry!'

Frances's nerves snapped. 'What do you expect me to say?'

The woman grabbed her up, her dress tearing and shoved her violently away. For a terrifying moment Frances was hurtling through the air, then she collided with something that gave her a sharp blow in her back. A chair clattered over and crockery broke.

'All right, all right.'

The man's tone was comforting but he was nowhere near her, nothing made sense, there was a pain when she breathed, she musn't take a deep breath, perhaps she would lose consciousness, but Clare, Clare, she must get up for Clare's sake!

He was helping her up, was he? Or was he going to hit her? She flinched.

'I'm not going to touch you. Here's a settee . . . We're a wee bit upset, you see, Mrs Carr. A wee bit upset.'

There was the sound of liquid pouring. 'Where did you get that from?' the woman snapped. 'Did you go out?'

'Willy got it.'

'Names, don't use names,' the woman shouted.

'All right, calm down, calm down.' The voice approached the settee. 'A wee bit upset Mrs Carr. Frances.'

'What?'

'Isn't that your name?'

She clutched at the torn edges of her dress, bewildered at his change of tone. She could smell him; her sense of smell had grown sharper in the cellar, his shirt had a rather greasy, petrol smell, which mingled with aftershave.

'Get on with it,' the woman said.

'Shut up will you!' The man leaned over Frances. 'Here. Drink this.'

She smelt whiskey. Were they going to poison her? Drug her? She kept her mouth rigid. He pressed the rim of the glass against her teeth, and tilted her face. Whiskey ran into her mouth and over her chin. She choked, swallowed. It tasted all right, in fact the warmth in her throat and her stomach was comforting, bringing her out of her daze.

'That's it, that's it.'

His arm was round her and he was squeezing her shoulder. At the totally unexpected tenderness she broke down, crying.

'I'm sorry, I'm sorry, whatever it is I've done I'm sorry . . . don't take Clare away, please don't take her away.'

The man hushed her, taking the spilling drink from her hand. 'She's safe . . . We've treated you all right, haven't we?'

'Yes.'

'We've been patient?'

'Yes, I . . . yes. Please let my daughter go,' she whispered.

'Jesus we want to let you both go! We don't want you here! I'm a prisoner here too! Once we have the money we can all go home!'

The adhesive tape bit the spectacles into her cheek, but she dare not touch them, for fear they would become violent again. 'He will pay,' she said.

'Ach, well now that's the problem.' The man was finishing off her whiskey. 'To tell you the truth, he won't. He's not terribly keen. I don't think your man appreciates the gravity of the situation. As you do.'

'He wants to negotiate! *Bargain*!' The woman sounded at the end of her tether. 'He wants to *bargain* for you! We haven't time to bargain, Mrs Carr, do you understand? You tell him!'

'Me?' She was overcome. They were going to release her? Keep Clare?

'You speak to him.'

She struggled to get up, hands groping out blindly. 'Speak to him? He's here? Geoffrey? Geoffrey?'

She blundered into the table, felt the wood. The man was laughing as he put something cold and metallic into her hand. A wire trailed against her, and she realised it was a microphone.

'Imagine he's here,' the man said. 'Imagine you're holding his hand.'

10 *The Price, Darling, The Price!*

If they had had this turn-out for a product, it would be worth a fortune, Geoffrey thought. The press conference was jam-packed. All the plastic shelled chairs were occupied, and they were standing at the back.

Lansbury had taken soundings among his friends and reported that all were sympathetic. They would accept without question that he couldn't talk about Frances and Clare or an imminent ransom demand, for fear of risking their lives. In a hushed silence he told them that Lefray-Eagle was going to purchase his personal holding in Carr Computers.

The room was with him. The questioning was gentle.

'How will this affect your position in the company sir?'

'Oh, I should think they might retain my services?' Geoffrey answered.

'I should think we might,' said Richard, who was on the platform with Tyndall and Lansbury.

Everybody laughed except Taylor, a dry elderly Scot who peered over half-spectacles at Geoffrey from the front row. He and Geoffrey had clashed before. Taylor regarded anything other than gilts as highly speculative.

'Mr Carr,' he said. 'What is the value of your holding?'

'Rather less than it was, Mr Taylor,' Geoffrey countered drily. There was laughter at his tone.

Taylor looked at his calculations. 'Assuming —'

'Please don't speculate about what I'm worth.'

'Of course not. All of us here appreciate your horrible predicament, Mr Carr.'

The murmurs of sympathy did not comfort Geoffrey. Taylor had the quiet stillness of a cat waiting to pounce.

'However . . .' Taylor's voice was regretful but insistent. '. . . we have a public duty to report what is going on in a quoted company. I'm not so concerned with what you're going to get, as with what he's going to pay.'

He pointed at Lefray. Lansbury leaned forward, putting a worried expression on his face. 'But Wally . . . have I missed something as usual? Aren't they the same thing?'

The laughter didn't perturb Taylor. '*Per share*,' he persisted. 'How much are you offering per share? Will you have to find five million? Six?'

Lefray and Tyndall looked at one another. Geoffrey was sure he detected something in that look. Or was this whole business making him paranoid?

'We can't comment at this stage,' Tyndall said.

'Will this undisclosed sum come from Eagle's own resources,' asked another journalist, picking up Taylor's tone.

The mood of the meeting changed. The sympathy disappeared as they smelt blood. Geoffrey tried to stave it off, tried to bring the meeting to a close, but what he feared happened.

'Is Katsushomo involved?'

'No,' Geoffrey replied. 'The Japanese deal is a separate one.'

'Is that still on, sir?'

'Of course it's still on!'

'You were in Dusseldorf yesterday?'

Taylor's eyes were unblinking over the half-glasses: this was the kill. Yes, you bastard, thought Geoffrey, I was in Dusseldorf yesterday, at the rain-soaked airport, waiting fruitlessly at the Park Hotel, refusing to talk to some junior Japanese executive they tried to fob me off with, going into all the restaurants in the Konigsalle in search of the men who mattered, trying to save this company so I can save my wife and child, while all you care about is a story for tomorrow's paper, grubbed out under the moral disguise of public duty.

'I understand the Japanese have visited Sonnencomputer in Dusseldorf,' Taylor said. 'Are you afraid they will do a deal with them instead?'

Geoffrey suddenly felt a great weariness, but managed to smile: never, ever show the bastards that you are bleeding. 'I have visited the Bank of England,' he said. 'But it doesn't mean I have done a deal with them. Unfortunately.'

Somehow he got through it. Tea was brought into the conference room, now bleak and empty, with full ashtrays and discarded handouts on the askew lines of chairs. At one end of the room, Tyndall phoned the company's brokers: it was approaching close of business for the day. At the other Geoffrey faced Lefray and Lansbury. Far from being downcast and depressed, they were at most philosophical. Geoffrey was beginning to get the picture. He tried to control himself, but the anger that had built up during the press conference burst out.

'It would have worked if you had answered the questions!'

'What exactly does that mean?' Lefray said coldly.

'No calls, absolutely no calls to this room.'

Although Tyndall's voice was quiet, across the room, they instantly stopped talking, and waited for him to come to them, pushing a couple of chairs out of the way.

'The share price closed below a hundred. Ninety-nine point five, to be exact.'

All were stunned. Geoffrey could scarcely believe that only a couple of days ago he had been secure, in control of everything. 'What is going on?' he said.

'They've decided the Jap deal is off,' Tyndall said.

'They've decided!'

'Self-fulfilling prophecy,' Tyndall went on. 'Do you

think the Japs will sign something that they've read in the papers isn't going to happen?'

Geoffrey walked a few paces and then turned to Lansbury. At least Lansbury always had a joke for the situation, even if he had no solution for it. But not this time.

'You've been at the top too long,' Lansbury said flatly. 'You're over the hill. The Irish Folly. Delusions of Research.'

Geoffrey stared at him, thunderstruck. Lansbury's face slipped into an apologetic smile, as he spread his hands.

'I'm expressing the media's point of view, of course, master.' He spoke in headlines, conveying what he felt in the disguise of other people's opinions. 'Terrible about the kidnap, but if it hadn't been that, it would have been something else. We built him up. Now we'd better pull him down.'

Geoffrey stood an inch away from Lansbury. 'I — built — myself — up!'

'Oh, of course, master, I was merely expressing their opinions . . . these things are entirely illogical . . . irrational . . .'

'It's not entirely illogical.' Lefray took up the demolition process. 'The company has always seemed to be you. Your inspiration. Your ideas. But — you must face this, Geoffrey — it hasn't been like that for some time now. If a man has one good idea in his lifetime, that's more than most. You've been lucky. Forget research. Rescue what you can, Geoffrey. You've just been through the pretence of selling to me.' He put his papers in his case. 'Why don't you?'

'You made it all too perfectly clear you can't afford to buy me out.'

'Not fully. But suppose instead of borrowing money from the bank on your remaining unpledged shares, you sold them to me?'

In the silence that followed Lefray shut his case and twirled the safety locks.

'That would give you control,' Geoffrey said.

Lefray shrugged, as if that had never occurred to him, and anyway was not really the point.

'On the cheap,' Geoffrey said.

'I'm thinking about the stability of the company. And Frances.'

'You're thinking about yourself! You could have made a full takeover bid sound plausible.' Geoffrey whirled on Lansbury and stabbed a finger at the front row of chairs, where Taylor had been sitting. 'How did he know I was in Dusseldorf? Stability of the company!' He strode back to Lefray. 'The company is perfectly sound! When this business is over the share price will recover! You know that! You want control. You always have. You want me to do what your mean, shortsighted, pennypinching mind tells me to do and live off our present products. That would *really* make the price fall. For good!'

'You're just being paranoid, Geoffrey!' Lefray shouted back. 'I know —'

Geoffrey pushed him to one side, contemptuously. It was only a small shove, but Richard staggered into a chair, which went over.

'Wouldn't you be bloody paranoid.' His gesture indicated the chairs, the departed journalists — the whole situation. Finally he turned to Tyndall, the solid one, always behind him in many battles. He was closing his case too, an old-fashioned one with brass clasps.

'Alan.'

The clasps were out of true, and Tyndall fiddled to fasten each one before replying.

'I think Richard's offer is the only course to take, Geoffrey.'

Geoffrey walked out. On the way home — if he could still call it that! — Janice phoned him to say that Greaves of the Three Cities Bank had been trying to get him all afternoon.

Geoffrey could picture the paintings of the three kindly old men on the wall as Greaves's painfully slow voice told him the bank could not lend him a million, let alone a million and a half.

Traffic was building up into the rush hour as they went round Regent's Park. A group of excited schoolchildren were leaving the Zoo. Geoffrey knew that at any moment Greaves would say if it was up to him . . .

'But you agreed, Peter!'

'Subject to my Loans Committee. The steep fall in share price has alarmed them so much, they feel there's insufficent security. If it was up to me . . .'

'I know, I know, Peter, you've been very kind.'

He walked into his silent house and made some coffee. It was a dark evening, but he didn't switch on the lights. The answerphone tape was full of calls, and he began playing them back. Jacobs, the estate agent of unshakeable principles, was sending someone called Appleyard. He ran on the tape. Everything seemed irrelevant now. Suddenly, into the dim room, came Frances's voice.

'What's happening darling, what is happening, they're going to kill us if you don't —'

At first he thought it was an illusion, a nightmare. He ran back the tape and heard Margaret's voice.

'. . . we've received a tape. I'll try and play it over the phone.'

There was a scuffling noise as the mouthpiece was placed against the tape recorder, and then Frances's voice came through the crackles, suprisingly cheerful and normal.

'Hello Geoffrey. We're all right. We . . . Oh, I hate speaking into these damn things!'

The cheerfulness vanished. The voice was cut off and then returned, hysterical, at a bigger volume.

'What's happening darling? Why is it taking so long? Why haven't you paid the money?'

Geoffrey's front door bell rang. He remained motionless as the tape rolled, static sighed, and Frances's voice went on, blurred now because she was too close to the microphone.

'This is a gun I'm touching . . . This is a bullet . . . the one they will use . . .'

The door bell rang, longer, shrill. Geoffrey got up.

'. . . just release Clare, give them what they want for Clare, she's been so ill, she nearly died . . .'

Geoffrey switched off the tape and, with slow, mechanical movements, opened the door. A couple in their mid-thirties were smiling expectantly at him. Both wore quiet dark suits which murmured money. Parked behind them was a black BMW.

'Mr Bolton?'

Geoffrey stared numbly at him, and then remembered this was the pseudonym he had told Jacobs to use for selling the house.

'John Appleyard. My wife. Splendid hall.'

'Yes,' Geoffrey said and then just stood there, while they waited, their smiles freezing on their faces. 'Look, would you excuse me?' he managed. 'I . . . I'm in the middle of something . . . Would you mind showing yourselves round?'

While they went upstairs he returned to his study. He sat, head in hands, listening to them move about above him, before moving slowly, in a trance, back to the tape recorder. Frances's voice was now as slow and halting as his movements.

'You have ten days to get the money if you. . . .' She stopped for several seconds. '. . . want to see us again. The deadline is twelve noon on Saturday, next Saturday . . . Please! Let me!'

It sounded as if she was struggling with someone. The door opened and Appleyard came in.

'I love you, Geoffrey,' Frances said, as the line went dead.

'I'm awfully sorry.' Appleyard backed out hastily. He left the door open and Geoffrey could hear him talking with his wife as he dialled a number.

'What do you think?'

'It's a splendid kitchen.'

'It's a good road.'

'It's a lovely road.'

'So what do you . . .'

'The other house has those wonderful fireplaces . . . much more character . . . we've measured up everything . . . I do prefer it . . .'

'Oh, so do I! But the price, darling, the price!' His voice dropped. 'You know who he is, don't you? We could probably knock him down even further.'

Geoffrey closed the door as the phone was answered by Lefray.

'Richard,' he said. 'It's Geoffrey. Can you possibly come round?'

11 *An Ulster Fry*

Frances ground the point against the stone floor, spat on it, ground it, and wiped it on her dress. It was as sharp as a needle now.

She had found the steel comb two days ago, buried in the rubble at the side of the ill-fitting cellar wall and floor, among cigarette ends and bits of paper. She had scraped away the brown rust and, wrapping a handkerchief round the teeth, made a crude but effective knife, sharpening the point while Clare, as now, was asleep.

She kept the weapon from her, as she had kept the knowledge that in six days time they would be shot. The only hope she clung to was that they would release the child. And that they would get careless. They now thought her so passive, so easy to deal with. She hid the knife behind a loose brick.

Was it six days? She got terribly confused. She picked up her marking brick, counted the clumps of three scratches and then worked forward, putting in the days to come. Yes. Six days. Less than a week.

She scored the line that marked the deadline day, again and again.

'What are you doing?' Clare was awake, sitting up in bed.

'Scratching a brick.'

'Why are you scratching that one? Where have all those days come from?'

'I'm marking the weeks. I'm making a calendar.'

'That week has only six days.'

'Oh. Has it?'

'You're going stupid.' Clare buried her head into the pillow. 'What's the point anyway? Each day's the same as the next, the same as the night — what's the point?'

'At least I won't have to hang it up.'

'What?'

'The calendar.'

Clare groaned and beat at the pillow with her fists. 'I hate it when you're trying to cheer me up.'

As Frances tried to sit on the edge of the bed, Clare rolled over to prevent her.

'Move,' Frances ordered.

'You smell.'

'So do you.'

Frances sometimes became as childish as Clare. What mattered in life had been reduced to childish things: food, how many times they had walked round the cellar, and how much room the other took up in bed. Frances tried to control herself but sometimes, like now, she momentarily lost her temper and grabbed Clare's wrists and shook her.

Clare kicked out viciously. Frances fell on top of her, trying after her initial burst of rage to turn the struggle into a game, but there was real violence not far from the surface. Didn't caged rats become violent and eat one another?

'You smell like mouldy cheese,' she yelled in Clare's ear.

Clare capped her: 'Old socks.'

'Old boots.'

'Pigswill.'

'Drains.'

'THE BUCKET!' Clare shouted in triumph, and they collapsed in laughter. 'I won I won!'

As her prize, Clare took a hunk from the secret store of bread — two slices — under the mattress, and began to eat it in spite of Frances protesting that they should save it. As she chewed she said: 'Is that when they're going to let us out?'

She pointed to the deadline brick which Frances had

scored heavily. Frances nearly broke down. She turned away so Clare should not see her face. Clare put her arm round her. It was sometimes becoming like this, with Clare supporting her.

'It's my period,' Frances said. 'It's just a bad period that's all.'

Clare squeezed her shoulder in disappointment. 'I thought you were going to have a baby.'

Frances gripped her daughter's hand. 'So did I.'

On watch, reading at the kitchen table, Kate found her head nodding until she had to go outside, where the air was a cold shock, and the limestone crags shone in the moonlight. Yet, as soon as she went to bed she couldn't sleep, and had to take two Mogadon.

At ten the next morning she had woken, muzzy and still tired, to find no bread and one tea-bag which spilt fine dust from a tear in its side when she lifted it out of the tin. Frank's door was shut: he always slept late. Under the sink was the empty bottle of Jameson's. He was drinking more.

Willy and she split the shopping, since Frank couldn't go out, with every guard in the twenty-six counties looking for him. Usually it was her, in her role of middle-class writer, who went out, but since Ronan had been shot she had grown increasingly nervous and hadn't shopped for days.

She opened the door leading down to the cellar. The woman was knocking on the door: knocking, not banging. She had become cowed, passive since she had made the tape-recording. Presumably they hadn't been fed. She poured boiling water over the tea dust and went to the window.

It was a clear, autumn day, windy enough to blow round the carousel of washing. They each did their own by hand, as the ancient washing machine had broken down. At first they had expected her to do it! Willy was running towards the house. He went jogging every morning.

If anyone passed, which happened rarely, nothing could look more normal.

A fine, ashy deposit floated on her tea. It was not until she was putting in milk that her muzzy brain, working uneasily on what she had just seen through the window, realised what was wrong.

Willy was there, the car wasn't. She flung open Frank's door. The room was empty.

Frank had the car window open, the fresh air smacking against his face. It was a wonderful feeling. He hadn't been out of the house for over a week. Even if he went out into the grounds she threw a scene. He knew that the real danger came from her nervousness, not his foolhardiness.

He'd been on the run before. With his hair cropped short and his moustache shaved, did he look like Frank Crossan? In his tourist gear of horribly flared blue jeans and T-shirt saying *All The Best People Come To Ireland*?

If you were brash enough, the police looked right through you. It was much more likely that Kate would do something stupid, like buying five loaves of bread in the same shop when there were only supposed to be two of them, her and Willy.

But it wasn't the shopping really. He needed air. And it was his daughter's birthday. It was safe enough to phone up Deirdre, and leave a message with her.

Mary was nine today. It would mean so much to her. He could picture her face. When he'd been away before she'd kept, from each mass, a small particle of wafer, hiding them in a handkerchief.

'What's that? Cornflakes?' he had said.

The traffic built up as he got into the town. Jesus, it was busy, far busier than he had expected! He looked for a supermarket with a phone near it. He passed one, but there was not a scrap of parking space. He began to worry. He thought he could nip out while she was under the Mogadon. She would go hairless!

There was a Quinnsworth — and there was a space. No! A bastard had just nipped in before him. He could just about squeeze in at the top of a bus space. He ran to the phone. Deirdre was engaged. And once that woman started talking! But he could do with a feel of her tits now, he thought as he ran into the supermarket and began hurling bacon, bread, tins into a trolley. Black pudding, that was the stuff, Kate never bought any.

He smiled at the check-out cashier as he gave her two twenties. Who would look for him in a bloody Quinnsworth?

He got the message through to Deirdre, timing himself fifteen seconds just in case it was tapped.

'Look after yourself,' she said.

His heart leapt. He bought a couple of papers, lobbed them on top of the huge carton of groceries and hurried to the car. There was something about the kidnap . . . He saw Carr's name on the headline . . . A ball bounced towards him. As it hit his legs he saw, above the bobbing line of the carton in his arms a guard crossing the street towards him. He had an instant to react. The Browning was in the boot of the car. He must get the boot open . . .

While he was thinking this he had trapped the ball and kicked it to the small boy who was playing with it, giving him a cheery grin. The boy ran back to his mother who was chatting at the roadside. Frank dropped the carton and had the keys in the hatch by the time the guard reached him.

As the hatch sighed up the guard said: 'Can't you see this is a bus stop?'

He was scarcely over the yellow line, half a wheel over but don't argue, Frank told himself.

The Browning, wrapped in oily rags with the jack, had been disturbed during the jolting ride into town. Frank could see the muzzle of the Hi-Power pistol. So could the guard, if he looked down. It was the gun he had used to shoot the chauffeur. Why the hell hadn't he got rid of it?

'Bus stop?' he said.

'Can't you read?'

In fact a bus was pulling in, and had no difficulty.
'You start, others come in,' the guard continued.
'I'm sorry, I didn't see that.'
He smiled apologetically, bending to pick up the carton. As he moved to put it in the boot, the guard stepped forward to wave on the bus, blocking Frank's way.
'There's a car park at the bottom there.'
'Thank you, thank you, I'll remember that.'
The guard stepped to one side and Frank, as if the carton was unbearably heavy and he couldn't hold it a moment longer dropped it in the boot and pulled down the hatch. He opened the door and was about to get in when the guard followed him.
'Aren't you from the north?'
Frank grinned. The grin was becoming fixed. 'I was from the black north but I'm a Dubliner now, in spite of the price of petrol.
'Can I see your licence?'
Frank fished out his licence with his left hand, keeping his right clenched round his keys. The guard's face was unmoving as he read: *Vincent Stephens, 18, Pearse Street, Dublin 2.* The guard had fine black hairs sprouting from his nostrils which trembled slightly as he breathed. He was either a very slow reader, or he had sussed him. Frank shifted position slightly. He could catch him with the door and smash the keys into his face.
Brakes screamed. The guard whirled round.
'Jesus,' said Frank.
The small boy had darted after his ball and a car had just pulled up in time. The guard thrust the licence into Frank's hand.
'Use the car park in future!' he said.
'I will, oh I will,' said Frank gratefully, jumping into his car, as the guard strode over to the mother to deliver another lecture. He found it difficult, as she was in full voice.
'You tell them till the words are worn out but you might as well talk to that pavement, look the man is

after putting your name down in his little black book, oh you're in trouble all right now!'

The guard did have his notebook out, but he was staring uneasily at where Frank's car had been parked, as if there was something he was struggling to remember. His face burned slightly. He should have taken the licence number. As the boy's mother went on, he wrote down 49, the only two digits he could remember.

The worst thing was when something was happening above them and they had no idea what it was. Frances squatted with her ear against the door. Usually they could hear nothing, but they must have left the door open at the top of the steps, for they could hear the woman, whom Clare called the witch, shouting.

Frances tried to get Clare to listen, for she had sharper ears.

'I can't hear anything mummy, I can't hear!'

'She said: where is he? Where's he gone?'

'Did she? I'm frightened of the witch, mummy.'

'It's all right. It's all right.'

Clare was terrified. They couldn't walk or do poetry, all they could do was listen. Frances's stomach rumbled. Surely it was long past breakfast. What was happening? Every possible scenario had gone through Frances's head. The thought of being rescued was almost as bad as any other. There might be a gun battle. If they were not shot deliberately, it might happen accidentally.

The witch was shouting at the man. A door slammed above. The outside door?

'He's gone out. The witch is on her own.'

Clare gripped her mother tightly. Frances went to the wall, took out a brick, and then took out the knife. Clare's eyes were large hollows in her pale face. 'Where did you get that?'

Frances didn't answer her. If the man was out they had a chance. She might be able to kill the woman, get her gun and wait for the man. She had worked out, in the long nights when she couldn't sleep, exactly where she would stab the knife, by probing at her own chest. She read in her daughter's face what she must look like, with her dirty savage looking face, her torn dress and lank hair hanging down the sides of her face.

'Just in case — don't cry!' she said sharply. 'We can't afford to cry! If I shout floor, drop there — there, behind the bed. Do you understand?'

Clare was shaking. She nodded dumbly. Someone was coming down the steps. Frances tried to conceal the knife in her clothes. It was impossible. She tried to put it in the band of her knickers but couldn't walk without the risk of impaling herself. Clare was laughing hysterically. At screaming point, Frances thrust the knife under the blankets as the bolts were slid back and the key went in the lock.

The door opened. Clare moved to her mother.

'Stay away from me!' Frances hissed.

'Why?'

Clare pressed against the wall. Frances stayed on the bed, near the knife. It was the witch pushing the tray into the room with her foot as she always did. On it was nothing but a few biscuits and two mugs of water. The witch's hand hovered near the gun in her belt.

'What's going on?' she said, the hooded eyes moving from the crouching girl to Frances. 'Aren't you hungry? Well go on! Pick it up!'

Clare moved.

'Not you!' The witch yelled, turning to Frances. 'You! Move!! Are you deaf?' She took the gun from her belt. The man was always calm when he had a gun, in fact it seemed to make him calmer, but it always pushed the witch nearer to the edge. The tips of Frances's fingers were under the blankets, touching the handle of the knife. The gun was in her face, its muzzle frighteningly large.

'Please don't point that at me.'

'Don't you tell me what to do!'

The gun caught the light as it quivered in the witch's

hand. It was just too far away for Frances to dive under it and go in with the knife. She brought her hand out slowly from under the blankets and bent to pick up the tray. A man's voice, the man they called Willy shouted from the top of the steps.

'What?' the witch shouted back.

There was no reply, only the sound of running footsteps and a door slamming.

'What? What?' The witch was half-out of the door, her over-wrought face twisted towards the steps.

Frances flung the tray then herself at the witch, shrieking: 'Floor.'

As Frank got out of the car at Annacloy, he saw Willy running towards him. Very muffled, there was a shot.

Willy stopped, turned. As Frank ran after him the fear hammered in his head: she's panicked, she's shot them, that bloody guard stopping me, I would have been back, she's shot them.

He and Willy entered the front room at the same time and collided at the top of the cellar steps. Kate was shouting and there was a horrific, animal-like snarling.

The woman was like a wild beast. She clung on to Kate's hand holding the gun, banging and scraping it against the raw brick wall until Kate yelled in pain and fury. The girl, sobbing, was wrenching at the blankets as the gun dropped from Kate's hand and Kate and the woman fell on the bed.

Frank and Willy pulled them apart. Frank hurled Frances away and picked up Kate's gun. The little girl was screaming. He went over to her.

'All right,' he said. 'It's all right now, it's all over.'

She backed, not taking her eyes from his face and he realised that he didn't have his hood on. Willy must have pulled his on as they came down the stairs.

Kate holding her bleeding hand, was almost incoherent. 'You went out you stupid fool, I thought they'd got you.'

The woman dazed, shaking with shock, appealed to

him. 'She was going to shoot me!'

'She threw the tray,' Kate yelled, then: 'Hood hood hood!'

'For God's sake,' Frank said, 'they know who I am! We've done it, we've done it!'

'Done it?'

'We've got the money!'

'You've collected . . .' Willy began.

Frank was now delirious. 'No no no, it's in the paper, he's sold up, in the paper in the car, he's sold out of his company, he's back here with the money, we've done it!'

He found himself hugging the little girl as if she was Mary. The woman was speechless, taking a step in one direction, then another. Willy cleared the debris from the thrown tray so she could sit down. Kidnappers and hostages were abruptly brought close together except Kate, who leaned against the wall, sucking her torn hand.

The plates had been piled high with bacon, eggs, sausage, mushrooms, tomatoes, black pudding and potato bread. Clare was slumped in the extra chair they had brought in, her jaws moving with aching slowness. There was little left on her plate but grease and egg-yolk. She sighed a deep sigh, her eyes closing.

Frances echoed her sigh. The best meal in the best restaurant in Paris could not have tasted as good as that. It brought back some of her old acidity: 'I knew they were the sort of people who would eat black pudding and potato bread.'

'I like it.' Clare forked bread from her mother's plate.

'There's grease all round your mouth.'

'I can see my face in yours!' As Frances wiped it, Clare laughed. 'There's no-one to see us!'

'There's you. Me. Each other. We mustn't let ourselves go.'

'You did.'

Frances brushed at her dishevelled clothes and didn't reply. She pushed up the sleeves of an old sweater they had given her and examined her arms, throbbing with bruises and scratches. The cellar looked more habitable. They were eating on a rickety card table, and a small table lamp and shade had been rigged up from the ceiling rose. The door at the top must have been left open again, for she heard a faint burst of laughter. Presumably they were celebrating after eating their own fry.

Frances took out the knife, which was still embedded in the blankets.

'We won't need that now,' Clare said.

'No,' said Frances. But she took the brick out of the wall and put the knife behind it.

12 *Do Not Pass Go. Do Not Collect £200*

From his study window at Kilnameath Geoffrey saw Margaret greeting Simon as he arrived, breaking off to shout up to workmen repairing the roof, which had proved vulnerable to the recent rains. Since the kidnap Margaret had spent more time at Kilnameath than she did at home, and Geoffrey had leant on her more and more.

He had a heavy cold. He plucked a tissue from a box and studied the heavy, crackling document in front of him, which was headed: *Deed of Sale Between Geoffrey F. Carr Esq. and Lefray-Eagle Finance.*

He read it from habit: he read all small print. There was little point in doing so. He had to sign it, transferring his shares and control of his company to Richard in order to get the money for Frances. And he would still be about 150,000 short. The only way he could raise that was by selling land to O'Leary, the farmer who had outmanoeuvred him at the auction.

He could hear Margaret telling Maire something in the hall, and then she came in with Simon. She'd probably been up since dawn, seeing to the farm, getting the children off to school, and now she brought fresh air and energy into the stale room.

'Could you phone O'Leary —' Geoffrey began.

'It's done,' she replied crisply. 'He'll see you this evening.' She smiled at him, her cheeks glowing. It was weird. Sometimes she looked so like Frances, as now when she said abruptly: 'Stay with us tonight after dinner. I can't keep on running after you!'

She went as Maire called her and Geoffrey poured coffee for Simon. Simon, too, looked well, fit. He was smoking, turning something over in his mind.

Geoffrey pulled out a chunk of tissues. His nose was really streaming. 'What is it?'

'They've come down from three million to two in ten days.'

'So?'

Simon looked for an ashtray. The room, the whole house was untidy. 'I would stick it out a bit longer.'

Geoffrey sneezed. 'I am not bargaining!'

'It's not a question of bargaining.' Simon's voice was smooth, assured. 'If you settle too easily they might try and squeeze more out of you.'

'There isn't any more!'

'They don't know that. To make sure of it, they might release your wife and keep the child.'

Geoffrey sat down. Mucus dripped on the contract of sale unheeded.

'This business is not only about how much you pay, but when. You must take them to their limit.'

'Limit?'

'The point when they feel they've had enough, the police must be closing in, and they must get out. Another week and they might come down another million.'

'But that's over the deadline!'

'That's a pressure rather than a serious threat. The police know who the leader is, so he's even less likely to kill them. Margaret can tell them you're having difficulties turning shares into cash. You'll pay a quarter-of-a-million for the child now.'

Simon's voice was rational, persuasive. What he said made sound business sense; it was the language of negotiation. Geoffrey walked about the room in a turmoil. What had seemed so settled a moment ago was all in the air again. He argued with himself as much as Simon.

'They know how much I have now! No they don't.

They only know I'm selling the shares. They don't know how much I'm getting for them.'

He picked up the deed of sale.

'Have you signed that?' asked Simon.

'Not yet. The bank's preparing the cash.'

There was a silence. He turned the pages. Legal clauses swam in front of his eyes. Simon put out his cigarette.

'I'm not minimising the risks, sir. But holding on and keeping our nerve is just as likely to reduce the risks in the long run and get them both out.'

Geoffrey closed the document. He looked at the calendar on the wall: one date was circled again and again. He rolled the document between his fingers and opened his mouth several times before actually speaking.

'I can't do it. I must trust the kidnappers. If O'Leary buys the land I'll pay them exactly what they're asking for.'

O Leary told Geoffrey that he might be seventy, but he could still do every job on his huge farm, and then, or so it felt, proceeded to demonstrate it. Geoffrey, in an anorak and a heavy scarf Margaret had wrapped him in, tramped round hens, pigs, silage and finally the new milking shed.

He was shivering from his cold, and only continued the tour from inertia. O'Leary had made it clear that he wouldn't buy any more land: if he had any more, they would be renaming it County O'Leary!

He sucked at his dead pipe while he chattered on about milk yields and butter mountains and how the English were killing the Irish farmer.

'I could just accept £140,000,' Geoffrey muttered, keeping at him on the assumption that O'Leary's indifference was simple bargaining. Of course the old bastard wanted the land. The people he'd had to crawl to! Richard, and now this bloody verbose farmer!

O'Leary didn't answer. He darted away, towards

the cows' swishing tails, uncoupled a cow's udder from the milking machine and crooned to the animal.

'They don't always like being milked by hand when they're used to the machine, but you know me don't you?' The cow turned a blank face and O'Leary laughed. 'She gives a higher fat-content when she feels my hands on her tits.' The milk frothed in the pail as he pulled steadily on the pink teats. 'For your wife is it? Easy now, easy!'

'My wife. Yes. It is.'

'Right-hand pocket. Cheque-book. Write it out. I can't stop. Rhythm. That's what counts. With women and cows.'

'Write out what?'

'A hundred and fifty thousand. If that's what you want to borrow. I'll phone the bank in the morning. I don't want the land. I wouldn't have sold a field for my wife, but it's your money.'

The cheque book had been used as a mat for mugs of tea. Geoffrey wrote his name and then asked, in a choked voice, about interest.

'You've paid me that already, Mr Carr, several times over. If you remember the occasion?'

For the first time since the kidnap, tears stung Geoffrey's eyes. O'Leary emerged from under the cow, wiped his hands on his trousers and signed the cheque. He unhooked a metal jug and pulled it through the still bubbling milk.

'Would you tell me what you think of that, now?'

Geoffrey clutched the cheque in one hand and the warm milk in the other. He swallowed. 'I think that's the best milk I've ever tasted.'

Margaret, who had insisted on driving him to O'Leary's in her Land Rover, picked him up. They were going over the heath towards Kilnameath when he shouted to her to stop. He had picked up from Frances the need to go the top of places, to the copse, or up here, where he could see the house, through the trees, blue with distance. The thin wind cleared his head and he felt a little better. He had done it. He had got the money.

Do Not Pass Go. Do Not Collect £200. Was that the title of Jim Slater's book, the one he wrote when he crashed? It had always been one of Geoffrey's nightmares; that one day he would be found out, and would lose everything.

In the fifteen years during which he had accumulated his power and his fortune he had never worked harder than during the last ten days when he had tried to dispose of it.

Well, what he had built once he could build again, couldn't he?

He smiled at Margaret. 'Everything must go. It's invigorating. A challenge.' When she grinned back he grimaced. 'It's appalling.'

'Make up your mind,' she said.

He found himself talking, rambling, the words spilling out as they walked back to the Land Rover. It was amazing! He had never talked to anyone about his feelings before he had met Frances. Now he couldn't stop.

'I had to have everything my own way before Frances . . . under my own control . . . I sometimes think now . . . what a relief it would be to go back to that!' He looked down at Kilnameath, at the remains of his little empire. Soon that would have to be sold to provide them with somewhere to live in London. He stopped and turned to Margaret. 'Sometimes I wish I'd never met her! Isn't that a . . . a dreadful thing to say.' The contradiction he immediately made seemed an essential part of his relationship with Frances. 'But I can't live without her! If anything happens to her . . .'

Now he was crying, really crying, he couldn't stop and Margaret's arms went round him and she rocked him like a baby.

Robert Healey laughed when he was told to put on a suit because Geoffrey was coming to dinner. It was evident even to a piss-artist like him that his wife fancied Geoffrey.

She was always over there because she cared that much about her sister? Not on your life! The suit had the indelible remains down the front of one evening at Mickey's bar, so he sat there in his shirt sleeves as usual, and why not, at his own table?'

Wasn't he richer than the Englishman now? He'd told them at Mickey's, he'd had a few, that when the wine was circulating — they'd laughed uproariously at that — he would make an offer for Kilnameath. Not that he didn't feel as much as anyone for his sister-in-law and the wee one, but you couldn't weep all the time now, could you?

She'd had the fire on all day in the best room, he could tell that. There was almost no smell of damp. The huge oak dresser gleamed with silver and there was even flowers on the table!

The sight of it sobered him and made him nervous and in need of a touch but she'd hidden the whiskey. There was a bottle of what on the table? Pouilly Fuisse?

Margaret stunned him to silence. She was looking grand, really grand in a black dress — where the hell had she got that from, it wasn't her sister's was it? — and a Celtic-style brooch he had bought her years ago, when their first child had been born.

She made him feel awkward, regretting the suit, he even went and sponged it but the stains wouldn't come out, it looked ridiculous. He became awkward, conscious of the grime in his nails and shuffled from the kitchen to the best room to lay the table.

He stopped in front of her, unable to find words, just wanting to touch her.

'Don't fool about, Bob please.'

Fool about, I'm not fooling about he wanted to cry, but he just grinned and hunted until he found the whiskey. He wouldn't drink it, he'd just put it on the dresser there, in case of emergency. The kids went to bed, and the three of them sat down to dinner. It was brown trout cooked in foil, lovely big mouth-watering fish, the butter dripping from it.

The other two were silent. He didn't like silences. He poured the wine and tried to think of something smart to say, or anything at all that wasn't foolish or jokey. He wasn't going to let her down, no he was not. He split a few drops of wine on the stiff white cloth, went to mop it up and nearly overturned his glass. He picked up his knife and fork. The silence continued.

Desperately he picked up a jug. 'What's this?'

'Garlic sauce,' Margaret said. 'You don't have to eat it. Don't put your nose in it.'

'She doesn't cook like this for me!' he grinned, 'and that's a fact!'

'Geoffrey's glass is empty,' Margaret said.

'More Polly Fussy? Or would you prefer whiskey?'

That slipped out, that was provoking, he tried to apologize with a look, reaching across the table for her hand, but she pulled it away. Anger filled him and before he knew what he was doing he was at the dresser picking up the whiskey. She said nothing. She poured Geoffrey's wine. He wanted her just to say something, anything, so long as she just didn't ignore him, and then he would put the bottle down. He wasn't jealous, was he? Jealous! After all these years! He laughed, first at himself and then out loud.

'She doesn't dress like this for me, and that's a fact, Geoffrey,' he said.

'Only because you wouldn't notice.'

'Ah but I *have*!' he said triumphantly, and then stared at the whiskey which he had somehow poured into the remains of his wine. Had they seen him? They were very interested in their plates. Ah, brave it out, he urged himself, raising his glass to the light and squinting at it critically. 'An excellent year. Just a hint of peat. She's attractive when she blushes, don't you think so, Geoffrey?'

'Shut up.'

Margaret was crimson with embarrasment. She dropped her knife in her lap. He was going too far, but it was impossible to stop. He chewed noisily.

'What will you do, Geoffrey, make another fortune? Fish is grand, Mags, A one.'

'Robert, please.'

'What?' he said, innocently.

The room was unusually warm, so warm that Geoffrey had taken off his jacket. Sweat was beaded above his eyebrows. He put down his knife and fork. 'I just want them back,' he said, 'I can't think beyond that.'

Robert looked at his sweating face and felt ashamed, reached for the whiskey, caught Margaret's eye and stopped. 'Ah no, no, no,' he stammered. 'You can't, of course you can't.'

There was a deep silence in which Robert cut out the bone of his trout.

'I won't make a lot of money again,' Geoffrey said.

Margaret was scornful. 'You're depressed! It's your cold saying that.'

Geoffrey shook his head. 'You need an idea. Luck. Energy. And a belief in your infallibility.'

Jasus, Robert thought, the man uses long words like a politician. And wasn't his wife hanging on to them!

'That combination comes once in a lifetime, as someone reminded me recently.'

Robert stared at him. Not another of those awful ponderous silences! Ah, he couldn't resist it!

'I'm still waiting,' he said.

They laughed, and for an instant at least he was sure Mags was laughing with him and not at him. He guffawed in relief, and reached for the whiskey.

Frank came in from the night and looked at his watch. One o'clock. He was on duty until three, when Kate took over. He was off the booze again, didn't need it, wanted to keep his mind sharp and clear for the most dangerous part of the job — the drop.

Picking up two million pounds.

Were they playing straight with him, or would the money be followed by the police?

He'd worked out a routine to cope with that. He

made tea in a flask, sweetening it liberally. The flask was an old habit, formed by many hours of waiting at night; the flask, and two or three chocolate bars.

Unlike Kate, he enjoyed the night hours, the shadows in the garden, the sound of sleep. He unscrewed the flask and studied the ordnance map. Willy had recced the place he had chosen for the drop and cleared it. It was lake country near the border. A good open approach during which they could see if the money was being followed. A choice of escape routes.

The police would be convinced they would try to escape to the north whereas that was the last thing he wanted to do. He wanted to buy the arms himself in Dublin. They demanded half-a-million up front. Then there was his cut and Willy's — for expenses. He hadn't really gone into that with Kate yet. There was plenty of time.

He had left the door to the cellar open and as he sipped the sweet tea and drew a sketch of the drop area there was a faint banging. At first he ignored it, but eventually went downstairs and told the woman to shut the bloody racket.

'The light's gone and I've upset the bucket . . . It is not funny!'

He went in, locking the door behind him, and replaced the bulb. Clare went back to sleep. He should go, but it was a long time till three and it was amusing to see the woman clearing up the mess, just as the POWs had to do in the Maze.

He stood leaning against the wall, tossing the old light bulb from hand to hand. She wore the V-necked sweater they had given her and had washed her hair and cleaned herself up a bit. Since the Ulster fry he had relaxed a bit more, too much Kate said, bringing in a few books, a jigsaw for the girl, but why the hell not?

'Bit there,' he said.

As she bent to clean near him, the sweater swung open, exposing for a moment her bare breasts. He stopped fiddling with the bulb. She looked up at him, a look of such bitterness and arrogance, that for a moment he glanced away. Then, hating her for that, he dropped the light bulb. The shell-like fragments sprayed up near her face.

'Oh, dear. Sorry.'

He stood over her. The stench was awful. The girl wheezed and coughed in her sleep. Again the woman's sweater parted. Her sleeve trailed on the floor and she jerked it away in disgust.

'Shit,' he said.

Again her black eyes. This time he didn't look away. He was without his hood, without his gun. He took out his handkerchief and offered it. She wiped her sleeve, offered it back.

'No thanks. My brother was on the blanket.'

Why had he said that? He had no desire to start a conversation with the woman! She was crouching below him, waiting for him to go on. He put the key in the lock.

'Are you from Derry?' she said.

He whirled. 'How do you know?'

'Your accent.'

'Brits can't usually tell.'

'I'm Irish.'

'That is a matter of opinion.'

She didn't shrink from him. There was even something contemptuous in the way she turned her back on him to take the bucket to its corner, something patronising, galling in the way she said: 'How did you . . . start?'

'Throwing stones,' he said and left, locking the door.

Her look, her veiled contempt stayed with him as he walked up the steps. Perhaps she wasn't afraid any more because she knew she was going to be released. It irked him that she retained her views, that she didn't realise his contempt for her and her kind, that it never entered her head that the kidnapping was fully justified, that she had no inkling what the Brits had done to the Irish, how they had imprisoned them in their own shit.

It was all very well Kate saying no talking but that bloody woman should realise why she had been kidnapped!

By the time he reached his flask of tea he was in such a rage he could not sit down but went right back down the steps. When he opened the cellar she was standing by the bed, about to get in it. Now there was a flicker of fear in her eyes and he realised it was because she thought he had come back to rape her, a flash of her breasts had turned him on, that's what she was thinking and his rage increased that for one moment she could imagine he wanted her.

He advanced on her. She backed to the wall. Yes, that's what she was thinking. She had swallowed the stereotype. He was a terrorist brute. He stopped in the middle of the cellar, the words coming out without any preparation.

'At four o'clock one morning there was a hammering at the door and the troops were thundering upstairs shouting William Crossan. My mother held on to my father and they threw her off him against the stairs. He'd done nothing. We weren't a Provo family, this wasn't the Bog or the Creggan. I was twelve. If she caught me throwing stones at the Brits, she belted me.'

He took a step towards her. She wiped her hands continually down the sides of her dress.

'He had bronchitis, he wasn't a well man. They ran him across the road in his bare feet across the broken glass. He was spreadeagled against a wall, the crucifix round his neck torn off — "You have a fucking cheek to wear that" — and when he collapsed he was batoned in the stomach or the balls.'

He snatched at her neck as if she was wearing a crucifix. Her head hit the wall as she reflexed backwards.

'And when he could no longer get up they stamped on his fingers and broke two of them. When he was released there were no charges. That night, it was the week before Bloody Sunday, I was allowed out to throw stones.'

He was very close to her, breathing jerkily into her face. Suddenly she was gazing past him, clenching her hands. He turned. Kate, hooded, was standing at the door, staring rigidly at them.

Frances prayed, kneeling by the bed in which Clare slept.

'Bless me father, for I have sinned. It is so many years since I have confessed, my sins must be so many. Only release us without more pain and I will be faithful to you, and to my husband, for the rest of my life, Amen.'

Geoffrey dreamed. He was walking back from the copse to Kilnameath and suddenly the leaves beneath his feet were shards of broken glass from the windows. The banisters were hanging loose in the hall as he tried to follow the sound of Frances's voice. First he thought she was in the big room where the floor was so rotten he put his foot through it. He wrenched it out and ran upstairs. It was the side-room she often went into, from which you could see the copse, that's where the voice was coming from.

Paper ballooned from the walls. The voice was there. The paper wrapped itself round and round him. He struggled, suffocated, and woke twisted up in the blanket. He half-expected the telephone to be ringing as it had on the night when the hoaxer had called. What made the nightmare worse was that he was in an unfamiliar room; it was a moment before he pieced the shapes together and remembered he was at Margaret's.

He took a fresh handkerchief from his overnight case. In it was the Deed of Sale between himself and Lefray. He still hadn't signed it. Why was he putting it off? He had already taken the decision. The dream was still vivid, her desperate, calling voice still echoing in his head.

He went to get his pen from his jacket, then remembered he had left it in the dining room, after that appalling dinner, where Bob had got paralytic and Margaret had insisted on helping him upstairs alone.

Two o'clock in the morning! And she had to be up at half-past-five. Margaret wandered round the kitchen with a kettle of boiling water looking for the glass in which she had put whiskey and a clove.

What a fool she had made of herself! She couldn't blame Bob, she'd known what he would be like. She tripped over the trailing belt of her dressing gown and nearly spilt the boiling water.

She sat down at the table and, as soon as she stopped looking for it, saw the whiskey concealed among the photographs she had pulled out. Among them were a number of herself and Frances as children. One showed them holding hands on the very edge of the stream at Kilnameath.

Had Frances been daring her to jump over it? Probably. She cradled the hot whiskey. She was only beginning to admit to herself that, dreadful as the last ten days had been, they had, well . . . given her life something that had been lacking for years.

She used to enjoy sex. The last time she had slept with Bob had been five years ago. She poured another whiskey, adding hot water and sugar. Somehow that made it not drinking. She had nearly had an affair with an accountant who did the farm's books. She had confessed.

'You must change your accountant,' the priest had said.

She had done so. Because she had wanted to avoid temptation, or because she had discovered he was having another affair? Perhaps Frances was right. Frances wouldn't have stayed with Bob. Normally, Margaret told herself, I can cope. It's only this last week, when I've been practically living with Geoffrey, that I've realised what I've missed.

She was gripping the whiskey glass in front of her face, and through it, saw Geoffrey distorted, standing in the doorway, like the genie coming out of the bottle in one of the children's story books she still kept. And wasn't it a fairy story, a whole load of nonsense she'd been thinking about him? She was thirty-seven! He sat down opposite her.

'Can't you sleep?'

'I always go through the family album at this time of night,' she said, reassured to find herself talking with her usual crispness. 'Can't you?'

'I came down for my pen.' He twirled it round on the scarred table-top.

Her dressing gown was open. She wrapped it round her tightly and knotted the belt. All those silly fancies! She was in her own kitchen, and it was business as usual. She picked up the whiskey bottle.

'Cold cure? Sugar? Clove?'

Bob would have been amazed at the size of the whiskey she poured herself. Oh well, she deserved it after this week and that dinner. Out of all the photographs on the table he had picked one of Frances and her first husband, Michael, both on horses, of course, they had lived on horses. He didn't look up when she placed the hot whiskey in front of him.

'Don't worry,' she said. 'She'll come through ok. She always does.'

The bitterness in her voice took her by surprise: she must watch the drink. He didn't notice, didn't take his eyes from the picture.

'Were they happy?'

'Idyllic.'

He didn't pick up the sarcasm, either. He nodded. 'She can't bear to talk about it.'

Not surprisingly, she thought. 'How can you be so clever — and so naive?' she said.

'What?'

She shook her head. She suddenly felt irritated beyond endurance with him, with his infatuation with Frances, for that's what it was. She drank. She'd not finished that huge whiskey, surely? She picked out a photograph and laughed.

'I won a beauty contest when we were children. She wouldn't speak to me for days!'

The two girls posed inside a Hula-Hoop, both in flowered dresses with big bows, Frances sullen and Margaret with a big smile on her face.

'I didn't often win anything! She might have smiled. A beauty contest!' She laughed in delight. 'I've gone downhill since, of course.'

She waited for at least his polite contradiction, but he was poring over other pictures of Frances. Her irritation boiled over into anger.

'Since no-one's allowed in there, I suppose you still have her bedroom as it was — spilt powder, pyjamas.'

Now he looked up. 'The sheets have been changed.'

She began to laugh. 'You're a literal romantic . . . or do I mean romantically literal?'

'What's wrong?' He got up.

'Nothing. Nothing's wrong,' she said in alarm.

'Margaret —'

She stood up, suddenly near to tears. 'Oh will you go away?'

'Come on, come on,' he said, squeezing her shoulders. 'It's been too much for all of us.'

'Yes, yes,' she said, shocked to find herself trembling like a young girl at her first dance. She pushed him away. 'Go to bed.'

'Have another drink.'

'I don't want another drink.'

'Come on. Here.'

He took her hand. His voice was so kind, gentle, she wasn't used to that. She was always the capable one, the one who looked after the others, she wasn't used to someone caring about her.

'Oh, it's only this last week,' she burst out, 'that

brute on the telephone and I thought it's over, it's nearly over now and I'll sleep tonight, and I haven't slept, that's all.' Then it came out. 'I don't even like her.'

'Frances?'

'I hate her! No I don't! Yes I — Oh holy mother help me, I've been clearing up after her all my life!'

She was crying. This was absolutely terrible! What an evening he'd had — first Bob, then her.

'This is stupid, I've had too much to drink, that's all, go to bed, Geoffrey, please, go to bed.'

She wanted to move from his arms but couldn't. Her face was on his chest. He was stroking her hair. She lifted her face, her eyes closing and her lips parting. The kiss was a brotherly peck on her forehead.

She pulled away more hurt and angry than she could ever remember and tried to recover some normality.

'I don't want your cold,' she said.

Then the bitterness of years came out, with no restraint. She swallowed the whiskey he had poured her.

'Idyllic! She killed him.'

The only movement in the room came from the edge of his tongue as it touched his upper lip, raw from his cold. Her voice became flat, tired.

'I'm just so tired of picking up the pieces for her.'

'He fell off his horse. Didn't he?'

'Yes yes yes. He fell off his horse.'

Now she moved, she wanted to go, but he moved with her. The curtains were undrawn and she saw herself briefly in the black panes as he put a hand on her shoulder. Outside the wind caught a bucket and rolled it backwards and forwards across the yard.

'She destroys men. Haven't you realised? I love men. There's something wrong somewhere.'

The drink hit her and the room lurched. She sat down abruptly, planting her elbows among the photographs, a whole life, two lives in snapshots. As she stared down dizzily at the outings, the holidays, the birthdays, she thought that only the young children showed their true feelings, love, hate, the happiness of sunshine, the absolute tragedy of a dropped ice-cream.

'They were pissed,' she said. 'To be charitable. Ah, not that pissed, to tell the truth. She was having an affair with Andrew. He mortgaged his farm for her. Well you *knew* that *surely*? Oh God, oh what am I saying, ah well I can't stop now, can I? It was in the big room at Kilnameath. It started off as a joke, a bet. But she was serious. There was that terrible gleam in her eyes. She told me she was going to choose between them.' She saw the disbelief on his face and shouted: 'It's the truth man, can you not hear her saying it?'

She looked at her clasped hands, almost as scrubbed as the table, and went on quietly.

'They saddled up the horses. They had a jump off for her up at the copse. She came here with Andrew afterwards. Of course. They brought the body here. I was quite fond of him too.'

Outside the bucket rolled. Geoffrey sat down quietly. She thought he was very calm. Perhaps he didn't care very much, it wasn't important to him. It was a while before he spoke.

'Is she still . . . with Andrew . . .'

'I don't know.' She looked up and saw his face. 'Oh God, oh no, you mustn't think that!'

He got up. 'You're right. I am somewhat naive in these matters.'

He gave her a twisted smile, but when she went to him his social face crumpled. 'Just leave me alone.'

She stopped him angrily. 'Oh don't be so stupid! She thinks you're wonderful! She does! But you mustn't put her on a pedestal. You must love her, not a fantasy . . . Come on! There's no need to be that upset!'

She had once been near a bomb going off in the north. People had had faces like Geoffrey's, that dazed, wandering look. She felt sick.

'Sit down.'

'I'm all right,' he said.

'No you're not, you're not. Oh God forgive me, what a stupid stupid thing for me to tell you. What's past is past. She's different. She loves you, you stupid man.'

'I'll go up.'

'Oh Geoffrey you're about a hundred and fifty intellectually, but fourteen emotionally. You look so frightened!'

'Frightened? Don't be absurd!'

'Stay and talk. Please stay and talk.'

'I'm tired,' he said. 'I'm just so tired.'

'Yes. Yes. I am. We all are. Take your drink then.'

'Thank you.'

'Shall I hot it up? . . . Sleep then, sleep.'

She held him briefly and kissed him. When she returned to clear up the photographs, she saw his pen on the table and caught him up on the stairs.

'Here,' she said. 'You forgot what you came for.'

The central irony, Geoffrey thought, is that if I'd never met Frances I would be able to cope with the situation much better. This morning he felt a little more like his old self. His cold was better. He stood by the tall windows of the big room, watching a horseman descend from the copse towards the house.

Maire came in with coffee and told him that the bedroom had been done. It had been getting on his nerves keeping the room the way it had been on the morning she was kidnapped. Margaret came in, followed by Simon, who was carrying two despatch cases. The horseman was Andrew, wearing the same hat, the same brown cords, which he never seemed to change. As he rode past the windows he saluted. Geoffrey raised his hand. We have good reason to salute one another, he thought.

The meeting went badly from the start. Simon opened the despatch cases and displayed used Irish banknotes, tens and twenties. He told Andrew and Margaret that the drop would be done in two stages; the first — this half-million — being paid for Clare.

Geoffrey sat impassive while the argument began. Andrew shouted; Margaret pleaded.

'That's not what the kidnappers are expecting! Please Geoffrey! I've talked to them. You haven't. They'll kill them. They mean it. They're desperate. I can feel it. They said two million and we must give them two million!'

'I can't,' Geoffrey said. His brain was ice-clear. He felt back in control of himself for the first time since the kidnap.

Andrew spoke vehemently, collectively, as if it was their money, their wife. 'Can't? We must!'

'We can't, or rather I can't because the money isn't there.'

'But you sold the shares!' Margaret cried.

'Yes. To O'Leary.'

In the bewildered silence that followed, Geoffrey recollected the last hectic twenty-four hours: tearing up the agreement with Richard, drinking in O'Leary's chaotic office. There had been no time to draw up a legal agreement. They had shaken on it, just as in the old days, shaken on one and a half million pounds.

'But we agreed to pay them two million!'

'No Margaret. We've never agreed on a specific sum. I agreed to sell the shares. We've never said how much we will get for them.'

'I don't understand! If the sale isn't worth as much, why did you do it?'

'O'Leary's a bloody farmer,' Andrew shouted. 'He knows as much about computers as you do about pigs. What's he going to with your shares? Feed them to his sodding cows? Ah, I smell it, I smell it.' He turned with disgust on his face to Margaret. 'The man's done some kind of a deal.'

'There is a buy-back option in six months,' Geoffrey said.

'He has to sell the shares back to you in six months?'

'If I can pay for them.'

'But they know from the papers about the deal with Richard!'

'No sum was mentioned. So far as they're concerned, this is a better deal.'

Simon lit a cigarette. Margaret sat hunched, staring out of the window. Andrew walked the length of the big room, passing the picture of the fifth earl. It was from this room that the three of them had gone out the night her first husband had died. Margaret looked up at Geoffrey. Was she too thinking about that night?

Andrew came up to Geoffrey. 'You have all the answers haven't you?'

'So far as I know.'

'You've saved your wretched company.'

'I might save it.'

'And sentenced them to death.'

The words stung Geoffrey. Simon was right. If they were going to free Frances and Clare it would be by a rational controlled approach, not by an emotional reaction; paying out as much money as they could raise might only lead to a demand for more.

'Don't be absurd Andrew,' he said. 'We've been negotiating now for three weeks under threats. Their demands have gone down sharply as they've realised the problems of forced selling . . . Margaret, you must see I have done everything I can.'

She nodded reluctantly, making Andrew angrier than ever.

'Not everything.'

'Everything has been sold!'

'I thought you loved her,' Andrew shouted. Margaret tried to intercede, but Andrew, his face wild and passionate, pushed her to one side. 'You love your company. Your money. Everything is figures! You said that the first night I met you, and you bloody well meant it, didn't you!'

Was he her lover, or merely her ex-lover? Oh Frances, Geoffrey thought, this is well-named a crisis committee: two men quarrelling over you, a sister jealous of you, and a loss adjuster. He winced slightly, which Andrew must have mistaken for a smile, for he spat the words out.

'That newspaper headline. "I Love You." Did you say

that, or did your man send a press release?'

'What do you want Andrew,' said Geoffrey contemptuously. 'Another jump off?'

Geoffrey jerked away as Andrew lashed out but the blow caught him on the side of the jaw. Simon pulled Andrew off him. Margaret came over with a handkerchief as Geoffrey sat down, shocked, with the warm salty taste of blood in his mouth.

Frank went to get another whiskey but there was nothing in the bottle. He hurled his glass into the sink. Pinned up behind one of the kitchen cupboards was a faded carbon copy headed: 'INVENTORY ANNACLOY. All breakages must be paid for.' Kate had, to his amusement, checked every knife, fork and spoon. He smashed another glass in the sink.

'That doesn't help,' said Kate.

'It helps me!'

Kate and Willy were sitting at the table on which dirty plates had been piled in the centre. They had been talking for over an hour. Each person kept putting forward the same points, and being met by the same objections. Frank had argued that they should accept the half million for the child, but the other two argued she had seen too much.

As the arguments went on, he thought about the child. Before the meeting he had given her another jigsaw. She had been so delighted. The woman must have picked up something from his manner, for she looked at the jigsaw as if it was a condemned man's breakfast. She picked up everything that was going on, that woman. She had pleaded with him to tell her what was happening, and he had had to wrench himself away.

At the beginning of the meeting he had had everything clear in his own mind. He couldn't stand any more of this place! It was worse than being in prison! Either they shot them or released them, one or the other. Call it a day. Release the girl and shoot the woman, that's what he'd worked out. Go back to Derry, back to his own, whatever the consequences.

But somehow Kate had bogged him down, made what had seemed simple complex. Every time he produced one extreme, she brought out the opposite point of view.

'A million and a half is still a lot of money!' he said.

'If they pay! I doubt if they intend to now. He's lied, Frank. He has! They'll keep offering less. They're buying time to find us.'

She enjoyed committees, he could tell that. There were plenty of people like her in Derry. They always produced objections, never solutions. She looked as if she could sit there for ever. He walked about smoking, sat on the edge of the table.

'What happens if they don't pay?' Willy said.

Kate looked at Frank. After she'd discovered him in the cellar that night she'd said some rubbish about him getting too close to her. Because he was trying to tell her some truth about the north, instead of the shit that had been put into her head. He got the Browning out of a drawer and checked the magazine. The heavy weight in his hand was a relief after all this talk.

'I will execute the woman if I have to. Do you want me to do it now?'

He spoke softly, quietly, his eyes never leaving her face. There was a long, long moment. Willy coughed, dropped ash in the remains of a plate of spaghetti.

'And lose everything?' Kate said.

'Christ! You've just said they don't intend to pay!'

'They will if we show them we're serious!'

'And how do we do that?'

He listened, and though he had been involved in worse things, felt sick. Perhaps Kate was right: he shouldn't have talked to her at all.

13 Needle in a Haystack

Margaret felt like a criminal. All the way down the mountains and along the vale to Rathdrum she had kept glancing in the mirror, believing that the police were following her. What did it matter to the police if they paid the money or not? People who wanted to get arms would get them somehow.

If only they *could* pay the money! If only they knew what was happening! Today at twelve was the deadline the kidnappers had set for payment and they had heard nothing since that horrific phone conversation with Tom.

'Half a million!' Tom had shouted.

'And a million later for —'

'You've just killed her, Margaret, you've just fucking killed her.'

He had slammed down the phone. She had gone on screaming into it until Simon forced it out of her hand. Wasn't that what she *had* done? Killed her? Would Geoffrey have pulled out of his deal with Richard if she hadn't told him about Frances and Andrew?

Geoffrey made it sound so logical, but the fact remained that they hadn't heard, in spite of putting three small ads in the *Irish Times* asking Tom to contact them.

The 'safe' phone, as Simon termed it, remained silent. They had established it above a shop in Rathdrum. It was always manned by herself, Geoffrey, Andrew or Simon.

She parked some distance away and walked down

an alley to get into the square. It was difficult for anyone to follow her without being seen. The shop had a yellowing piece of plastic inside the glass to protect the display from the sun, which today was shining only fleetingly, pale lemon among growing clouds which suggested it would rain before lunch.

In the window were cheap plaster statuettes of Christ, The Sacred Heart, printed cards saying: *Jesus Is In this Workplace.*

She opened a door at the side of the shop and went up stairs covered with cracked brown lino.

It was just after half-past-nine.

Andrew was still asleep on the camp bed when she went into the tiny office. She didn't need to ask if there'd been any calls. He opened one eye.

'Did you bring milk?'

She put a carton on the desk and followed it with a copy of *The Irish Times*. There were papers from two days last week, each folded at the small ad, *Tom Ring Diamond*. Andrew sat up.

'Oh well. We did get three insertions for the price of two.'

She was beyond any form of joking. 'Andrew, the deadline is twelve o'clock!'

'They always extend it.'

'Simon says.'

She made tea on the solitary gas ring. The previous tenants of the office had sold agricultural chemicals. Calendars and posters advertising sheep dip and worming chemicals were curling away from the walls. Andrew dressed but wouldn't go. She was glad of that. She kept on thinking that there must be a limit to what her nerves would take, but this endless watching, waiting kept stretching them until she was ready to run out into the square screaming.

At just after ten the phone rang. It was Geoffrey.

Geoffrey replaced the receiver. He shouldn't have phoned. Over the past two days he had kept Margaret going. He had been quite certain that Simon was right: the gang were professionals who would negotiate; to them, killing Frances and Clare would be killing one and a half million.

Of course he wouldn't hear anything. He had told himself that. That was part of the technique of negotiation: making the other side sweat it out. But by phoning he had just conveyed to Margaret his fear of miscalculation, a fear that had chilled him from the moment he had woken up at dawn.

As he walked from the bedroom, he heard Maire zealously cleaning out the bathroom. He wanted the whole house tidy, as his house in St John's Wood used to be. He passed a wastepaper basket full of nearly-empty shampoo and old medicine bottles. Maire dropped in another handful. He stopped and picked up a bottle labelled: *Miss Clare Donavon. Ventolin. Take as Instructed.*

He went over again the scene in the bedroom, on the day they had taken him to the airport.

'Maire, weren't Frances and Clare collecting pills, Clare's asthma pills, the day they were kidnapped?'

She shook her head blankly.

'That's right! Frances asked me to remind her. There were some things found in the car . . . shopping . . . parcels . . . what happened to them?'

'The police kept them.'

He sat in front of his computer in a state of excitement. Hadn't Frances said in her tape message that Clare had nearly died? Might that have been an asthma attack? If so, how had they coped without medication? Really, the police had stopped thinking about finding them, if they had ever started. They were concentrating on the family leading them to the kidnappers.

When Simon came at eleven o'clock, no doubt expecting him to be at the end of his tether, he was half-way through a computer programme.

'Trying to find Frances and Clare is like trying to find

a needle in a haystack,' he said to Simon. 'It sounds impossible, but it may be merely difficult. Thank you Maire.'

He took the post from her. There were a number of letters and a small parcel.

'If you can identify where in the haystack you were plying your needle and use a magnet then —'

'Don't open that!' Simon shouted.

Geoffrey's hands jumped away from the parcel. It was wrapped in brown paper, about two inches square, with a printed label sellotaped to it.

The parcel had been checked for explosives and now McLaughlin, in the police laboratory in Dublin, carefully slit the sellotape with a scalpel. He was a chatty Dubliner in his late forties, with fingers plump and wrinkled from constant washing. The fingers, now encased in rubber gloves, teased aside the wrapping, exposing another wrapping, which he handed to his assistant, Fox, a man in his twenties.

Fox wrote the details on a form. The parcel had been posted in Navan at noon the previous day.

McLaughlin drew out a white cardboard box, like that used for cheap jewellery. Inside the box, on top of a folded piece of paper, was part of a finger. McLaughlin grunted. Fox swallowed and looked away.

'Get a sterile dish,' McLaughlin said.

Later he reported to Kearney, O'Hanlon and Watson.

'It was severed, not very skilfully, above the second joint. We haven't a good left little finger print, but it's from a mature female unaccustomed to rough work. She's about five feet eight, judging by the bone length.'

Mrs Carr, Kearney remembered from the police description, was five feet nine.

'Is she alive?' O'Hanlon asked.

'Well, now then. The skin was retracted over the bone and so —'

'Spare us the details,' Kearney said sharply. He felt

responsible. They knew the man, he was probably near the border, they ought to have made more progress. On the other hand, they'd had no cooperation from the family.

'She was alive when this was done,' McLaughlin said. 'There was also this ring at the bottom of the box.'

Kearney took it. 'Anything under the nail?'

'Blood. Tissue. Hairs — she certainly scratched someone. Particles of whitewash . . . brick dust . . .'

Watson spoke for the first time, his heavy Belfast accent cutting across the lighter southern voices. 'Is there a postal address under there, Mr McLaughlin?'

'Analysis might suggest an area. We're working on that now.'

Geoffrey and Margaret went to the incident room at Ballyglen. He hadn't been there for several days: when they had been setting up their safe phone the police had appeared to be more hostile than the kidnappers.

The kidnappers had come to seem reasonable people, people who could be bargained with.

The pictures of Frances and Clare were still on the wall. The files were bulkier. The phone was still ringing, but less so, he thought. There was a feeling of stalemate, of people settling in; on one board there was even a list of Garda football fixtures.

It was bewildering, these scraps of normality contrasting with the ring Kearney handed to him.

'Yes,' he whispered. 'That is hers. Is she alive?'

'We don't know.'

'Can't you tell from the . . .'

'We think it was done when she was alive,' Kearney said.

He surprised them by bursting out: 'Thank God! I thought I'd killed her!'

Margaret squeezed his arm. Watson's chair creaked as he shifted forward. 'Why did you think that, Mr Carr?' His tone was conversational.

Geoffrey sipped the water they had given him. It was

ice-cold against his dry, cracked lips.

'You've been negotiating with the criminals?' asked Kearney, also conversational.

Geoffrey looked resentfully at him. They were so obvious, trying to get at him now he was vulnerable. 'You would know if I was. You're tapping my phone.'

Kearney shrugged. 'There are other phones.'

'Geoffrey. We must work together.'

This was O'Hanlon, earnest, honest, but not very bright. I could trust him, Geoffrey thought, but not the others, or their bosses. There was an idea at the back of his mind, and he teetered on the edge of exploring it with them. They could see him hesitating. Watson puffed on his cigarette, his eyes permanently squeezed together against the smoke.

'You've got precisely nowhere,' Geoffrey said.

Kearney went on to the attack. 'Because you won't tell us what you're up to!'

'Mr Carr,' Watson said. 'Even if you pay the money, you have no guarantee these sadists will fulfill their part of the bargain. Judging from their behaviour, they will not.'

'You're from the north, Mr Watson,' Margaret said.

'I am. I know these people. Including the man who has your sister.'

There was a silence and Margaret got up. Geoffrey followed her. Watson coughed, his voice remaining casual, almost sleepy. 'Personally, if someone had done that to my wife I would want justice.'

Geoffrey strode back to him. 'Justice!' he shouted. 'I want them found! I want them shot!'

Watson stamped on his cigarette. 'Then for God's sake help us, man!'

'You want Frances,' Margaret pleaded. 'Not revenge! What's the point of that?'

She tried to draw him away, but he shook her off, turning on the three policemen. 'You're still in the steam age! How the hell can you hope to find them with a card index system? If I thought you were at all competent . . .!'

'If you thought we were at all competent, what, Mr Carr?'

Kearney touched the silky flap of hair falling over his forehead. Geoffrey thought: he must make that gesture when he is fishing, patiently waiting for a bite.

He turned his back on them and went out. The sun was still shining, but a thin drizzle met their faces. They got in the Land Rover but didn't start it. The sleeve of her anorak was patched where barbed wire had caught it. It seemed quite natural that he should want to hold her. They had been so through so much together — more, in a way, than most couples go through in a lifetime.

He put his arm round her, and her head went on his shoulder.

'It's my fault,' she whispered.

'What are you talking about?'

'If I hadn't told you about Frances and Andrew this wouldn't have happened.'

'Nonsense!'

'The day after you went back on your word.'

'I sold the company.'

'For *less*! So you could buy it back!'

'It made no difference!'

She pulled away from him. 'It did! They cut off her finger.'

Her eyes were as wild as those of her sister. In fact, it was as if these events had drawn out of her some long buried passionate part of herself that longed to be Frances, to break away from the hum-drum predictable life she led. He felt as if he was going back to the rows he had had with Frances in St John's Wood, and on their second honeymoon.

'All right it did,' he cried. 'It made the difference. Oh it's all such a mess! I wish I could sleep. I wish I could work. I wish I could get back to normal.'

He kissed her. Her lips parted. She was Frances. He took her hand. She had all her fingers. It had never happened, this nightmare, they would go back to Kilnameath and he would hold her . . .

She was pushing him away. 'I'll take you home,' she muttered. The wildness was sinking back into her face, the dour practical Margaret re-emerging. 'That didn't happen.'

As she started the Land Rover and swore at the wind-screen wipers for sticking, it was impossible to believe it had.

Frances no longer had any sense of time. They had taken Clare to another room. She lay in bed shivering with cold for a period, then awoke burning hot. She tried to get to her wall to make the scratches, her life and Clare's life seemed to depend on that, but she fell on the floor and screamed when the witch picked her up.

She was a real witch, who appeared through the wall, who slept with the devil, who was here to punish her, she would cut her again, no it was the man who had cut her but the woman was worse, she was evil and this cellar was hell, the walls were red, burning red, she was on fire! Her flesh crackled. Her scream shuddered on and on until she wasn't sure it was a sound or a quivering orange mist.

She came to her senses with the witch being sent out of the room by Frank, Frank, yes, that was his name. It was impossible to tell whether she had been awake or in a nightmare. Shapes were running back to where they belonged: the door, the bucket, the scratches, they were shimmering, dancing on the wall, they had stopped moving. His words were making sense — what was he saying?

'Why scream at her? She never touched you.'

He was changing the bandage on her hand, winding it round the stump of her finger. The dirty, discarded bandage lay on the blanket. She winced and pulled away.

'Keep still, keep still will you!'

She flailed out. The bandage unwound. 'What's the point!'

'You've been ill! You've had a bloody fever!'

She laughed hysterically. She never thought he could be so funny. 'Oh, you're worried about me are you? I've been ill.'

He slapped her across the face. She laughed and went on laughing. She sat up. They had taken the sweater off and her breasts were visible through her torn dress, the dress that seemed as much a part of her as her skin. Odd. Once she would have cared about something like that. He really was making a mess of the bandage, he was all fingers — that was something she could never be again! She began giggling and he stopped trying to bandage her. He was going. No, he was turning back at the door, looking strangely at her. She remembered him telling her about his father, the crucifix being ripped from his neck.

'Are you a Catholic?' He didn't answer. 'Can I have a priest?'

'You won't need a priest. He's agreed to pay.'

'Again.'

'He'll pay. This time.'

She didn't believe him. She didn't want hope. Hope was the worst thing. Somehow he fumbled the bandage round her hand. 'You should have let her do it.'

'You're not cruel.'

He laughed at her in astonishment. 'Jesus Christ! What do I have to do!'

'You do cruel things, but you're not cruel.'

Perhaps it was the fever in her saying that, although she felt better, still very weak, but clear in her mind. He got up, sat down, got up again rubbing his bitten-down nails through his cropped hair. She could see the angry words in his eyes for a minute before they came out of his mouth.

'You're a bloody case. I've never met a woman like you. You should be smashed. Broken. You're contemptible. It doesn't hurt me to hurt someone like you, let me tell you that. I watched you at the house you bought.' He became extraordinarily excited, hammering his fist into his palm. 'I watched you fill it with all that junk as if there'd been no Bloody Sunday no 1916, no famine, I watched you at your party in your black dress and jewellery and I said I'll have all that!'

He sat on the bed, ducking his head between his hands and rubbing his cropped hair violently, mumbling his next words so that she wasn't sure what he had said until he looked up at her.

'Can I touch your breasts?'

His words stilled them both. They didn't avoid each others' eyes. The indifference she had felt about her nakedness abruptly left her. She combed back her hair with her good hand, a gesture Geoffrey would have recognized, as he would the contempt in her voice.

'You don't have to ask.'

He stood over her, shouting so she could see the back of his throat. 'I am bloody well asking!'

Paul Getty Junior lost an ear, Baron Empain, head of a French steel and nuclear consortium, a finger. Both kidnap victims got out alive. Simon recited the facts to himself, all culled from lectures by Bennet to his men, as he drove to the safe phone in Rathdrum.

There was the money graph, dipping in almost every case to thirty per cent of the original demand after two weeks.

'The closer you come to an agreement over the price, the more threats you get . . .' Simon could hear Bennet's dry voice as he parked and walked down the alley to the square. 'The kidnappers say he's very ill . . .'

Or they cut off a finger.

Simon ascended the brown linoed steps. She was alive, that was the main thing. The amount had been agreed. All they had to do now was to deliver the one and a half million.

He entered the office and opened the black despatch case he was carrying. Inside was what looked like an eloborate radio receiver. He walked slowly round the office with the case, covering every square inch of floor. He rested at intervals. If there was a bug, they would realise what his careful pacing meant. He drew a blank. He frowned and lit a cigarette. It was unlikely that someone as unsophisticated as Margaret had not been followed here. If so it would be very odd if the room wasn't bugged. It would also be very inconvenient. He needed to know exactly what the police knew.

He found it in the wall, where he assumed there was a ventilation shaft. The red light in his case flashed on and off. Yes, there it was. He arranged the blackboard and chairs for his lecture so that the police would have no trouble hearing it.

By the time Geoffrey, Margaret and Andrew had arrived he had drawn a map showing the road from Longford, through Cavan to Butler's Bridge and the border. He shaded in Lough Erne.

'Sorry about all this teacher stuff, but we must all be clear about what's happening when. The treasure trail the kidnappers have given us starts at Longford where you, Geoffrey, will draw the money . . . A million and a half weighs just over six hundredweight and will take two men fifteen minutes to load . . . Tom has told us to drive in a white Cortina to a phone box outside Ballinagh to get instructions. You must be at this box Margaret, not later than —'

'Me?' She sat bolt upright.

An argument began, Andrew bitterly protesting that it was his job, but Simon stuck to saying that Margaret should do it because she had the kidnappers' confidence.

So far so good. Simon took Andrew in his car, leading Geoffrey and Margaret in the Land Rover. He swerved off the road and into a field. Cows at the top of it wandered over as he assembled his selfconscious little group. Like most civilians they couldn't take it seriously, expressing disbelief about the bug until he showed them his case.

'So I'm *not* delivering the money,' Margaret said.

'No. You're the decoy.'

'That's a relief!'

'Sorry about the little charade, but you wouldn't have been convincing if I'd told you. There will be *two* white Cortinas. Margaret will go to Longford with Geoffrey and appear to be drawing the money, but Andrew will draw it from Kells, on the N3.'

It was a beautiful autumn day, the best for weeks. They had a burst of optimism, forgetting the anguish for a while, enjoying being conspirators. The cows browsed near them, big Friesans, udders swinging, occasionally lifting their heads to stare at them.

'Sir!' Andrew stuck up his hand.

'Yes Andrew,' said Simon.

Andrew seized Simon's detector case and took it over to the startled cows. 'I think this big black one here is bugged.'

Simon joined in the laughter. They needed it, needed more comradeship — there hadn't been much in this group, God knows! — if they were to mount a reasonable operation.

'Anything else?' he said.

Andrew's tone was still facetious as he slapped his brown cords. 'Do I carry a gun?'

'Not unless you want to be shot.'

They smiled, made more jokes, but the atmosphere of a game had gone, and when Simon took back his case, they walked back to the cars in silence.

14 *Murphy's Law*

Nobody said anything, but Frances sensed that this was the day when the drop, as the man called it, would take place. He was collecting the tray — he always brought the meals and collected the tray now.

Clare was squatting on the bed, blankets round her, reading a book, but Frances felt her eyes as she talked to him. She told herself that the more she talked to him, and encouraged him to feel that she desired him, the more chance they had of getting out alive. He hadn't slept with her. She could stop him short. He wouldn't rape her. He's had plenty of opportunity. He had kissed her and sucked her breasts. He was a boy. He was easy to flatter — full of delusions! Now, with an unawareness of the effect it was having on her which made her shudder, he was telling her about the first person he had killed.

'. . . It's like your first woman. You want to get it over. Get in the pub. Tell them about it. You know. Jesus! The bang, the jump of it! His wife came running out. I wasn't sure he was dead and I had to fire twice more. That was hard. You have to remember what the man has done, why he has to be executed.'

He looked at her to see she understood and she found herself nodding. She even managed a sympathetic smile at the occupational hazards of killing. He nauseated her but didn't he fascinate her too? He had spoken in an undertone, but she wondered if Clare had caught some of it, the way she was looking across at them. He must have thought so too, for he snatched up the tray.

'I'll do that,' she said.

He ignored her, piling dishes on the tray.

'You're going to collect the money?'

'Yes.'

'You and the other man?' He didn't answer. 'Please don't leave us with her.'

'She won't touch you.'

'Please.'

He pushed her to one side surlily, and locked and bolted the door. Clare turned a page of the book, but Frances knew she wasn't reading it. As Frances approached, Clare shifted round until her back was to her.

'What are you staring at?'

'I don't stare with my back,' Clare said.

'You know what I mean.'

'I don't!'

Frances lost her temper and snatched the book away. Clare tried to grab it. Frances flung it into a corner, breaking the spine. She closed her torn dress, as if there were marks her daughter could see.

'What else can I do?' she said.

Clare shrugged, muttered, picked up the book and smoothed down the pages. 'It's what you always do.'

'What? What did you say?' she gripped Clare's shoulder.

'You're hurting me!'

'I will hurt you! If you believe I want to touch that, that —'

'You do!' Clare shouted.

Frances hurled Clare from her. She hit the edge of the bed and fell dazed on the floor.

'I am trying to save our lives and even if I have to sleep with that scum I will do so but don't you ever dare say that to me again!'

Border Country. There are as many twists and turns in that insane border as in the mind of the man who put it there — Lloyd George. Kearney thought of his grandfather, a staunch Republican, who used to say that to him, and wondered what he would think of his grandson, here — hopefully — to catch the gunmen.

It was impossible to seal the border, which ran for a hundred and fifty miles, from Derry to Warrenpoint. Only the main and some minor roads could be contained. Attempts had been made to close others by blowing craters in them, or planting huge girders. But indignant farmers, faced with long detours in everyday journeys, filled in the craters and uprooted the girders.

Much of the border snaked through hill farms, which were run by Ulster's Catholics. The British could pursue as far as the border, but not cross it. They ran the risk of running into mines planted on the Ulster side, which could be detonated from the Republic.

Kearney and Watson had to keep tight on the tail of the money. If they lost it for a moment, it was as good as over the border. Fortunately, the bugged 'safe phone' office had given them all the information they needed.

The phone box at Ballinagh, where Margaret Healey would make her first contact with Tom, was tapped. The kidnappers would probably keep her on the road for a couple of hours, so they could observe her and make sure no police were following. They would be careful — and with any luck, always a jump ahead.

Kearney guessed that the drop would be somewhere between Clones and Cavan, and had established another incident room at Scotsbridge, at an army observation post in a desolate, boggy area. The Irish Army and the police were on full alert, although there was no evidence of it — there were no Garda cars. Between Ballinagh and Clones there were twenty unmarked Special Branch cars, driven by picked men.

God help us, thought Kearney, if there's another major incident in Ireland today. Yet Watson was not happy. Kearney wished he would stop smoking. The air was poisonous. Watson lit another one and pored over the ordnance maps pinned to the walls. The R/T crackled on the specially established frequency. O'Hanlon was in a car in Longford.

'Control, alpha 2 . . . Carr entering Longford bank . . . Cortina is white estate, roofrack, brown suitcase, registration number . . .'

Other calls came in. Every eye was on the maps. Kearney picked up his coffee, but it had gone cold long ago.

Watson started to speak but his throat was hoarse from smoking. He spat in his handkerchief and started again. 'We cannot be sure Crossan will direct her to this part of the border.'

'We're covering every road to the north! And we're tailing her.'

'Suppose we lose her? We can't watch every field! One helicopter . . .'

'And scare them off?'

Watson would have had half the British Army there. Kearney had done a delicate operation. When you cast the bait, the fisherman must not be evident. There couldn't be too many people, or the kidnappers would be warned. If there were too few, the trap might not close. He asked a sergeant for a fresh mug of coffee with cream. He would soon know if he had got his sums right.

The charm of Kells, the woods coming down to the Blackwater, the church with its copy of Ireland's most famous book, was entirely lost on Andrew. He had come down the evening before D-day, only to find the white Cortina Simon had ordered was not ready.

On D-day itself he arrived at the garage in plenty of time. It would be an hour and a half before Simon drew the money from the bank's vaults. The assistant in his tiny portable cabin looked up from a muddle of forms and receipt books and smiled.

'Cortina Estate?'

That was more like it! After all this waiting, hanging about in that grim office, he was at last going to do something. Free Frances. He would deliver the money, not Geoffrey. She would remember that. And that

Geoffrey had bargained. And then who knows what might happen? His daydream vanished. He stared at the car in front of him.

'In Wicklow we call that red.'

'The white one's still being serviced.'

'Jasus! When I came to collect it yesterday you *swore* it would be ready.'

The assistant had a sheaf of service forms, another customer waiting, and looked as if he dealt with this sort of problem all day long. 'This has the same wheels. The same engine. And less on the clock.'

'It's red!'

Andrew was so vehement the clerk backed away slightly, and indicated to Andrew to follow him. The white Cortina was a forlorn sight, jacked up with its front wheels off.

'Dermot,' said the assistant and first a pair of black hands, then a placid, oil-streaked face appeared from under the car.

Simon's plan revolved round exact timing. At Longford, parcels of guillotined newspapers had been transferred by Geoffrey's company to the safe deposit. At one o'clock he was to draw them out and Margaret was to drive them in her white Cortina to the phone box at Ballinagh.

She would tell Tom to phone another box at Kingscourt, on the L14 from Kells, where Andrew would be waiting with the real money. If he wasn't there the whole plan would collapse. Frances might lose her life. All because of a bloody oil leak!

He offered Dermot twenty. They thought he was mad. He said it was for a wedding. The white was a mark of respect. Dermot was an agonisingly slow mechanic.

'I need to put new gaskets in . . .'

'Just put the wheels on and get it on the road!'

It was approaching half-twelve. He kept on feeling he should jump in the red car, but then thought he can only take another five minutes. The five became ten, the ten fifteen. The assistant came over to query something with Dermot. Then the mechanic lost one of the nuts for the wheel.

'Funny . . . I always put them in the cap . . .'

It was nearly one by the time he screeched out of the garage, down the main street, into the bank. Simon was at the back with two security guards, who wheeled out the money. He cut short Andrew's explanations.

'Load! We must be at that phone box in ten minutes!'

Andrew was staggered at the weight and size of the packets of money. 'It'll take us twenty minutes to get there!'

The money filled the back of the estate so they could scarcely see out of the rear window. As they jumped in, Andrew thought, not for the first time, that it had to be significant that Murphy's Law had been discovered by an Irishman: if anything can go wrong, it will.

The man was so small he scarcely came up to the phone. He had old, seamed cheeks, and his nose and mouth fitted into the receiver as he gabbled on, almost appearing to be part of it. Once Margaret opened the box. He wasn't a bit put out.

'Ah, there's someone wants the phone, shan't be long, shan't be long . . .'

Margaret paced up and down the street. Two children stared at her. A curtain twitched. When they'd loaded up the money, one of the parcels had burst, exposing part of the *Irish Times*. The look the security guard had given her! A couple of cars passed. She hadn't seen any sign of the Garda. Was that good or bad?

'Did you want the phone?'

The little man was holding open the door. And the phone was ringing. As he moved to pick it up she pushed past him and pulled the door behind her. The box smelt of the man's tobacco. She dislodged orange peel as she snatched up the receiver.

'Tom? Margaret. Ring Kingscourt 483.'

The familiar, soft Derry voice sounded in her ear. 'Hang on Margaret. I tell you —'

'Kingscourt 483.'

It took an enormous effort to do so, to break contact, but she put down the phone as Simon had instructed her to do. When she left the box, the little man had joined the children, staring at her. There was no-one else in sight.

Now the police would be confused and alarmed. Or that was Simon's theory. She had the money, but apparently no instructions. She was to proceed towards the border, Simon said. As she got into the Cortina her legs were shaking. The little man disappeared into a shop, the children following him. The street was deserted. She started the car and took the road to Cavan.

The road from Kells was a never-ending serpent, twisting and turning through fields and wooded lakeland with a grey sky hanging over it. Simon wanted rain. And a delivery at night — if they ever got that far.

When the Cortina skidded on to the pavement at Kingscourt, Andrew could hear the phone ringing through the broken windows of the box. He scrambled out, ran to the wrong side of the box, and pulled at a non-existent door in his anxiety. By the time he reached it, the phone had stopped ringing. Simon joined him. Andrew shut his eyes, panting. He felt as though he had run the whole distance from Kells, to no purpose. The phone clicked, and the receiver was at his ear before it rang.

'Hello? Hello? Tom?'

'Who's that?'

'Andrew.'

'What the fuck's going on?'

'I'm delivering. Quick! Before the line's tapped!'

'Tapped! I told you no fucking police!'

'We're trying to avoid them! Where do I go?'

Static sang down the line. Andrew could feel Simon at his elbow. When Frank did speak, it was quickly and precisely.

'Go to Clones. Take the Monaghan road until . . .'

Andrew drove fast towards Carrickmacross. The main risk was that, although the police could not have tapped the Kingscourt phone in time, they might radio cars in the area to pick up whoever was taking the call. He pulled off into woods near the town, and he and Simon disguised the money with fertiliser bags. They had a couple of drums which they placed at the back. They liberally splashed the car with mud, as though its normal habitat was farmyards.

Andrew looked under the car. The brakes were getting sluggish. He pulled a face. Dermot had been right: oil was still leaking and the gaskets needed replacing. But they hadn't too far to go — fifty miles perhaps?

He and Simon put on battered trilbys and dirty sports jackets. They tied a piece of metal tubing on to the exhaust to give it a convincing rattle. Between Carrickmacross and Clones there is a bewildering network of tiny roads running through the boggy county of Monaghan; a countryside of small farms and miniature, tree-surrounded lakes, whose sedgey mud swarms with dragon-flies, and where even the locals are sometimes not sure which side of the border they are on. Into this warren, where roads double back on themselves without warning, and there are few signs, rattled the one and a half million pounds.

Kate saw the white Cortina at Rockcorry and again, as it followed the twists and turns Frank had given them, near Newbliss. Through the powerful glasses she could see right into the back of the estate. No-one concealed. No-one following.

The sky showered and cleared, showered and set into a steady, persistent rain. To get to the drop she passed through a wooded area where the birds were settling for the evening. She flashed her lights. A torch blipped twice from a building blurred in the failing light across a couple of fields. The building was a deserted barn, now used as a dump for old cars and decaying farm machinery. Frank pulled back a door, which scraped protestingly along the floor, and she drove in.

She reported the car was clear and he, in high spirits, produced his inevitable flask of coffee. This was the moment they'd worked for for over a year, yet all she could feel was a nagging, corrosive bitterness.

'One and a half million,' he said. 'That's a lot of rustle. They should listen to that in the north all right.'

'If they get to hear it.'

The words were out of her mouth before she could stop them.

'What do you mean?' He gave her a slow, incredulous grin. 'I'd keep it for myself?'

'And her.'

He leant back against a pile of sacks and laughed until she could have thrown the hot coffee into his face.

'Don't put ideas into my head.'

'You're screwing her.'

'I haven't touched her!' he shouted. 'Not now, Kate, not on the bloody job. Jesus Christ here we are and you . . . .' His anger evaporated a little and he grinned again. 'I'm raising her political conscience.'

'Consciousness,' she said, aware she was being petty. 'God, you're as thick as ever.'

There was an uneasy pause between them. The rain drummed on the tin roof and dripped through various holes on to the floor and some sacking near her. She peered out across the darkening field. Frank had chosen the place well. It was too open for them to be taken by surprise. A track round the back of the barn would take them into the north. Or they could double back towards Dublin.

He touched her arm, hesitantly. 'Sorry Kate. You're not jealous of her, are you?'

Jealous! They all thought they were God's gift to a woman!

But then he said, looking straight at her: 'You're

worth twenty thousand of that woman.'

She began unloading from the car the camping equipment which had been their cover. Why, if she didn't care what he thought, did she get such a lift from that look, those words? But here he was again, unable — like her — to leave it alone.

'That would be the big laugh!' he said. 'If I took his money and his wife!'

The other man brought Frances and Clare their next meal. So the witch had gone with Frank — her pleading had worked. Frances expected Clare to be relieved, but instead she grew more and more sullen and morose, as minute after minute dragged by.

She tried to get Clare to do the jigsaw, which she had completed seven times already, or was it eight? Eventually Frances tipped the pieces on the table and began it herself.

Enthusiastic reports on her progress — 'I've got the roof on!' — met with no response.

'Come on, darling,' she said gently. 'I'm sorry I shouted, I'm sorry for everything . . . We're going to be released!'

Clare's face was white and frightened. The wick in the oil heater was burning low and gave off fumes which made her cough. Frances struggled to adjust it, without losing the flame. Clare muttered something.

'What? What's that darling?'

'We'll never be released.'

Frances held her. 'Don't be silly. Don't be silly. He's gone for the money now.'

In the control room at Scotsbridge there had been turmoil since Margaret Healey had switched the kidnapper to another phone. Kearney frantically tried to switch cars to Kingscourt, but it was twenty miles over a countryside of narrow, twisty roads. Officers shouted into phones, the R/T crackled, and all the time Kearney had Watson's face, shrouded in cigarette smoke, at his elbow.

'Control, Alpha 2.'

'Two go ahead,' said Kearney.

'She's through Cavan, heading towards Butler's Bridge.'

'Stop her,' said Watson.

'And blow the whole thing?'

'She hasn't the money.'

Kearney suspected in the depths of his sinking heart that Watson was right, but he put up an argument, then suddenly caved in. As they waited, he thought bitterly that there would be more time for fishing in the future: this had been his big chance, his big operation, unless . . .

'Alpha 4, go ahead,' he said as the car called.

'We've stopped the lady at Ballyconnel. She's carrying a large number of parcels.'

'Containing?'

'Well . . . chopped-up newspapers, sir . . .'

Clones is an agricultural town built round a large triangular market square. Farmers and farm workers are common, and no-one glanced at the battered white Cortina, with drums and sacks in the back, as it parked near the post office. Not that there were many people to glance: like most Irish towns of its size, it was dead after five o'clock.

Simon looked through the film of rain being pushed away by the wipers, at the old cross in the centre of the square, corners all smoothed to curves. It was impossible to believe that a few miles away was Britain, where the road signs changed, the pillar boxes were painted red instead of green, the whiskey and petrol were so much cheaper the Irish went over in droves for it, and people were killing one another, buying the weapons with money such as he was delivering. Although, of course, he had nothing to do with it. Neither did Bennet. They simply gave advice, which the family took or not. .

'This is as far as I go,' he said.

'Lloyds never deals with criminals,' Andrew said.

'I don't even work for Lloyds,' Simon said. 'Sure of your route?'

'No.'

They looked at the ordnance map and the scribbled instructions Andrew had taken down on the phone.

'The gate must be there. What's the marker?'

'Warning. Poison.' Andrew said. 'In red letters.'

'You've half-an-hour. They'll wait twenty minutes. No more. Good luck.'

He got out of the car and shook hands awkwardly, guiltily: he was the soldier, he should be doing it. He walked away quickly before he did anything foolish. Andrew shouted. Simon turned, the rain blurring his vision.

'Mine's a large Jameson,' Andrew said. 'No ice.'

They were still in with a change, Kearney reckoned. The border went up roughly like an inverted 'U' from Cavan to Dundalk on the coast. Dundalk was heavily guarded and led to the 'bandit' country of South Armagh — Crossan might not be sure the money would get into the right hands.

The Cavan area was where they picked up Margaret Healey. They could assume that since she'd drawn the Garda there, Crossan was unlikely to be in the same spot. That left Clones, Monaghan and Castleblayney.

They knew certain things. The money was being driven either by Andrew Pagett, or the man called Simon. They would need a truck or estate car to carry it. Loading time would be ten minutes, so he'd have to drive off the road.

Local knowledge poured in to the control room at Scotsbridge, about farms, tracks and smugglers' routes. At any one time Special Branch cars were following up to fifteen suspected vehicles. They were ordered not to intercept unless a contact was being made.

Kearney's hopes were raised twice. The first time twenty crates of Johnny Walker Black Label whiskey were picked up near Castleshane on their way south and turned over to Customs. At Hooklough, a fifty-year-old married farmer was jumped on while meeting a woman with whom he was having an affair. He had a heart attack and had to be rushed to hospital in Monaghan, where his condition was said to be satisfactory.

'Which is more than can be said for mine,' Watson said.

It was six o'clock. He had run out of cigarettes and, he believed, out of time.

Andrew was lost. He tried to calm himself by muttering Frances's name, but panic was not far off. The roads were black as pitch and the steady drizzle had turned to a downpour. The brakes must have got oil on them because they were getting frighteningly sluggish on the bends.

When a sign came at some crossroads, he stopped. It was difficult to see which way each arm was pointing. But at least he couldn't be far now. He had ten minutes to find the drop.

He glanced in his mirror, trying to see over the piled-up money. A while back he had thought a car was following him, but it must have turned off.

He decided to go straight on. When a farm, and then a couple of houses appeared he knew he was wrong. He had to go up to a gate and reverse. Six minutes to find them. He shot off back the way he had come. As he passed the farmhouse he took the bend very fast. Before he was round it, he saw the glint of oncoming headlights.

The brakes scarcely responded. The car was approaching very fast. Andrew pumped the brakes and crashed the gears. He glimpsed the approaching driver's face, rigid with fear, as he wrenched his car off the road. The off-side of the Cortina caught it, hurtling it into the hedge: the bang was tremendous: Andrew, dazed, held by his belt, thought a petrol tank had gone up.

That made him scramble out. He was bleeding from a cut on his forehead, and there was a ferocious pain in his knee which made him hobble. The rain cleared his head. The raindrops seemed to hang, motionless and sparkling, in the criss-cross of three headlights: one of the Cortina's had gone.

Across the fields, a dog was barking, on and on. The front lights of the farmhouse had come on.

Andrew stumbled across to the other car. The driver's head was lolling forward. As Andrew opened the door, broken glass fell and tinkled. He pulled the man's head up. He was unconscious. Someone was shouting across the fields. Andrew started to run to the Cortina when a radio crackled in the other car.

'Alpha 7 . . . Alpha 7 . . . confirm suspect Clare Road heading *south*?'

Andrew leant into the car, over the inert driver and found the microphone.

'Alpha 7? Alpha7.'

'Negative Clare Road,' said Andrew. 'Suspect has rejoined N54, direction N12.'

The voice rebuked him. 'Listen out, seven.'

Andrew rubbed the microphone on his sleeve. 'You are intermittent,' he said, wrenching out the cord and throwing the microphone into the bushes. A torch was dancing towards him down the road. He ran back to the Cortina. Stopped. The back had burst open and two of the packets had been thrown out, one spilling bundles on to the soaking grass. He just had time to hurl them back in before the farmer came panting up. Andrew indicated the unconscious driver.

'Can you look after him?'

The farmer's mouth was a vacuous, blurred oval behind the shimmer of his torch.

'Here! Where are you —'

Metal twanged as Andrew wrenched open the Cortina's door. Miraculously, the car fired straight away. The farmer shouted. Andrew yelled back.

'Get out of the way! My wife is ill! Dying!'

She might be ill, dying, she might be, might have been, might be my wife. The thoughts hammered through his head as he drove back down to the crossroads. They could arrest him, do what they liked with him, so long as he got the money through. A sob escaped him. He still couldn't be sure which road it was! It was so bloody dark. Then, as he turned the wheel, the single eye of the headlight caught it.

WARNING. POISON.

The gate was coming off its hinges and it caught in the mud as he dragged it back. He peered into the pouring rain. He could see nothing. To the left were dark shapes where the forest began. To the right, miles away over flat bog-land, brief flickers of light marked a road.

There was a track. The car churned mud, then lurched forward. He peered over the wheel. He felt as if he was driving into nothing. The wheels spun, and gripped. If he stopped, he would never get going again. They must have gone, if they had ever been here. The track seemed endless. Her face was in his mind, he saw her as she had been on the night of the jump-off. He had won. He had done the jump and won her! Her wild tongue had been in his mouth. Then Michael had jumped and died.

He cried out as a hooded figure appeared and then another. His foot slipped off the clutch and the engine stalled. For a moment he couldn't find the handle to wind down the window.

One of the figures was pointing a pistol straight into his face. He swallowed before he spoke.

'Tom?'

The voice had the soft cadences he knew so well from the phone.

'What kept you?'

The man in the crashed car was coming round, moaning. The farmer's wife, Mary Stephens, an old coat of her husband's belted round her against the rain, was comforting him. Stephens kicked broken glass off the road. He trod on something half buried in the ditch. It was a parcel, the paper wet and soggy. The farmer's torch showed a familiar purple colour.

'Mary!'

She glanced round, and stared in astonishment at a thick bundle of twenty-pound notes.

Andrew struggled to reverse the Cortina in a half-circle so that it backed up to the kidnapper's car. The bent wing caught on it, and the wheels spun. Frank swore and ran to his car. They were working without lights, and he caught the barn door as he drove out. They switched off the engines and listened.

There was only the soft fall of the rain. Lights winked on the distant road.

Tom picked up a packet of the money. 'Make a chain.'

Andrew threw to Tom, who threw to the other figure in the car. A packet slipped from his cold fingers into the mud and the next one hit him.

'Come on come come on!' Tom cried.

'You will release them?'

'Not if you don't get a move on!'

Kearney found the grid reference of Stephens's farm. O'Hanlon and a Special Branch Officer, McGraw, were nearest. They picked up the injured man and Stephens told them about the track to the north, by the deserted barn. The Cortina had gone in that direction.

Cars arrived at the crossroads without lights. McGraw positioned men armed with rifles and sub-machine guns. As they crept forward, they reached the open gate. There were recent car tracks, still not washed away. They could see nothing through the driving rain.

McGraw and O'Hanlon consulted with Kearney, then men pushed a Garda car, equipped with a powerful roof light, through the open gate.

The farmer pointed out the position of the barn, as the car edged slowly forwards.

'Fire after my warning, unless they fire first,' McGraw said.

So faintly at first that it was impossible to tell which direction it was coming from, a siren sounded. As McGraw dived for the R/T the farmer slapped his side as he remembered 'My wife sent for an ambulance.'

Men collided with one another as McGraw shouted instructions. Kearney's voice went unheeded on the R/T. The siren grew louder across the dark fields. Ahead in the blackness a car engine fired.

'Lights,' shouted McGraw impotently, 'lights lights lights!'

'You bastard,' Frank snarled.

'I lost them', Andrew cried, 'I swear to God I lost them.'

'Down!' yelled Frank as a beam of light shot yards to the left of them.

Andrew threw himself down by the Cortina. Kate was in the other car, shouting incoherently to him.

'Out! Keep the engine running!' he shouted back.

The back was open. About half the money had been transferred. Some was in the mud, inches from his face. The beam, sparkling with rain, had swung the wrong way, but was now on its way back and would find them in seconds. He aimed, forgetting the mud, the rain, everything but the moving white finger, now illuminating a decaying tractor, the rusty-red side of the barn . . . He expelled his breath, becoming part of the rifle, the bullet. Three shots rapid. As he rolled from his position towards the car he thought: the first would have done.

Sub-machine fire rattled back. In the air. The idiots should go for the kill. Never give anyone a fucking chance if you want to live.

A loud hailer boomed out. 'No further warning Crossan! Come forward! We're all round you!'

Like hell they were, but they soon would be while the loud hailer kept echoing round the field. He motioned Kate to crawl back to the front of the car. He thought he could glimpse a car being pushed into the field.

'That track is . . .' The loud hailer stopped as Frank shouted. 'That track is mined.'

He ran, doubled up. No time to shut the back doors. He was in the driving seat.

A voice behind him was shouting: 'Don't kill her.' Andrew.

Mud churned as he careered off. A bullet smashed the wing mirror. Others hit the chassis. Money was sliding from one side to the other.

In the rear mirror he glimpsed Andrew falling. He was driving without lights. He just missed an old car dumped by the side of the barn. Now the barn was between him and the bullets. In a few minutes he would be over the border and they could switch cars.

They rigged up a light to illuminate the scene round the white Cortina. Kearney and Watson arrived. Men were going over the ground round the barn inch by inch. Watson was examining the muddy brown packets of money in the Cortina.

'We seem to have got most of it,' he said.

Kearney didn't answer. He was standing over a doctor who was examining Andrew's body. The rain still drizzled on his upturned face. The doctor pulled a piece of plastic sheet over it and rose to talk to Kearney.

15 *The Gamble*

'I do not want a receipt! I want the money returned!' Geoffrey was standing in front of the portraits in the big room at Kilnameath, facing Kearney and Watson. Margaret was huddled in a chair near him.

Kearney held out out a slip of paper and, when Geoffrey did not take it, put it on the table. 'That's what we recovered, sir. One million, two thousand and twenty pounds'.

'It is my money, and I want it!'

'It has to be held in evidence, I'm afraid.'

Geoffrey could see that Watson, far from being afraid, was pleased to have something over the family. The police could freeze the money until the inquest on Andrew.

'You're keeping the money so we can't get her back! You're going to kill her and her little girl, just as you killed Andrew!'

Margaret became hysterical. Geoffrey sat on the arm of her chair and comforted her. He could bring a High Court action but that would take time. The police were still looking for Frances and Clare, but clearly were putting their main hope on trapping the kidnappers, as they had trapped the hoaxers on the day after the kidnapping — which now seemed months ago.

He had been vulnerable then. Incredibly emotional and weak. Now he felt, overcoming everything, even his love for Frances, a slow, controlled anger, a hatred for the kidnappers, a contempt for the bungling police.

They were idiots. He should have taken matters into his own hands from the beginning.

'I'll find them,' he said.

'Just like that,' said Watson.

'Just like that. How many reports have you filed on the case?'

'Over a thousand.'

'All in a card index?'

'Yes.'

'Useless. You're still in the steam age.'

'We are following every lead, Mr Carr!' Kearney's cheeks burnt a dull red.

'You can't see for paper. The police had the same problem with the Yorkshire Ripper. If they'd used a computer, three or four lives could have been saved.'

'You're talking about Miriam, Mr Carr,' Watson said. 'That's still experimental.'

Geoffrey knew all about Miriam — Major Incident Room Index and Action Management — as his company had been developing some of the techniques in the field. It would take years for a practical police computer for big investigations to develop from it — not because the knowledge wasn't there, but because of red tape and lack of money.

The police were also reluctant to allow computer experts from outside to handle sensitive material.

'We can make our own Miriam,' Geoffrey said. 'I've got the know-how, the computers. You've got the information. Give me access to it.'

'Impossible,' Watson said.

'Then I'll go to the courts and get the money and I'll pay. And next time it will get through.'

Kearney tugged at his flap of hair. 'You can't ask us to open confidential police files to a member of the public.'

'I am not a member of the public! It's my wife they've mutilated!'

'You'd be taking the law into your own hands,' Watson said.

'Nonsense. You'd be in control.'

'And we've seen some of the results of that,' Margaret put in bitterly.

Kearney wavered. 'It's not our decision . . .

'You're gambling, Geoffrey!' Margaret said.

She started to get up, stopped and put her head in her hands. She looked finished. On the other hand he now felt full of energy, convinced he could find Frances. And he wanted to see the people who had done that to her, he wanted, all right, he did, he wanted revenge. That was the driving force now.

'Agree,' he said, 'and I'll tell the kidnapper I can't deliver until my High Court application succeeds. That gives us — maybe a week. If we haven't found them in that time, then I'll fix a drop at which you can lay a trap.'

Margaret shuddered. He put his arm round her. Her eyes were closed as if she was asleep.

It had gone wrong. Frances could see that in his eyes. It must have been very late at night when he came. Clare was asleep. He'd been drinking. Was drinking. He had a glass in his hand with which he motioned her out of the cellar. The corridor was silent, lit from a bulb at the top of the steps. There was a long fresh gash on his forehead. He held out the glass which was full of whiskey. Still he said nothing.

She licked her dry lips. 'Did you get it?'

They were like conspirators, criminals together. His face moved into the shadow.

'Some of it.'

Did he mean that Geoffrey had cheated again? She didn't pursue it: what was the point? She saw in her mind Geoffrey's face, his smile, heard his bargaining voice. She remembered the auction: he'd had no idea of her feelings then, and she'd been sitting next to him. She drank. They finished the whiskey together.

It was because she was so tired, more than for any other reason, she was tired and she no longer cared. He slipped his hands round her breasts and put his tongue in her mouth. She responded. He was just like any other man, after all. No he was not, he had the power to end her life, to stop all this warm movement, which was exciting her, disgusting her but exciting her, he could stop it as he could just switch off the light. She sobbed as he went into her, he was everything, her hold on life. He gave a little snarl and she could feel him coming inside her and she dug her nails into him and he didn't seem to care if she hit him or kissed him and when he was spent he picked up the empty glass and went up the steps without a word or a look back. She had nothing to dry herself or clean herself with. What did it matter. The smell of sex would drown in all the other smells. When she got into bed she knew Clare was awake. And when she touched her and Clare moved sharply away, she knew that she had heard.

Geoffrey thought: That was a very successful lie to Watson. Of course they'd lost control. Now he was playing the cards. Hadn't he got RTE to broadcast the news he wanted the kidnappers to hear?

'Speculation that the mysterious shooting of Andrew Pagett is connected with the kidnap of Frances Carr, increased today when her husband began a court fight to regain possession of the million pounds found in a car near the incident, which he claims is his money . . . There is now open warfare between Carr and the police over their month-long handling of the affair.'

Astonishing what journalists and the public would swallow! Exactly the opposite was true. For the first time he was working closely with the police — or, rather, they were working with him.

He explained his theory that when Frances said, on the tape, that Clare had nearly died, she could have been referring to an asthma attack. Kearney produced tablets and an inhaler which had been found in the back of the car from which they had been abducted.

Had the kidnappers got fresh tablets, an inhaler? They were available only on prescription. If they searched through recent chemist break-ins . . .

Breaking and entering cases were stored in the Garda computer in Dublin, which was simply used for statistics. Geoffrey copied them on to disks, which he could use with his computers, a number of which were now installed in another incident room.

Next he turned to holiday homes. If they were a gang on the fringe of the IRA, it was unlikely that they were holed up with sympathisers. The most likely bet was a holiday cottage. It must be detached and remote. It probably had an outhouse or a cellar, so that the hostages could not be detected by a casual, unexpected visitor.

The flaw in all this was whether the kidnappers had got the place through an agency. Geoffrey gambled on that. All the agency information had to be processed on to disks. There was a daunting amount of it. But the computer could sift out many of them immediately: the kidnappers must have taken the place on a long let of at least two months.

And they were even getting a picture of the house. Fresh whitewash had been found under the fingernail, as well as old brick dust — unusual, as most older Irish houses had been built of stone.

'No idea of the age of the house, I suppose?' Geoffrey asked McLaughlin, the police scientist.

'Oh, yes,' said McLaughlin, as unmoved as if he was giving Geoffrey the time. 'The kiln making these bricks shut down eighty years ago.'

Kate had been for cutting their losses. With half-a-million they could claim success, contribute to the movement's funds and have the capital for another attempt. But the packets of notes, far from satisfying Frank, made him greedy. He argued that the money was proof that the family was willing to pay another million — hadn't they practically had it in their hands?'

The news on RTE confirmed that. Were they going to

throw it away? Kate only agreed to negotiate another drop on condition they moved. Every day it felt more dangerous to stay at Annacloy. There'd been the chemist's break-in, Frank's escapade in town . . . there were too many pointers to the place.

Two days ago they had sent Willy to look for another safe house, giving him money to pay in advance. He hadn't returned. Eventually Kate checked the money. There was sixty, or perhaps as much as seventy thousand missing. And the car. She didn't normally smoke, but she took one of Frank's cigarettes. He was down in the cellar. As usual.

She put a spoonful of instant in a mug, and then left it without making the coffee. When Frank came upstairs she was packing a case. She told him about the money.

'I know.'

'You *gave* him it!'

'Of course I fucking didn't! I found out he took it!'

'And you didn't tell me?'

'You can't leave me here!'

She put her gun in the case and packed underclothes round it. 'You're free to go.'

'And leave a million?' He stopped her closing the case. 'I need you Kate.'

She turned away to pick up her jacket, annoyed to see her hands were trembling, and to find she was actually pleased he had said that.

'I can't be here,' he continued, 'and picking up the money at the same time, can I?'

That sort of need, she thought, and the words came out before she realised how bitter and angry she was. 'Perhaps you should ask her to help you.'

He threw the case on the floor. She grabbed at the gun, her other hand moving to the safety catch. She could shoot him. She had never been so angry. The room seemed to shimmer as the blood thudded in her head.

'Money for arms! What an idiot I've been. You wanted it for yourself! You want her as much as the money, don't you?'

'Don't be bloody stupid! I hacked off her finger! I hate her more than I've ever hated anyone in my life!'

'Then why are you screwing her?'

'I don't know, I don't know.'

He sat on the bed, his hands clasped, so bewildered, lost that she laughed. He was vicious, violent, but an adolescent still, a boy.

'I want you,' he mumbled.

He was putting it on, while she held the gun — he was so transparent!

'I want you! Don't go Kate! You're part of me, you are, you are, the head on my thick bloody shoulders you are.'

He kissed her. She still had the gun in her hand. The butt scraped the back of his head. She pushed him away. The pulse in her head was still thumping like a drum. She knew perfectly well he was lying, but she put the gun back in a drawer and began to pick up her clothes from the floor.

She had kept the agency lists. Within a few hours she had found another house. They cleared up and burnt anything incriminating, and wiped all surfaces for prints. It took much longer than they thought, for she insisted on going over every square inch. It was late, they were exhausted, and so they decided to spend one more night at Annacloy and start at first light next morning.

Geoffrey dozed for an hour or two at a time in the computer room. A number of operators had been flown over from his company. The research project he had dreamed of setting up in Ireland was now happening — but in a much grimmer context than he could ever have anticipated.

Whenever his eyes flickered open, he could see the green glow of the monitor screens.

The chemist break-ins had easily been handled. They had imagined that the kidnappers would smash the place up, take other things to disguise what they were after.

In the week before the tape had been recorded by Frances, there were four break-ins which fitted the pattern: two in Dublin, one in Limerick, and one in Roscommon.

From that point the difficulties began. Geoffrey constructed a programme which extracted all the sightings and reports within a forty mile radius of these centres. He amalgamated this with data on holiday lets which fitted the profile he had drawn up. What held them up was getting the data from agencies and transferring it to disks.

He stared at a screen as an operator tapped the keyboard: CASTLE HOUSE. 1912. 15 acres. Outhouse. Lets 2 wks 3 wks 2 wks 6 wks. He was nodding off again when someone shook his shoulder.

'I don't know if there's anything in it,' Kearney said.

'What?'

Someone had seen Crossan. Geoffrey couldn't follow it. He hadn't had much more than cat naps for two days. He followed Kearney to the Garda car and sat between him and Watson in the back. Immediately the dark trees and hedges began slipping by. It was two o'clock.

'Where are we going?'

'Carrick.'

All that work, and a policeman had knocked at the right door, that was all he could think of. The car was hot and the swish of the tyres on the empty road had a hypnotic effect. He awoke and stumbled into another Garda station in some strange town he had been unaware of entering.

In an interview room, clasping and unclasping his hands nervously, was a man introduced to Geoffrey as Garda Twomey. At the table a police artist was retouching a photograph of Crossan. Geoffrey watched, bemused. It was like a child inking a moustache on a newspaper picture. The artist sprayed out the hair, cropped it and gave it a reddish tint. Carefully he brushed in dark glasses.

Before he had finished, Twomey was pointing excitedly. 'That's him! That's the fella!'

Kearney picked up a card. 'How can you be so sure? When you only ". . . glimpsed him in a passing car?" '

Twomey had a habit of narrowing his eyes, which made him look cunning and uneasy by turns. 'Well now, it was a good glimpse, it was a bit more than a glimpse of the man I had.'

'A bit more?'

Watson smiled: the pinched reluctant movement of someone who does not smile often. A small shiver of excitement went up Geoffrey's spine.

'I thought he was passing through. It was only when the note came yesterday that he might be in the area that I . . . I did report it sir!'

Kearney gave him a puzzled frown. 'I know you did. What are you trying to say?'

Twomey's head dropped miserably. 'I apprehended him sir.'

'You apprehended him?'

'For parking at a bus stop.'

Kearney's mouth opened, but nothing came out. Geoffrey turned away so no-one could see the smile on his face. At the same time his heart was going at such a rate he rubbed his chest and told himself to calm down, calm down.

'Then there was an interruption sir, a child in the road, sir, if you have children yourself —'

'Get on with it.'

'And it was only when he was driving away that it clicked sir and feeling I would —'

'Look like an idiot you wrote you'd glimpsed him in a passing car. Stay in the station.'

'Yes sir.' They waited for him to go but he said, apologetically: 'I have the man's address, sir. I asked for his driving licence.'

Clare got both hands round the loose brick in the wall. It grated as she tried to pull it out. She stopped and looked at the bed. Frances hadn't stirred. Carefully she removed the brick and took out the steel comb, brushing away the red dust that pattered on her.

She walked past the table. The jigsaw was half-done. There were a number of roof and sky pieces missing. She squatted in a corner and gazed at the dirty white walls which had been their home for three weeks, according to mummy's calender. Mummy. Making love. Fucking, the man called it. The word you saw on walls. Walls like this one. She was never sure whether it was fuk or fuck, but it was exactly the right word for the grunting, the sharp breathing, that cry, exactly the right word she thought as, curiously calm, she held out her wrist and stabbed downwards with the sharpened steel comb.

She had worked out quite carefully that she would plunge in the knife and draw it straight across without making a sound. But the sharp pain and the blood shocked her into crying out. The knife clattered on the floor. Her calm vanished and she began crying hysterically.

'Oh mummy, mummy, mummy mummy!

The pieces were falling into place. Kearney ran a check on all cars hired in the name of Vincent Stephens, 18 Pearse Street, Dublin. Descriptions were circulated of a woman who had visited there, and checks would begin when cottage agencies opened.

It was six o'clock in the morning. The forecast was fine, with rain later.

Geoffrey had a mug of tea and a hot bacon roll. He had been on the phone for an hour to his computer operators, who were extracting all cottage lets within a forty mile radius of Carrick.

Kearney wouldn't wait for the list to be completed.

'We'll pick the rest up on the R/T,' he said. 'The best time to get these people is before they wake up.'

He held out his hand for Geoffrey's list.

'We'll recce them house by house as they come in.'

'I'm coming with you,' Geoffrey said.

'Mr Carr, they have already killed two men.'

'She's my wife. I have the list. Either I go with you, or I go on my own.'

They bandaged Clare's wrist and gave her one of Kate's sleeping tablets. They told Frances they were all leaving. Clare dozed. Frances sat by her, rocking backwards and forwards in agony.

'What have I done,' she whispered, over and over again.

The man came in and touched her on the shoulder.

'All over then,' he said.

She stood up and gave him such a look of steely contempt that he backed to the door. 'All over,' she echoed.

'It was only superficial.'

She laughed. She drew him out into the corridor so as not to wake Clare and she brought out every word as if she was thrusting it into him.

'What you have done isn't superficial. She's been in this hole for weeks, she needs air, sunlight, people to love and care for her. If she was your daughter, what would you feel? Don't tell me you don't feel, you do care, I know.'

The woman was coming down the steps, but she didn't care; she went on in the same tone.

'If you have any feelings for me, let her go. You've had half the money.'

'A third,' the man corrected.

'You sound like my husband,' she said.

His faced crumpled, dipped away, as if this was the worst insult she could have paid him.

'She can go.' He ignored the exclamation from the woman. 'We can drop her on the road.'

Tears sprang into Frances's eyes. 'Thank you, thank you,' she said, and went back to Clare.

16 *Shamrock Special*

Seven o'clock! They'd wasted two hours messing about with the girl! Kate was standing outside the cellar while Frank went in to hood her.

He was actually arguing, explaining the necessity of doing it to the woman!

'She'll see the place, tell them. They might trace us from it.'

All this pussyfooting around was making it worse. Now he was giving the hood to the woman!

'Let me put this on darling.'

'No no no no no no!'

'They're going to release you.'

She was working the girl up into a panic. Perhaps she meant to, the clever bitch. The whore had got him eating out of her hand. Kate rubbed her temples. The dull thumping that now seemed to be always with her had given her a splitting head.

'They're going to kill me,' the girl was screaming.

'No darling, no no no. You'll soon be in the sun, the fresh air. Then later they'll free me.'

'I'll suffocate! My asthma! I don't want to leave you! I want to stay with you!'

Kate moved to intervene but Frank pulled her away to the steps where he sat down and lit a cigarette.

'Let her calm down.'

Her eyes throbbed painfully. 'You think she's fallen for you. The woman from the big house falls for the big man! She's laughing at you, Frank! She's got you exactly where she wants you. Who do you think the knife was for?'

Frank had had enough. Enough of Kate, enough of the woman. Ignoring the girl's screams he forced the hood over her face and lifted her over his shoulder.

He ran out to the waiting car and dumped the girl in the back. Kate brought out the woman. He took the gun she was holding so Kate could close the back doors of the estate. Kate yelled a warning. As Frank's hand went on the door handle he saw a blur as two men rushed him. Beyond them he glimpsed other men with guns pointed.

Frank rammed the car door forward into one of the oncoming men, and lashed backwards with his gun at the other. Kate was yelling and biting as she was overpowered at the rear of the car. She'd managed to partly close the back doors. He pushed his gun into the hood covering the woman's head.

'Back or they'll be shot! Back back back! Leave her! I mean it!'

He clicked off the safety catch.

One of the Special Branch officers, a man with a bald patch called out: 'Get back! Return to the fence.'

'In the car!' Frank yelled to Kate. 'Take the gun. Keep it on them. And keep your head down!'

Frank got out and looked round the men encircling him. The one with a bald patch stepped forward.

'Detective Inspector Kearney. You've no chance Crossan. Be sensible and release them.'

They always thought they had the bloody cards! Be sensible Crossan! As if he was a fucking kid! He'd not come this far to be fucking sensible!

'Shut up!' he screamed. 'I'm telling *you* what's going to happen! Get rid of those guns for a start!'

Kearney signalled and the guns disappeared. There would be others on him, but it made him feel better to see them vanish, to make them realise who was cracking the whip.

'I want a plane at Dublin airport, fully-fuelled, ready to fly. The hostages will be released, unharmed, at our destination.'

Libya, possibly. Anywhere in the Middle East where they could use half a million pounds and a highly trained guerilla.

'I'll have to consult.'

Consult. The man was a poor bloody office worker like the rest. Drinking tea and consulting.

'You can have half-an-hour.'

'It will take at least an hour.'

'Then move! No tricks, no interference, or they'll be shot.'

He looked down into the car. Kate held the gun at the woman's head. She had that mad look on her face. For a moment he was more concerned about her than the police. She might get jumpy and loose off a shot and that would be curtains for both of them. He showed none of this dilemma as he gazed back at the men round him, leaning back against the car and reaching for his cigarettes.

The three men observed Crossan and the hostages through binoculars and then talked near the black Mercedes which had brought them to Annacloy. Behind them clouds were building up over the limestone crags at the head of the valley.

Doherty, a tall grey-haired man, had the distinguished features and the beautiful suit usually only found on actors playing politicians. He was an assistant head of the Special Branch, with special responsibility for 'politically sensitive incidents'.

With him was Colonel Mahon, an expert on terrorism and a man called O'Connor, who gave his profession as 'courier'.

Doherty handed the car telephone back to the driver and turned to Mahon.

'Right. They will be allowed to ascend the ladder to the plane, but must not board it. First foot on the ladder, we're off the hook and the army takes over. I understand they'll be vulnerable to snipers on the airport roof?'

When Mahon nodded, Doherty turned to O'Connor, who had greased, wavy hair, and who was peeling the cellophane from a small cigar.

'O'Connor is a marksman, won a number of medals, haven't you O'Connor?'

O'Connor was secure enough of his prowess to show no interest in it. He looked anxiously at the cigar, which was a little bent. 'Yes sir,' he said.

'See if you can win another.'

Crossan was shouting. It was two hours since the abortive ambush.

'I'll try and talk some sense into him en route,' Doherty continued, 'but if at any time you can shoot *both* of them without endangering the hostages, you are to do so, do you understand?'

'Yes sir.'

'Shoot them in the head. One of them may appear to be unarmed. It makes no difference.'

'I'm driving off now,' Crossan was shouting.

The tone of Doherty's even voice did not alter. 'You must take them *both*. And you must be sure. Clear?'

'Yes sir.'

O'Connor lit his cigar to discover that his anxiety had been well-founded: it did not draw well.

Crossan was pulling open the door of the estate and getting in when Doherty approached. Still Doherty did not hurry. Keep calm, consider all requests, talk and keep on talking, treat the man courteously, sympathetically, as an equal — that was the only formula that worked.

'Frank Crossan,' he said. 'Jimmy Doherty.'

He might have been meeting the man at the Shelbourne, except that he was holding a walkie-talkie.

'Ah,' said Frank. 'We're into the big stuff now.'

'You have your plane.'

Frank flashed a triumphant look to Kate in the car.

'We will escort you to the airport.'

'Like hell you will!'

It was beginning to drizzle, but Doherty showed no sign of noticing it. He thrust his hands into his pockets. 'Listen Frank! You may meet roadblocks, police, army who know nothing about you or the hostages. They may shoot. We'll clear the way for you.'

Frank pulled out his cigarettes. The packet was empty. Doherty looked behind him, and a packet appeared.

'Thanks.' Frank rolled a cigarette between his fingers. 'A police escort.'

'That's right.'

Frank gave a sudden grin. 'Ok. Why not?'

'You'll need this.'

Doherty slid the walkie-talkie along the grass between them.

Frank had seen it before, but only at the pictures or on television: a cavalcade, traffic cleared before it. Two motorcyclists rode before him, and two after him, followed by the majestic black Mercedes, and other cars. And it was all for him!

Far from being afraid, he was exhilarated! He gripped the wheel and grinned in pure delight. 'Beats a package tour, eh girls?'

Clare was wheezing. Kate was grim-faced, keeping the gun into the woman. Ah, she probably spat out her mother's milk, Frank told himself. Frances was different. Frances would enjoy it.

'Take their hoods off. Come on! Give the girl a drink.'

Frances put her arm round Clare and gave her a drink from a flask. They huddled together, blinking at the unaccustomed light, their skins a blotchy, almost luminous white.

'I know you like travelling in style,' Frank said.

The walkie-talkie crackled. 'Frank.'

'Yes. Jimmy.'

'We're going left on the N55 to Athlone.'

'That's not the Dublin road!'

'The plane's at Cork!'

'I said Dublin!'

Clare began to cough and wheeze as the exchange got angrier. Frances offered her the flask but she pushed it away. Kate had slid down in the back corner, so her head was not visible from the cars behind. She kept the gun trained on Frances.

'I'm sorry Frank, but the only serviceable spare plane is at Cork.'

'Sod. Bloody Shamrock special is it?'

'You are flying Aer Lingus, Frank.' Doherty put the R/T down and glanced at Colonel Mahon. 'Buys time. And he'll have to do a petrol stop.'

On Doherty's other side, O'Connor put out his unsatisfactory cigar and stared out of the window. As they passed the huge bulk of the church of St Peter and St Paul Doherty picked up the R/T again.

'This is from the Taoiseach himself, Frank ... release the hostages now, and it would very greatly influence the length of the sentence you would serve, do you understand me?'

There was no response. Perhaps he wasn't listening out. That would be a problem. Sirens sounded as the procession went over red lights and headed towards Birr. Doherty tried again.

'There will be no extradition to the north. That's a promise from the Taoiseach himself.'

Doherty's voice was as well-cut as his suit, sober and sincere. Two tiny notches appeared in his forehead as he repeated the statement. Frank's voice boomed out suddenly, making Doherty pull the walkie-talkie away from his ear.

'I can't hear you, Jimmy. I have the Pope on the other line.'

Pine forests rose up to the Galtee Mountains, scarcely visible through mist. There was just enough rain to make the wipers squeak. There were bits of Donegal like this, thought Frank, remembering Danny. If only Danny could see him now! He'd planned to do something really big — now look at him!

The girl was in a very bad way, coughing and wheezing without stopping. It got on his bloody nerves. Frances was shouting in his ear.

'I gave the pills, everything to you!'

'Where did you put them Frank!' Kate was throwing things about.

'I didn't pack them.'

'Sit down!' yelled Kate to Clare.

Frank glanced in the mirror. The gun was up. If Kate wasn't careful, she'd be a target.

'She can't sit down!' Frances yelled back.

'I can't breathe,' sobbed Clare.

'Frank please!'

Frank glimpsed in the mirror Kate's distorted face when Frances used his name. He was pleased. As well as this procession, he had a woman like this! Nevertheless he shouted at her: 'She always has bloody convenient attacks.'

'Because you always produce them!'

She was so close to him that her spit hit the side of his face. He saw a layby and went into it, telling Kate to look for the pills while he held the gun. The motorbikes waited ahead, engines running. The black Mercedes was parked at the other end of the layby.

'Let her go,' Frances pleaded.

'Hush your noise.'

'You said you'd let her go! You promised!!'

'Keep still or this'll go off. The hold-all!' he said to Kate.

'I've looked there.'

'Jesus Christ!'

One of the motorbikes revved. Doherty was standing motionless by his black car. He'd called on the R/T to ask what was happening, but Frank had ignored him.

'Look at her, look at her, look what you're doing to her Frank. Frank!'

The gun was between them. Her face was close, he looked at the shine of her tongue, her wild pleading black eyes. She got so close, her hair brushed his hand. Beyond her he could see Kate, rigid, no longer searching for the pills, and beyond Kate, Doherty. He picked up the R/T.

'The wain's sick,' Frank said.

'How sick?' Doherty replied. He could see only a confused picture. Crossan had the gun at the hostage's head. The woman terrorist was crouched in the back of the car. The small girl fell, got up, was obscured.

'She's coming over,' Frank said.

'Right, Frank.' Doherty clicked off the R/T. 'Stretch your legs,' he said to O'Connor. O'Connor walked round the back of the car, studying angles. The woman was no problem. He had already judged that she was the simpler proposition. The man was different. He had a marksman's instinct for knowing when he was a target. It was an interesting problem. He had to sight his weapon without having it in his hand. If he gave Crossan any indication of his role, the man might shoot. Doherty had tried to calm him, but, O'Connor judged, he was unbalanced, on a high, he might do anything. He needed a minimum of two seconds to get out his gun and take them both. He flexed his fingers, and put his hands in his pockets to keep them warm and dry.

Clare was confused: she didn't understand what they were all shouting at her to do.

'Can you walk, darling?' Frances said.

'Yes. I don't know.'

'You must know whether you can bloody well walk or not,' Kate said.

Clare had another spasm and as Frances moved to her, Frank gripped her. 'You stay close to me darling.' His hand gripped her, just under her breasts.

'One person only!' he shouted to the group round the black car. There seemed to be an argument going on. 'Move!' he shouted to Clare. 'Before I change my mind, for Christ's sake!'

'Mummy —'

'Go on Clare, please please.'

The child took a few stumbling steps away from the estate car, and then turned back towards Frances sobbing.

'Go on go on,' Frances shouted.

A man had broken away from the group. Frank saw that it was Geoffrey Carr. Doherty was protesting, but he broke away towards Clare. The idiot! I'm an idiot too, Frank thought, I could have exchanged the girl for him, I could perhaps still get him.

But, even while the idea was going through his head, the opportunity for putting it into practice was slipping away from him. The girl was staggering towards Geoffrey. She stopped, doubled up with coughing. Geoffrey moved closer towards Frank, squatting down and holding out his arms. As he was about to move Frances looked at him: perhaps she read his mind. Did she move closer against him? Was that all a pretence?

The moment passed. Geoffrey scooped Clare up in his arms and ran with her back to the black car. Now Frances was leaning right against him, her eyes closed.

The procession went up and down the hills of North Cork. In about an hour they would be at the airport. The petrol gauge marker swung around E. Frances, huddled up, her arms clasped round her knees, saw Frank glancing at it.

The witch registered every movement and kept the gun pointing steadily at her. Frances knew she would shoot her if she had any excuse at all. Why hadn't Geoffrey paid, why hadn't he simply paid?

'Where are we going?' she muttered.

'You wanted sun. Fresh air. You'll get plenty,' Frank said.

Hadn't he seen it all on television? Perhaps that's where he thought he was. And perhaps he was: once she thought she glimpsed a camera.

'They won't let you go,' she said.

'You're our first-class ticket,' Frank said.

'They're fooling you.'

'Tell me.'

'There are a lot more planes at Dublin than Cork.' She judged from his silence, from the set of his back, that the same thing had been going through his mind. 'They're planning something and we'll all be killed!'

He laughed. 'Not if we stay close together, darling.'

The knuckles of Kate's gun hand were four spots of white.

'I need petrol,' Frank said on the walkie-talkie.

'Right, Frank —'

'I'm choosing the garage!'

Frances could take no more. With Clare there she had been forced to keep a grip on herself; now she could feel her control going. The road was bad and every time a wheel went into a pothole, the gun jerked.

'Put it down! Tell her to put it down! You want to kill me don't you,' she shouted at the woman.

Part of her was still rational, calculating. If the woman did lower the gun, would she have time to throw herself across the back of the car! She would have no chance. The car turned sharply, throwing her to one side. They were going into a garage. She saw the open-mouthed face of an attendant. The motor-cyclists were roaring up, clearing the pumps. She felt totally alone, deserted, vulnerable. The police didn't care, nobody cared, so long as they got the kidnappers. Someone was filling the tank, a youth of about nineteen with spots and gappy teeth. He stared at the gun, at her. Nobody was going to do anything! She became hysterical.

'They shoot hijackers. We'll all be killed. Who's

going to give you shelter? Give yourself up Frank! I'll come and see you!'

He laughed. 'In the Kesh?'

'I will, I will!' She meant it, every word of it. She couldn't stay cramped up in that box a moment longer. As she moved, the gun twitched.

'I need a lavatory!' she said.

'Go in the plane,' said the woman.

She started getting up. Frank's hand pushed her down. Her face fell on his hand, sobbing.

'Calm down calm down,' Frank said. 'I need a pee myself. No problem.'

He picked up the walkie-talkie.

Doherty watched the three get out of the car. There was not an inch of space between them. They might have been one grotesque animal with six legs making its ponderous way past the garage shop towards the peeling red door marked TOILETS.

Doherty looked at O'Connor, who was standing by the car, his hand in his pocket. He drew his tongue over dry lips and spoke to Kearney.

'What's the woman's name. The hostage?'

'Carr.'

'Her first name!'

'Frances.'

Water dripped from the overhead cistern and formed a rusty patch in front of her. As she sat he kept the gun in her back and her body between him and the door. The witch was near the door, looking out.

'I thought you were bursting.'

It was ridiculous. For what seemed an age nothing would come out. He gave the gun to the witch and she watched with indifference as he pissed, squirting it like a small boy to bubble the water.

He zipped up his jeans, wrapped his arm tightly round her and the witch shoved the gun into her spine.

They moved slowly, a six-legged creature again, out into the open.

The group of men by the black car were standing like curious onlookers. There was no urgency or concern about them. One even kicked idly at a stone. The drizzle had petered out and the edge of a weak sun appeared behind liverish-coloured clouds. Frances stared at it, the first sun she had seen for three weeks, and stopped.

'Talk to them,' she said.

'Come on!'

The gun stabbed into her back. She twisted her head to look at Frank. 'Talk to them.'

'Their promises are shit.'

'I'm a witness! I'll fight for you! You can do a deal!'

She thought she saw a trace of hesitation in his face, then the gun stabbed her back again so she cried out and staggered. 'She'll kill me.'

'Give me the gun,' Frank said.

'She's fooling you.' Kate moved from Frances for a moment.

'Stay close!'

Frances let her legs crumple. Now they were dragging her towards the car. Kate was shouting.

'She got the girl out! We need *two* for shields at the airport! She only has to look at you and —'

Just as the hostage and kidnappers were one body, so were the outwardly casual Doherty and O'Connor. Both saw the argument begin, saw Frances screaming, dragging her feet. A sliver of the red toilet door appeared between the hostage and the male kidnapper. O'Connor twitched. The three came together again, like clumsy formation dancers. The kidnappers were arguing. The man grabbed the gun. For the briefest of instants he was off-balance, and the hostage staggering sideways. His hand was actually grabbing out for her when Doherty roared with such force that he was bent double, like a football manager shouting from the crease.

'Down Frances!!'

* * *

The next moment, probably half-a-second, lasted for the rest of Frances's life. Had she any control over it? Of course not. She was falling towards her right, flinging out her left arm to regain her balance when Doherty shouted. She sensed rather than saw Frank's grabbing hand and ducked away, pitching forward. The jar of her head and shoulder hitting the concrete coincided with the explosion. Her dazed eyes saw Frank on his knees. She thought he was going to make a joke, but when he opened his mouth, blood poured out of it. On her other side there was a curious mewing sound and she twisted her head to see the woman, half-crouching, flinging her hands in the air. Two more shots spun her half round and she fell inches from Frances. It was then that Frances began screaming incessantly, for she was sure they were going to shoot her too.

She was still convinced of that when they carried her off on a stretcher, for it was all of a piece with the way they covered the bodies. She only stopped screaming because her voice went. The screams went on inside. A man in a beautiful suit with a beautiful smile walked with her to the ambulance.

'I hope you didn't mind me calling you Frances, Mrs Carr,' he smiled. 'You were brilliant!'

'Brilliant,' echoed Geoffrey, as he held her hand in the ambulance. 'The way you got those brutes out of the car.'

It was at that point, deep, deep down under the shock and the exhaustion, that the debate about the half-second began.

17 *The Road to the North*

Normality had become unreal. For Frances, the first bath, sinking into warm water up to her chin, was a delicious fantasy. So were doctors, nurses, drugs, stiff clean sheets in a hospital bed.

The police were real, asking their endless questions, apologetically but immediately. Geoffrey, who, whenever she looked up was always there, ready to hold her hand, was not. Neither was Clare, already out and about, as if nothing had happened to her.

It was better when, after a week she returned to Kilnameath. They walked by the stream. She had missed the end of summer, and leaves were thick by the bridge. Clare took her arm on one side, and Geoffrey on the other. Behind them was an armed security guard. It was cold and fresh and they told him about the bucket, the walking, they were actually joking about it.

Then he squeezed her tightly, and they were ploughing through the leaves, their six legs moving in concert, and she was suddenly back at the garage, with the gun in her back.

'What's the matter?'

'Nothing.'

The trees seemed to be watching her, bird calls were unnaturally loud. He put his arms round her, but she twisted away. Sometimes she couldn't bear anyone too close to her now. Nevertheless, that night he made love to her, tentatively, gently. He held her hand, her poor finger and kissed it.

'Oh my poor darling.'

She smiled and kissed him. They handled each other so carefully, they might have been made of the most delicate glass. She felt remote from him, but it was going all right, things were gradually returning to normal.

It was about ten days after her release. It was not premeditated. It was as if part of her mind had been working on the idea, underneath the baths, the walks, Geoffrey's constant attentions, and presented it to her as a decision, fully-formed.

They had finished tea. Margaret, Robert and their children had come over and were playing with Clare. Margaret had made scones, and they were finishing off the crumbs.

'Can Clare come over tomorrow?' Frances asked.

'Of course. What are you . . .?'

'I shall be out for the day.'

It was the first positive thing she had said since her release. In fact, until she said it she did not feel released. Just as the kidnappers had imprisoned her, so had the doctors, the police, Geoffrey, telling her when she could get up, go out, what she was feeling.

'Where are you going?'

Geoffrey sat up. There it was: his look of tense concern. She teased up a currant and some crumbs between her finger and thumb.

'To a funeral.'

At first he thought it was a sick joke. She made no attempt to convince him she was serious. She'd told him, and that was enough. It was when she ordered the car for six o'clock in the morning that the row began. She was unwell, she had been too frightened to go out, what was all this stupid nonsense?

In the end, he humoured her and told them to get the car ready. She knew her Geoffrey. He was going to 'handle her'. This was some silly fantasy that he would gently draw her out of.

She was on sleeping pills, and he probably thought she wouldn't be up until ten. That night she took no pills, and drank nothing. She was dressed at five, in black, which emphasised the chalk-white pallor of her face.

Sitting on the bed in his pyjamas, his head in his hands, he finally lost his temper.

'I have never heard of anything so bloody stupid in all my life!'

The violence was a relief after the deadening carefulness of the last ten days.

She wanted to be free, in the car, on the road. On the road to the north. She had been in the north twice, but as a girl, never as a woman.

He sprang up as she got to the door and she realised after it had happened that her hand had come up, her fingers crooked, ready to scratch. This was like the cellar!

'You are not coming!' she blazed at him.

'Then I will phone Watson at the RUC and they will escort you.'

'Excuse me.'

She could not escape, any more than she could from Annacloy. A security guard, Eddie, followed her outside. It was very cold now in the mornings. She drank in the air eagerly and watched the rooks, wheeling and cawing in the pink sky. For the first time since her return, she had an urge to go up to the copse. She knew Geoffrey must be phoning the police. She didn't care, so long as she got to Derry. The car appeared as Geoffrey came out of the house.

'You're practically asking to be kidnapped again!'

'Morning Tom,' she said to the driver. 'Cold.'

'It is cold, madam. Morning sir.'

They got in with Eddie. It was not until they were on the other side of Dublin that she began to be frightened. Perversely she began to hope he would object again, but he dozed, seeming now quite unconcerned. Was he expecting her to panic, order the car to go back?

She huddled in a corner, staring at the bleak, flat

landscape. In Ardee they stopped at a garage and she found herself shaking uncontrollably. Geoffrey awoke and began chatting as if he noticed nothing. They drove through Monaghan and Derry was signposted.

Tom and Eddie were now silent and tense as they joined the queue waiting to cross the border at Aughnacloy. She stared at the notices saying: *One Vehicle at a Time. Is your Insurance valid for Northern Ireland?*. The lights went green and the car in front drove through. They bumped over the ramp. There were grey pillboxes and two British soldiers carrying rifles. She suddenly felt a great surge of anger and, before anyone could stop her, got out of the car.

'Don't point that rifle at me!'

The soldier was about twenty. He brought his rifle up.

'You! I said don't point that rifle at me!'

Geoffrey's calm voice came from behind her. 'I'm sorry. My wife is not very well.'

'Not very well! I am very well, Geoffrey, very well!'

They pulled the car into the side and led her back to it like a child. Now he tried to persuade her to go back but she refused to go in the car unless they went on.

Strangely, the fear went as soon as they were in the north. She gazed eagerly out at the towns, at the people as if looking for something. The battered, graffiti-sprayed streets of Strabane slipped by, and then they were approaching Derry. It had remained cold and clear, and across the river Foyle she could see the housing estates of the Bogside and the Creggan, sprawling up the hill, beyond the spire of St Stephen's Cathedral.

The funeral mass had begun. On Geoffrey's face there was indignation at the priest's words. She felt curiously at peace: he was voicing the debate inside herself.

'Our brother Frank was a violent man; but we can find penitence at the last. He released the child.

Perhaps he would have released the woman also, had he not received such summary violence himself.'

The looks began. Near a stone pillar, tinged red by the huge windows, was a woman of about thirty and a girl about ten. The girl had Frank's truculent lower lip. Frances could not keep her eyes off her.

She managed to stand directly opposite the girl at the graveside, although Geoffrey and Eddie flanked her and kept her well back. Behind them were police. Frances picked out Frank's mother, a grey-haired woman crying bitterly. The girl didn't cry. Her hands were clenched as tight as the stiff single plait that bound her hair. The grave-diggers eased the coffin down on the creaking straps. The hillside wind pulled at the priest's cassock.

'Let us call trustingly upon Thee, O God, the Almighty Father, who raised Christ Thy son from the dead, for the salvation of the living and the dead.'

The ritual words quietened Frank's mother, until she picked up some earth. Then the soil in her hand provoked more grief, and she stood staring stupidly at the stones and dirt, tears dropping on it. Frances stepped forward. The priest stopped speaking, his cassock flapping like a sail, and there was a moment's silence. Whatever, if anything, Frances had intended to say had gone from her head.

Earth hit her coat. The police moved forward.

The thrower was the girl, his daughter. She had another clod in her hand, arm drawn back to throw it, hatred on her face. Her mother shouted angrily at her. Frances stared at the small figure, dropping the earth but still defiant, and tears stung her eyes. The girl's mother spoke quietly.

'Please leave us alone.'

She felt ashamed of herself. This was an indulgence. She had no right to be here. She could not mourn for him. They were spurious, sentimental feelings she had been having about him. She had not betrayed him or was in any way responsible for his death. After what they had done to her? The very thought was ludicrous! The priest's mutterings, blown by the wind, followed her for some way as they walked back to the car.

18 *The Price*

While they searched for another house in London, Geoffrey rented one in Hampstead, near the heath. He no longer wanted to live at Kilnameath. Neither did Clare. At some stage, Frances knew, he would suggest selling it. Perhaps she would agree.

'I'm Irish,' she had said.

'That is a matter of opinion,' Frank had said.

She would recover, settle down in London, accept the life she had lived before. Geoffrey spent a lot of time with her, and was incredibly gentle and understanding. He bought her a new dog and she did little but walk it on the heath, round the ponds — always with the inevitable security guard.

She was frightened of going mad.

The journey north to the funeral had shown how unbalanced she was; so had feeling responsible for Frank's death. Geoffrey had found a psychiatrist, Dr Palmer, who had explained it all to her.

She had been forced to form a relationship with Frank to survive, Palmer said. She had become dependent on him for everything: food, love, life itself, just as a baby is totally dependent on its mother.

There was even a name for this dependence: the 'Stockholm Syndrome', after the city where a Swedish bank robber formed a relationship with a girl bank clerk he was holding hostage; for a long time after her release and his arrest she continued to feel close to him.

Talking helped. She confessed to Dr Palmer that she

felt she had been abandoned by Geoffrey, and it turned out that this was quite common in kidnaps too, although no-one had yet thought of a name for it.

She felt well enough to agree to a dinner party which Geoffrey wanted to hold for some of the people who had helped him most during the kidnap: Lansbury, Alan Tyndall and Richard Lefray. Geoffrey was on top form: that day he had completed arrangements for buying back control of his company from O'Leary.

Frances drank a fair amount, weathering the period when everyone said how brave she was. It was amazing how the cellar could be reduced to a few well-worn party stories — people couldn't take it, they wanted to hear, their eyes would stand out, and they wouldn't drink or eat while you were talking, and they would look down, and shake their heads slightly, and their mouths would wince, but they wouldn't accept the full horror of it, Frances had discovered, they didn't want to believe that such things could happen, they needed touches of humour or stoicism, like the bucket, the calendar — did you really?, how wonderful, how marvellous — in order to make it palatable, and reassure them that humanity had survived.

She was drinking too much. That must be why she was having this feeling of betrayal again. Her stories were also a betrayal . . . of what? She was thinking nonsense again. She picked up an apple, polished it and smelt it. There were shouts of laughter from the other end of the table. She had been glad when they had finally stopped talking about her, but she resented the fact that they could possibly talk about anything else.

Ah, she didn't know what she wanted! Her glass was empty. Geoffrey filled it and smiled at her before trying to get into the conversation.

'Do you remember —'

Lansbury wouldn't give way. 'Eight television producers and five newspaper editors are clamouring for your exclusive story, master.'

'Do you —'

Lefray gestured giant headlines. 'Husband Saves Wife Using Advanced Computer Research.'

As Geoffrey opened his mouth again, Tyndall raised his glass. 'Today our closing price went above the level it was when all this business began!'

There were cheers and glasses were chinked. Geoffrey thumped the table and shouted above the din. 'I am determined to say this! Do you remember —'

The sudden silence and the expectant faces turned to him momentarily drove the words out of Geoffrey's head.

'How can we remember, master,' Lansbury said with a shrug, 'if you have forgotten?'

When the laughter had died down, Geoffrey pointed a triumphant finger at Lefray: 'A man has only one idea, one fortune in his life.'

'It's still the same fortune,' Lefray said. 'You haven't made another.

Frances was about to cut into the apple. She put down the knife. The atmosphere was a little tenser. Lefray was playing with the stem of his glass.

'I still think you should have sold,' he said.

Geoffrey laughed in delight. 'Of course you do, of course you do!!'

'Sold what?' Frances said.

Geoffrey was too intent on Lefray's discomfiture to notice her expression.

'They were going to have me,' he said to her. 'This lot, weren't you? You thought I was finished.'

'Not I master,' said Lansbury. 'That was the press. Curs. Lickspittles.'

'Sold what!' Frances shouted.

Every face turned, smiles going. Geoffrey's hand reached across the table towards her. She started to apologise then stopped, hating the solicitousness in the faces. She was tired of being treated like an invalid.

'Sold what?' she asked. 'What should you have sold?'

Geoffrey smiled. 'Shares. Richard wanted to pick up some more shares in the company.'

'Oh.'

She was lost. She realised she was twisting her wedding ring, a nervous habit she had tried to stop as it drew attention to her mutilated little finger. In a moment someone would rescue the conversation. She struggled to find words, frightened of appearing stupid.

'Why didn't you sell?'

'Because I got the money from O'Leary.'

'I see.'

He took her hand and Lansbury began talking about poor farmers. She pulled away and broke in.

'No I don't see, I don't see at all, we were going to be released. Something happened.'

Wasn't there something in Geoffrey's eyes, in the way his smile had become fixed, and in their general shiftiness round the table? She looked at Lansbury.

'Are you going to tell the whole story, John?'

'Oh yes, of course Frances, and nothing but the story.'

'Then you will want to know how they cut off my finger.'

The only sound was a car passing outside. It changed down at the corner, as they always did. The light above her glinted on her glass as she pushed it away over the polished table, and on the knife as she picked it up.

Geoffrey half-rose. 'Darling I don't think —'

Frances seized the apple and hammered it down on the table. A glass fell over and broke.

'They held me down on the table. They had to do it twice, three times. Like chopping a dead rabbit.'

She hacked savagely at the apple. Pieces of apple spun, fell on the floor. Grooves appeared in the polished mahogany table.

'Put that in. But the man who did it was more honest than you are. Put that in. Put that in!!'

* * *

After they had gone she broke down and wept. He wanted to call Dr Palmer and she let him get as far as dialling before stopping him. She couldn't talk, she didn't want to see anyone, all she needed was sleep, oblivion.

He wouldn't let her take pills because she had drunk so much. He sat on the bed and held her hands while the tears streamed down her face.

'I'm sorry, I'm sorry, that was the most appalling after-dinner story ever!'

'It was the most appalling experience —'

She gripped his hands. 'I keep telling you, it's not the experience, it's you! I felt close to you. Loved. Then you stopped bidding.'

'Bidding? What are you talking about?'

'It was like the house, the auction, there was a price, and when you reached it you stopped bidding.'

'Darling, that's all in your imagination! I sold everything!'

She looked round the beautifully furnished room. 'But it's all still here. Your company. Everything.'

'Because we found you.'

She wandered round the room, confused. 'Yes. Yes.' Of course, that was right. He was being so patient and she was so pathetic, painful.

'Sweet, sweet, my darling. You know what Dr Palmer said. People who have been kidnapped often feel rejected, bargained over —'

'Yes, yes.'

'It's common.'

'Yes. You never left me.'

'I never left you.'

He kissed her gently, led her to the bed, and began to undress her. When her breasts were exposed she stared down at them as if they didn't belong to her. Her voice was matter-of-fact.

'He raped me.'

His hands left her. 'Why didn't you tell me before?'

She shook her head dumbly. 'Don't you want to touch me?'

'Of course I want to touch you!'

'I feel so *dirty*!'

'Oh my poor darling.'

'You don't understand.'

'I do I do!'

'Dirty *now. Then* I was clean! Dirty now! Now! Dirty dirty dirty dirty dirty dirty!'

'Darling you're not well, you're really not well, you must go and see Dr Palmer tomorrow. Promise?'

She nodded and cried while he held her tightly to him.

She knew now why she had gone to the north, why, in a sense, she had never returned. She knew too that if this was madness, she must struggle to hold on to it. He wanted her to take a pill now but she refused and, at the first opportunity, flushed them all down the lavatory.

The wind blew through the broken panes. He ran again up the stairs with the broken banister, and heard her voice calling tantalisingly from room after room before waking up in a sweat with the feeling that the phone had just stopped ringing.

It was as if the whole nightmare had begun all over again. He shouldn't have gone to work that day, the day after the dinner party! He regretted that, nothing else.

She had gone without saying anything or leaving a note, only a message with Ida.

'Where did she go?'

'I don't know.'

'She took Clare?'

'Yes. She said she would contact you.'

'When?'

'I don't know.'

Once more he couldn't work. Once more he woke in the middle of the night and couldn't get back to sleep. He walked round the heath, going to her favourite spots round the ponds, just as he had walked to the copse at Kilnameath.

He tried to find an explanation for it, he even tried to feel guilty but he could not. He had done nothing wrong.

He had done all that he possibly could for her — hadn't he sold everything? Found her? If he hadn't worked day and night on that computer programme, would she and Clare ever have been seen again?

Although it was cold, he sat by the pond for over an hour without a coat on, his anger building up. It was the way she had gone, the cruelty of it. She had always been like that. He remembered her taunting tongue in his mouth.

Then as he walked home, he felt remorse at these thoughts. She was deluded — scarcely surprising after what she had been through. Unless . . . the fear struck him that she really had been kidnapped again. Exhausted with his thoughts, he walked to East Heath Road and stopped a taxi, giving an address in Tufnell Park.

Dr Palmer's consulting room was in a Victorian house with polished banisters and plants hanging in the hall. It was late evening, and Geoffrey had to wait for a Spanish looking woman who drew up her collar as if she did not want to be seen there.

While he waited, he thought that the terrible thing was that he loved her so much, whether she was mad, whatever she was. It was a physical hurt. What would he do if he never saw her again?

Palmer had a quiet, dry voice and hands that were neatly folded when they were not taking notes.

'Have you told the police?'

'No.'

'Why not? If you think she's been kidnapped again?'

'No no I don't mean . . .' What had been crystal clear in the waiting room was difficult to grasp in front of this mild-mannered man, who sat without fidgeting. 'I mean . . . it's happened before.'

'Before the kidnap?'

'Yes. There's a pattern. Somehow . . . it's absurd! . . . the kidnap fits in.'

Palmer seemed to take this quite seriously. Too seriously. 'Are you saying she invited herself to be kidnapped?'

'No no no! Of course I'm not, of course I'm not.'

The silence stretched. He willed Palmer to ask him another question but he remained silent. He wanted to say: the trouble is I love her, that is the real problem, what do I do about that? Because I am so inexperienced in love, it is something I have avoided, for one reason or another, and I believed first that love did not exist, then that it wore to a comforting friendship, then that it meant happiness, and I found none of these things were true, oh there has been happiness, more happiness than I ever dreamed of, but more pain, much more pain, and I cannot take any more of it, what can you do about that?

Because he could never dream of saying this, his mind groped for a familiar, if totally inadequate commercial analogy.

'It's as if she wants to make me pay.'

'Pay?'

'And go on paying.' He got up with a sudden decisiveness. 'I'm not prepared to do so.'

When he got home he phoned the police. That produced nothing. It was five days before he heard. Again, Ida had a message for him. He stared at the sheet of paper she had torn from the phone pad: *Orchard Cottage, Stone's Down, Kent.*

'Is that all? Not even a phone number?'

'There is no phone.'

Geoffrey always found Kent a strange country. Urban sprawl could give way to flat marsh or downland as isolated as any in the country when the wind brought the snow in from the sea. It was cold enough to snow when he left the M2 at Whitehill and entered the web of small roads covering the North Downs.

He remembered now that she used to borrow a

friend's cottage here, before they were married. He went through several small woods and got lost twice before a girl on horseback directed him to what was little more than a track running past a farm.

Orchard Cottage was an old black and white building which from the front looked delerict. The eaves drooped over the dirty white plaster. The sun was at the back, and there was still frost on the drifts of fallen leaves which crunched under his feet as he walked from the car.

The car standing outside was splashed to the bonnet with mud. Inside, wellingtons, sticks and chocolate wrappings suggested, to his surprise and resentment, a normal life going on.

When there was no reply to his knock, he felt first irritation — they might have expected him, left a note — and then fear. Fear that something had happened, he didn't know what. He'd come too late. He hurried round the back, squeezing down a narrow, musty-smelling path, brambles scratching at him. The dog, Terry, heard him first. Clare shouted at it.

The place looked bigger at the back, an overgrown lawn leading to the orchard which gave the cottage its name.

Clare's voice came from an extension fitted with dusty, cracked panes like a greenhouse. Still half-fearing that something was wrong he pulled at the door.

'You really have to pull it!'

He thought the extension would collapse. The dog bounded round him, putting mud on his trousers. The room was misty with steam. There was a smell of baking. Clare glanced round as if she'd seen him only minutes before.

'Oh hello. I'm making jam.'

She pulled the scum from the surface of a huge bubbling pan with a wooden spoon, transferring it shakily to a saucer. A line of drips on the tiled floor marked similar journeys.

'Where is she?'

She licked the spoon before pointing with it. 'In the orchard.'

He tried to shut the door, gave up, and walked across the yard to an overgrown path that led to the orchard. On the way he passed a shed through the open door of which he could see apples stacked, separated by sheets of newspaper.

She was at the bottom of the orchard, trying to light a fire. When he was still some distance away she turned briefly and smiled. She was wearing her old riding trousers, boots and a thick blue and white striped sweater.

He stopped. The last time he had seen her tears had been rolling down her face and on to her bare breasts.

'Hello,' she said.

She dug a stick into the base of the fire, attempting to draw air through a clump of smouldering leaves. Her cheek was smudged with soot.

Of all things, this was the last he had expected. He had imagined she had been kidnapped again, had an accident, killed herself. Not this. All the concern, fear, love he had been through finished up squeezed inside a hard ball of anger.

'Is that all you have to say?'

She looked up at him, vaguely, uncomprehendingly, and coughed as smoke wreathed round her head.

'I'm trying to light this bloody fire.'

Even at this moment he could not help seeing how incompetent she was. The fire was a carelessly built structure, with too many large twigs at the bottom. The leaves piled up in the rusting wheelbarrow were damp.

'You need petrol.'

She flashed him a look of scorn. 'That's cheating.'

'Frances. Can we talk?'

'Talk? Of course we can talk.'

She sounded surprised he had asked such a silly question and returned to poking the smoking pile of rubbish. He knelt down to shout angrily at her and then snatched up a twig and broke it into small pieces.

'You'll have to rebuild it.'

He had a can of petrol in his car, why didn't he use that? What was he doing here, fetching newspapers, showing her how to make chips as his mother used to: nowadays with all the central heating, nobody knew how to make a fire properly.

'You have to fold the paper tighter than that.'

He found himself watching her old habitual gestures: combing her hair back with her fingers, sticking out her tongue as she concentrated.

'Is that better?'

'Yes. Not bad.'

He painstakingly removed all the wet leaves and built a pyramid to his satisfaction.

'One match,' he said.

He stood up and watched while the flames caught and spread. Twigs spat and crackled. His trousers were filthy, and he dashed at them with his hands.

'Thanks,' she said.

Enraged at her casual tone he went right up to her. 'You promised you'd go to the doctor.'

'I did.'

'You did not, Frances. I saw Palmer.'

'Oh. I thought you meant Whitemore. I saw him.'

'What's the use of seeing him?'

'I'm pregnant.'

She went to the wheelbarrow, took up an armful of wet leaves and asked him if it was all right to put them on now. When he didn't answer, she dropped them on. Clouds of smoke surrounded them. Coughing and spluttering, they retreated.

'I thought you wanted a child,' she said.

'I do, I do.'

'Good. That's all right then.' She began to walk back.

'Is it mine?'

She rubbed her smarting eyes. 'What?'

'Is it mine?'

'Of course it's yours!'

'How can you be so sure?'

'The date. When it happened with him I'd just had a period.'

He stood without speaking, knocking his hand incessantly against the trunk of a tree. She picked a windfall out of the long grass. A soft brown patch was just beginning to spread over it. She rubbed it against her sweater, and began to walk slowly towards the cottage, touching each tree as she passed it.

'And honoured among wagons . . .'

He followed her zig-zag path. 'Perhaps . . .'

'I was prince of the apple towns.'

'You see, I will always think . . .'

She broke the windfall and smelt it. 'Time held me green and dying . . .'

'Perhaps you'd —'

'Though I sang in my chains like the sea.'

'— better get rid of it.'

She turned on him. 'What? What did you say?'

His voice came out, slowly, haltingly. 'You see . . . I'll never be able to get it out of my head, you see, that it's not mine. You see.'

She smiled. 'That's absurd. It's all in your imagination, darling. It's just as nonsensical as me imagining that there was a price, that you wouldn't sell your company for me.'

Her broadening smile, underlining the absurdity of this proposition, produced an automatic smile back. She went inside. The dog was barking, and Clare was going on about something not being her fault. Inches from him was the path with brambles snaking over it — why didn't she clip them? — which led to his car, to certainty, to knowing when he was going to work and sleep. But he had said nothing that he had come to say.

There was a strong smell of burning in the lean-to kitchen. The dog jumped at him and the door stuck when he tried to close it.

'Pull it,' Frances said. 'I'm afraid I've burnt the scones I made for you.'

'For me?' he said.

She nodded. 'At least there's new jam and cream.'

She cut away the charred top of one of the burnt offerings, made a face and combed her hair out of her eyes.

He turned away. Through the dirty cracked panes he could see the leafless trees of the orchard. The smoke must have really got into his eyes, for they were smarting badly.

She came up behind him. 'What's wrong?'

Her voice was quite gentle. He turned. Now she was willing to talk, but was he? He would never know whether she was smiling at him or mocking him. Whatever it was, he wanted it. If he had to pay, he would pay. The pain would come back but, with that acceptance, for the moment at least, it had gone. A kind of peace stole over him. She brushed against him as he picked up a scone; they touched, as it were, by stealth. The scone was as brittle as a biscuit.

'Have you any shears?' he mumbled through the crumbs.

'Shears?'

'I thought I'd cut those bloody brambles on the path.'

'Oh would you,' she said. 'I've been meaning to do that since I got here.'

THE END

THE SALAMANDRA GLASS

A. W. MYKEL

The heart-stopping novel of international suspense and intrigue by the author of *The Windchime Legacy.*

Michael Gladieux thought he'd finished with The Group, a highly specialised unit he'd served with in Vietnam . . . until his father is murdered, his body found with a note accusing him of Nazi collaboration during the war and a glass pendant anchored to his heart with a shiny steel spike.

Who was Michael's father? Why are Washington and The Group so interested? Michael's search for answers leads him on a terrifying quest – to find his father's killer. What he uncovers is far more deadly, as he becomes the one man capable of stopping the twisted legacy of THE SALAMANDRA GLASS

Rivals Ludlum at his best!

0 552 12417 6 £2.50

CORGI BOOKS

GIRI 義理

MARC OLDEN

"Ludlum, look out, Marc Olden is here'
Walter Wager, author of *Telefon*

GIRI
to the Japanese, a term meaning duty or loyalty, the most binding obligation of the samurai warriors. But to an American, it means something else – revenge!

Combining international intrigue, Oriental philosophy, deadly violence and burning passion, *Giri* is a gripping, fast-paced thriller in which East clashes with West, and the ageless code of the hunter versus the hunted is put to the ultimate test.

"Anybody who loved *Shibumi* and *The Ninja* shouldn't miss it"
James Patterson

0 552 12357 9 £1.95

CORGI BOOKS